Soper, S. I.
Hot metal

DATE DUE

HOT METAL

Center Point
Large Print

Books are produced in the United States using U.S.-based materials

Books are printed using a revolutionary new process called THINKtech™ that lowers energy usage by 70% and increases overall quality

Books are durable and flexible because of Smyth-sewing

Paper is sourced using environmentally responsible foresting methods and the paper is acid-free

Also by S. I. Soper and available from Center Point Large Print:

Remittance Man

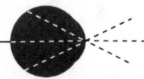

This Large Print Book carries the Seal of Approval of N.A.V.H.

HOT METAL

A WESTERN STORY

S. I. Soper

CENTER POINT LARGE PRINT
THORNDIKE, MAINE

This Circle Ⓥ Western is published by
Center Point Large Print in the year 2019 in
co-operation with Golden West Literary Agency.

Copyright © 2019 by S. I. Soper.

All rights reserved.

First Edition
September 2019

Printed in the United States of America
on permanent paper.
Set in 16-point Times New Roman type.

ISBN: 978-1-64358-337-2

Library of Congress Cataloging-in-Publication Data

The Library of Congress has cataloged this record
under Library of Congress Control Number: 2019943654

PART ONE

Chapter One

"Your name is Ben Hawthorne!" The hooded man thrust a smoking running iron at the prisoner crouched as far away as possible against the back bars of the rusty iron cage. Where the cage had come from and what its original use had been was unknown, but it was so small that though the captive—naked but for pants and boots—wasn't exceptionally big, slimly built and perhaps five ten-and-a-half or eleven when standing up, he'd had to be crowded into it, folded with back and knees bent and boot toes outside the bars. His bowed head was supported by the crooks of arms whose wrists were secured to the top bars by metal bands. The chains were locked to rounds with a big well-oiled padlock. There was no room inside the cage for the man to maneuver and avoid the red-hot iron.

Bare skin over ribs sizzled when heated metal touched it. The prisoner flinched; almost screamed: "Yes! Yes! My name is Ben Hawthorne! I told you that yesterday! I told you that the day before yesterday! My name's Ben Hawthorne! Why . . ."

"You're twenty-five years old." The rod touched again. The prisoner choked on pain but finally got out: "Yes! Yes! Yes! My name is

Ben . . . I'm twenty-five! I was born on a ranch outside Nacogdoches, Texas! The Comanches killed my family and took me when I was ten! I lived with the Injuns for five years! I went to work as a horse wrangler for Mister Hosea Inman when I was fifteen, and . . ." He jerked desperately at the manacle chains linking him to the cage and his voice rose. "Why do you keep tellin' me things I admit? Things that are true! Why? Why? What d'you want from me?"

"And then, you rode with Bert Holland and his men. You killed three innocent wimmen during a bank hold-up at . . ."

"NO! No, I never done that! No, I never rode with H-Holland's gang! No, I never killed no women! I never h-held up a bank! No!" Panting, the prisoner looked around the hole as if searching for some way out of this.

The place was a root cellar. A short, sturdy ladder led down from a thick trap door in the roof near the right wall. Beyond, shelves held food. Bins were full of onions, potatoes, apples, and squashes. Smoked hams and muslin-wrapped bacon slabs hung from rafters supported by earthen walls and a thick cottonwood center post. The cellar should have smelled of soil and salt-cure; instead, it was rank with the stench of pain-sweat, urine, and blood. The prisoner had been kept there for almost a week, hurt there nightly during that time.

The hooded man thrust the running-iron back into the blacksmith's coal pot brought down here to facilitate these activities, replaced the iron in his hand with a short, heavy whip, black with old blood, and turned to look at his two companions. All were dressed in regular range clothes. All wore salt-sack hoods with eye and nose holes cut out of the cloth. The other two had merely sat quietly on their heels while the first attacked the prisoner, but now they nodded and rose when he said: "Well, looks like it'll have to be this again." He flourished the whip toward the cottonwood support where stripes of blood on pale wood made the post look like it, instead of the prisoner, had been flogged.

The man in the cage again dropped his face into the crook of an elbow, shut his eyes, and gasped: "Yes, my name is Ben Hawthorne! Yes, I was born outside of Nacogdoches! Yes, my Injun name is Newcomer! Yes, I worked for Mister Inman . . ." —the two men had keyed the heavy locks and raised the cage top, attached to the bars by the manacle chain, Ben was half lifted with it— ". . . but I never rode with Holland! I never killed women! I wasn't there! I haven't . . . I didn't . . ."

The trap door in the ceiling crashed open. Their guns spurting lead and fire in the lantern-lighted dimness of the hole, four men by-passed the ladder and dropped one after the other into the cellar.

The man with the whip sprawled against the cottonwood post, three bullets in his chest. The two men by the cage let go of the top to grab at their own weapons. The invaders didn't hesitate. One hooded man bounced off the wall and slid down between it and the cage when bullets hit him. The other had his sidearm only half drawn when four slugs nearly tore him apart—he collapsed across the bars and began to bleed all over the man inside.

One of the invaders lunged to shove the corpse off onto the floor before he scowled at the captive staring wide-eyed back at him. He raised his six-shooter again and ordered: "Don't move, Seth." Two more shots shattered the chain that secured Ben to the bars.

The man grabbed the cage top, and hinges squealed when he leaned the frame back against the wall. "Oh, gawd almighty, look what they done to him! Everett! Al! Help me, here! We gotta git him outta here *pronto*, and I don't know if he can walk on his own in his condition, much less make that ladder. Murry, see if it's clear up yonder!"

While one man slammed his pistol back into its holster and hurriedly climbed the ladder, and one man watched, the other two seized Ben's arms, lifted him over the top edge of the cage and half walked, half carried him to the foot of the ladder. Above, the one called Murry leaned to scowl down: "Ain't nobody comin' yet, but hurry it up!"

Hands hurt old wounds and fresh when the men grabbed at Ben to support him, then palms against his buttocks shoved him up the ladder rungs. Half-scabbed whip cuts split and bled when Murry seized the broken manacle chains still at the prisoner's wrists, hauled him over the edge and out into a clear, starry but moonless night.

Immediately, the others pounded up the ladder to join them. One paused long enough to close the root-cellar trap and seat a wooden peg to lock it before he dashed to follow the others rushing Ben toward five saddled horses, merely darker shadows against the landscape sleeping beyond corrals, barns, and bunkhouses.

The men lifted Ben onto one of the mounts. Their leader looked toward the big square house at their left, saw a light flare in an upstairs window, and breathed: "Oh, shit, somebody's up. Hang on to the horn, Seth, so you don't fall off! You'll be all right now, son."

The inside of Ben's head seemed to be swirling around and around like water eddying past a stone in a stream, but he knew that man had called him Seth twice, now. No, his name was Ben . . . Ben Hawthorne . . . or Newcomer. He had been born on a ranch outside of Nacogdoches, Texas. He was twenty-five years old, had been . . .

Who was Seth?

He opened his mouth to ask the question, but the horse under him lunged into an instant gallop when the man beside him slashed at it. Because of the unsteadiness in his brain, it took everything Ben had left just to hang on. He did hear shouts and gunshots behind them, but, presently, they stopped. Or vanished into the distance.

Then ensued a headlong race through the night, the only sounds the horses' heavy breathing, their hoofs pounding packed dirt, the creak of saddle leather, and men's voices yelling—"Yah! . . . yah!"—to urge mounts to greater effort. There was wind in his face and stars blurred beyond tree branches. Then, an open prairie. Fingers wrapping his arm when he started to slide out of the saddle.

After ten minutes or so of hard riding, his rescuers slowed the horses to a canter. Another half hour brought them across a river ford. On the far bank, they headed eastward between the fringe of trees lining the river and where endless prairie started again.

Finally, the leader lifted a hand. "Hold up. I expect this is far enough tonight. Seth bein' in the condition he's in, we'll set up camp here and give both him and the horses a rest. Besides, we got to doctor the boy up some . . . now's not the time for him to die on us."

They guided the horses through river-edge

trees until they reached the bank, found a likely campsite with water rippling at their left and brush shielding them from prying eyes at their right, and dismounted. The leader ordered softly: "Ev, build us a fire so we got some light. Keep it small . . . we don't want to draw attention to ourselves.

"Al, get a blanket from your roll. We shouldn't lay him . . ."—he indicated Ben slumped over the saddle horn—". . . on bare dirt. Hurry it up, men, we got to get some food and water into this boy and let him rest some tonight or he ain't goin' to make it home." He patted Ben's thigh, saying gruffly: "Hang on, son. Set just a minute longer."

Ben couldn't do anything other than merely sit the saddle and continue hanging onto the horn. Light from the tiny campfire the man called Ev built was a hazed blur to him. He was cold. He could feel himself shivering, yet something deep in his gut made him not want to go close enough to that fire to warm up—fire was used to heat the irons they burned him with while they yelled words at him, and no matter what he said in return, they just kept at him and at him. . . .

Al spread a thin brown blanket on the ground near the fire before he hurried over to help the leader lower Ben from the saddle. They supported him while he made it across the short space between the horse and the blanket, and eased him when he collapsed onto his side on it. The leader wrapped the cloth around him before tucking it gently under his chin.

"You just lay quiet for a while, Seth." Fingers brushed hair back from Ben's forehead. "We're fixin' some food for you. Want a drink of water?"

"Yes . . . water . . . please, water. . . ." Ben's lips were so numb he could hardly force words past them.

Al brought a canteen, knelt, and held it out to Ben. Chains clattered when Hawthorne lifted his hand to steady the flask.

The leader touched one of the thick manacles, saying: "I'm sorry, but we can't get them off, Seth. You'll have to wear 'em till we can see a blacksmith. I s'pose we could shoot 'em off, but not here. We ain't that far away yet."

Ben was accustomed to them by now; they didn't bother him that much at the moment. What *did* confuse him was why the man kept calling him Seth.

He lowered the canteen and asked: "Wh-Who are you?"

The leader sat back and fished under his duster, brought out a paper and a cinch bag of tobacco, proceeded to roll a cigarette. He licked the paper edge, sealed the cylinder, twisted ends, and lighted up with a burning twig from the campfire. The smell of tobacco smoke mixed with that of whiskey from the bottle one man had gotten from

14

his saddlebags, and coffee beginning to boil over the flames.

He said: "My name's Reuben Bettiger, Seth. This here's Albert Hoffs. That's Everett Ribble . . ." —Ribble lifted the bottle in salute—"and him there is Murry Harding. We were hired by your daddy to find you."

No, my pa was killed by the Comanches when I was ten. The vision that had lingered in the back of his mind of the Indian attack cutting down his parents fifteen years ago swam again behind his eyes. He blinked it away and scowled. "No. You . . . got the wrong man. My name is Ben Hawthorne. I . . ."

"No," Bettiger said somberly around the cigarette. "Your name's Seth Locklin. Your daddy is Arch Locklin, and he . . ."

"No! No!" It seemed to Ben that everyone and everything around him had gone crazy. What was happening? He didn't understand any of this at all! He had ridden into town to buy horseshoe nails for Mr. Inman. It was the 4th of July; town had been all decked out with bunting and flags . . . there was a band playing down at the end of the main street . . . he'd gotten the nails from the hardware store and then had headed toward the saloon for one drink before returning to the ranch. As he'd walked past an alley, something hit him. He had come to, in a cage in a cellar, and then those men had told him he was who he knew he

15

was . . . who he had always been. Except for the part about some bank hold-up and killing three women, everything else they'd said to him was true, yet for some reason they kept him prisoner, burned him and whipped him as though they were trying to get him to be someone he wasn't.

Now, the men who rescued him told him he was somebody he knew he wasn't. He was so grateful to be out of the cage, out of the hole, he nearly wanted to cry over it, but who was Seth Locklin? Who was Arch Locklin who was supposed to be his pa?

"No," he whispered. "You got it wrong. My name's Ben H-Hawthorne. I was born on a ranch outside Nacogdoches." He wanted to stop saying that. It seemed he'd said it over and over so many times that the words were becoming visible, like they were printed on the air in front of his eyes. "M-My Comanche name is Newcomer. The Injuns killed my folks when I was ten. . . ."

"Jesus Christ," Ribble gritted softly. "They did a number on him, didn't they." He swigged from the bottle again.

Ben's rescuers didn't argue with him. They fed him beans and bacon and a cup of coffee, washed his face with cool water from the river, tucked a saddle under his head as a pillow, then while Murry Harding stood watch, spread their own bedrolls around their charge and slept off what remained of the night.

In the dawn, Ben was able to sit up and eat grits, more fatback, and drink another cup of coffee. With the help of Al Hoffs, he relieved himself in the bushes. He asked Reuben: "What makes you think I'm this . . . Seth Locklin, Mister Bettiger?"

"This." Reuben took a leather folder from his duster pocket, opened it, extracted a two-by-four inch rectangle and held it up in front of Ben's face. It was a daguerreotype, a portrait of a young man with fair hair and dark eyes. He was dressed in fringed and painted Indian leathers. His long hair was decorated with a single eagle feather. Bettiger said: "Your daddy had this taken of you just after he got you back from the Kiowas. You were nineteen."

Ben squinted at the picture, discovered that his eyesight was some blurry this morning. The face could have been his. The coloring was right. But what little showed of the leather shirt wasn't Comanche work, it looked more like Kiowa or Kiowa Apache. He shook his head. "You say this . . . Seth Locklin also . . . lived with Injuns at one time?"

"Yep." Bettiger nodded and returned the picture to its folder. "From ten to near twenty."

No, Ben thought, *that was too much of a coincidence! Me taken by the Comanches at ten years of age, likewise, this Seth taken by the Kiowas at ten. . . . No. No, there's something*

*real strange going on. Something too strange.
Someone's lying. Something is down-deep wrong!*

That picture could have been of him at that age.
But he knew who he was . . . didn't he?

The first shades of doubt brought a cold clench
around his heart. He didn't resist, didn't yet have
enough strength to try anything, and he knew it.
He let them lower a colorful cloth *zarape* over
his head in place of a shirt before they helped
him back astride the same horse he had ridden
during the escape last night. Today, they bound
the chains still around his wrists to the saddle
horn.

Bettiger said, while he was doing it: "This is
so you can't fall off and hurt yourself worse than
you already are, Seth. We got a long way to go.
It'll be a hard ride for you, all things considered,
but your family's waitin' on you up north."

"Where?" Ben asked. "Where are we goin'?"

"Home, son, home." Bettiger turned away and
also mounted up. He led off, northward.

Ben twisted in the saddle to look back. *Home*
was south, not north, he knew it. He tugged at
the chains. They were tight and well-secured
to the saddle. Had he been rescued from those
unknown men who had held him for days,
perhaps weeks? . . . or was he now some different
kind of prisoner?

He didn't know. Hurting from his wounds, he
bowed his head and applied himself to surviving

18

the day. He had to live until he could escape his "rescuers" . . . until he could get back to the ranch and let Mr. Inman know he hadn't merely stolen the horseshoe nail money and run off . . . until he could go *home*.

Chapter Two

Ben hadn't talked much yesterday, he had merely tried to stay upright in the saddle and last the day out. They had ridden hour after hour ever north and slightly west, not particularly fast, but steadily, keeping the horses at an easy but ground-covering canter.

In the evening, just at dusk, they had forded yet another river to camp on its northern bank. His rescuers? . . . present captors? . . . had seen to it that he ate and rested well—freshly killed prairie chicken broiled over the flames, a salted raw potato to crunch on the side, and coffee spiked with a small shot of whiskey from Ribble's fresh bottle. For all of it, conversation had been minimal.

This morning dawned summer warm. Hawthorne watched Murry Harding snag the coffee pot from over the fire and pour his own cup full before he swigged, finished the cup, and shuddered. "I got the end of last night's dregs. Aw, shit, but that's awful bitter brew!"

"Jez Christ!" Al retorted. "Well, if you'da just waited till I got fresh made . . ." Hoffs grabbed the pot and headed for the river.

Ben looked back at Bettiger and asked what day it was. Reuben pondered that a considerable length of time. Finally, he said: "I believe it's right around the Eleventh of July, give or take a day or two either way. Why?"

Ben was stunned. "Six or seven days! They had me more than six days! Who were they, Mister Bettiger? Why'd they do that to me? What was it they wanted?"

Bettiger slid a look around before he sighed and dug into the saddlebag he used as a back rest. "That was the Wharton Ranch, Seth, but whether the Wharton family was in on it or not, I dunno. We didn't wait to find out who it was we killed gettin' you out of there. As for the *why* of it . . ."—he produced a twice-folded paper and handed it over to Ben, seemed to assume that Seth read—"all's we can figger out is that they wanted to cash in on that."

Ben took the paper and unfolded what turned out to be a Wanted poster. The picture was a bad representation of a fair-haired man of undetermined age—it could have been of anyone. But the caption below the drawing read: **Wanted, Benjamin Hawthorne, Bank Robbery and Murder. $1500.00.**

Ben shook his head. He watched Al Hoffs dump ground coffee into fresh river water in the pot and set the boiler into campfire flame before he murmured: "I'm Ben Hawthorne, but I didn't do that. I never robbed a bank . . . never killed anybody. I been workin' for Mister Inman for . . ."

21

He twitched the broadsheet. "This don't make sense! If *they* knew I was me, why didn't they just turn me over to the local sheriff instead of doin' what they did? Why tell me I was me and do what they did to me? I don't understand!"

Bettiger also shook his head. "This whole mess is as much a puzzle to us, here, as it seems to be to you. Best I can tell is that maybe they knew you was innocent and wanted you to think you weren't. But, you see, you aren't Ben Hawthorne, Seth." Ben flourished the poster.

"Are you goin' to turn me in for the bounty?"

"Nope. We work for your daddy."

"But fifteen hundred dollars is a lot of money."

"Not as much as your daddy's payin' us to locate you and bring you home to him, son."

Ben leaned forward. "And how much is that?"

"Forty thousand, son. Forty thousand dollars."

Ben's mouth dropped open. He thought: *No one has that much money!* Blurted it.

Bettiger laughed. "Your daddy does, son. Why don't you go take a quick bath in the river, then let me look at you to see nothin' is festerin' before we go on today. Besides, I gotta confess that I find you somewhat rank when the wind turns."

Numbly, Ben nodded. He rose slowly and peeled out of the tent-like *zarape*. Reuben had to help him take off his boots and socks, but then he shucked out of the stained, stinking pants and underings, and naked, eased down the narrow, steep bank into the cool river. He took it slow while washing, both out of necessity and by design, using that time to try to sort out all he'd heard, and by the time they helped him back up the bank, he thought he had it pretty well figured.

He knew he was Ben Hawthorne, but forty thousand dollars was enough to make anyone who even faintly resembled this Seth Locklin *into* Seth Locklin in the eyes of greedy bounty hunters. Still, unanswered questions remained. There was that business about both him and Seth being taken by the Indians at age ten. That was too much. There was a Wanted poster carrying his name for something he knew he hadn't done. There were those men who had originally captured him and had tried to convince him that he was who he was as though they knew he was someone else they wanted to make over into Ben Hawthorne.

God, it made the inside of his head hurt just to try to think of it all!

Ben stood shivering with pain but silent while Bettiger doctored burns and whip cuts with smears of some kind of ointment from a jar he'd taken from his bags, then he helped Hawthorne dress in the underclothes, light shirt, britches, and socks they gave him. The duds didn't fit well, but they were clean. They flung Ben's old pants and underings into the river and let them float away; they were beyond washing.

They ate a quick breakfast. As Murry jittered about the camp and sent worried looks toward the northern plains, and Hoffs washed things for Ribble to pack, Hawthorne held out his hands to present the manacles dangling their broken chains. "Can't you shoot these off for me now, Mister Bettiger?"

"No!" Harding looked like he had a haunt riding his shoulders. Again, he flashed a look around. "No! The noise! Who knows who or what it'd bring on us! No, we gotta cat-foot it from here on in." He hissed at Ribble: "Hurry it up, Ev! We gotta git goin'. We . . . this . . . I . . ." He lapsed into an almost panic-stricken silence.

Reuben sent a puzzled look at Harding, but essentially agreed. "We're in Injun territory, Seth. We took enough of a chance bringin' down dinner last night. I don't want to let them redskins know we're comin' through, if I can help it. No, you'll just have to put up with 'em a little longer. We might even have to wait clear till we get to your daddy's ranch to . . ." He jerked around and scowled at Harding when Murry abruptly groaned and clutched at his belly. "What's eatin' *you?*" But then, he leaped to support Harding when the man started to sink to the ground. "Murry!"

Ev Ribble, looking considerably hungover this morning, also hurried to Harding's side. Down at the water's edge, Al Hoffs dropped the empty coffee pot into the river and scrambled up the bank to likewise kneel beside Murry. He asked: "What the hell's the matter with him?"

Ben sank to sit on a fallen log. He watched a violent spew of vomit wash away flecks of foam on Harding's lips before the man convulsed and died while the others looked on helplessly. Finally, Ribble gasped: "What could have kilt him like that? Somethin' he et?"

"I doubt that," Bettiger scowled morosely. "We all ate and drank the same things this mornin'." He moved to pull up the corpse's sleeves, then the pants legs to examine the skin. "Don't see no bug bites or fang wounds or nothin'. Maybe he had a heart seizure or the like." He sat back on his heel. "Damn! Ol' Murry was a good man. Shit!" He sighed heavily and looked around the campsite. "Well, nothin' left to do, I guess, but bury the poor bastard and git on with it."

Water hemlock, Ben thought as he continued to sit on the log and watch while the three men interred their deceased partner. He recalled seeing the plant growing on the marshy edges of each riverbank all along the trail, and he had also noted it here while he bathed earlier. He hadn't given it any thought then, mostly because water hemlock was common and more deadly in the spring than this time of year. Nevertheless, he was sure that man had been poisoned. He wondered if the price on his head was divided at ten thousand dollars per man to equal forty thousand, or whether the forty thousand was a total now to be divided among only three?

He didn't say anything about it. He concentrated on his own inner being, checking for signs of unease, and found none. He was tired and weak, and he hurt, but that was from items other than poison; his innards were all right. He did notice something else, though, a vibration jittering from the soil up through the soles of his boots into his feet.

"I expect you should stop buryin' for a minute and hunker down, Mister Bettiger."

Reuben shot him a frown. "What?"

"There's a large herd of horses, probably Injuns, goin' by up north."

"How do you know?"

"Stand still a minute and feel. It's either a raiding or a hunting party. They're travelin' too fast to have women, children, and all their household gear with 'em, so they're all warriors goin' some place in a hurry. Unless you'd like me to talk to them, I think you oughta just set a while till they pass."

Ribble lifted brows at Bettiger. "Could be the boy's right. But if them Injuns is Kiowa, we should be all right with him along."

"Unless his Injun pa, Medicine Shield, is leadin' them. That redskin might try to rescue his so-called son from us. No"—Reuben settled to a squat—"we'll just wait till they pass. After us searchin' for seven months for his boy, Mister Locklin ain't goin' to notice another hour."

Seven months? These men had scoured the landscape for Seth Locklin for over half a year. Why now? Why not sooner or later? What had happened to start such a search? Ben looked from man to man, studying them.

Reuben Bettiger was maybe pushing six feet tall, and thickly built through the arms and shoulders as though he had done heavy manual labor over an extended period at some earlier time. He had gray-streaked hair and a walrus moustache bushing below a hawk-beak nose, sprouted between crow's-feet-edged, light-blue eyes.

Everett Ribble was nearly as tall as Bettiger, but stoop-shouldered, sunken-chested, and stringy-thin, with large red knob-knuckled hands. For all that he drank, what Ben considered to be in excess, his eyes were dark blue and sharp in his weathered face—he was a cowpoke who had ridden into the teeth of many a prairie storm.

Albert Hoffs was shorter, about five-foot-eight, and compact beneath his trail duster. He seemed to be so nondescript—brown hair, brown eyes, small hands and feet, no distinguishing scars or features—that no one would probably have recalled seeing him at the local whiskey mill had they drank up an hour beside him.

Murry Harding had also been an ordinary man.

27

He was now merely a dead man, and a corpse had no personality.

Ben asked: "How much farther is it to where we're goin'?"

"'Bout another four-day ride. We could make it in three, I expect, were you in better shape, but we're takin' it some easy, all things considered," Reuben answered.

Ben nodded. "You said you had been lookin' for . . . Seth Locklin for seven months?"

"Yup."

"H-How long had he been gone from home before that?"

"You been gone near five years." Bettiger squinted from early-morning tree shadows out into the grassland. "I don't see nothin' out there. You sure there was Injuns passing by, Seth?"

Ben sighed heavily and twisted the manacle on his left wrist. The halves were secured with a chain link hammered shut through holes in the flange. He said: "They're passin' on east. I reckon you can finish your buryin' now. Why, after five years, did Mister Locklin suddenly send you out lookin'?"

"He has good reasons, but I figger he's the one ought to tell you. Come on, boys, let's finish up here and get on our way."

Ben continued to sit and watch them work. Presently, he asked: "Why did Seth . . . uh . . . I leave in the first place?"

"I expect that's something you gotta settle with your daddy as well, son." Bettiger turned away to help the other two men. The matter was obviously closed.

They finished the grave, and as they packed up, Hoffs moaned: "By damn, I dropped the coffee pot into the gawd-damned river when ol' Murry died. Lemme go see if I can find it." He clambered down the bank to the water's edge and peered around for a moment before he returned. "Damn! I don't see it nowhere! It must have floated downstream before it sank!"

The poison was in the coffee, and now the evidence is gone, Ben thought, yet he wondered how—when they had all drank—Murry could have been selectively poisoned in plain view of everyone else? Maybe he *was* dreaming. Maybe the man *had* suffered a heart seizure or the like.

He rose and mounted stiffly while Reuben held the horse for him. Once again, they headed northward. A half hour on, they came to a trail where grass had been flattened by passage of many unshod ponies, and Bettiger nodded at the sign. He said to the others: "Seth was right. War party or the like, headed east."

By late afternoon, Ben was again swaying in the saddle, the inside of his head blurry with weakness, and from pain of shirt material chaffing raw wounds. He decided he had about one more mile left in him before he perished, but his companions didn't let him rest. They halted only long enough to give him a drink of water and for Bettiger to once again bind him to the saddle, then leading "Seth's" mount, they moved onward, deeper into the northern plains, deeper into Kiowa country.

"That boy ain't said nothin' for three days," Hoffs scowled to Reuben. "You don't s'pose he's fixin' to die on us, do you?"

Bettiger looked hard at Seth. Their prize sat the saddle, his wrists bound to the horn by thongs close around the broken chains at the manacles, his head bowed. His eyes were open, but shadowed, as though he thought things far back in the deepest parts of his mind. The rest of his face was expressionless. During their night rests, and even when they halted briefly midday to eat and ease the horses, he merely accepted with a nod of thanks what food they offered him and ate in silence. In the evening, he finished his dinner and promptly rolled himself in his blanket, closed his eyes, and slept. He didn't try to escape, didn't argue with them, didn't resist, wasn't quite glum-sullen, yet he seemed to have withdrawn into some other world. Or, perhaps, he was trying to lull them into a careless moment. Or maybe all this had addled his brain to the point that there was nothing left inside him.

"We're only about a hour's ride from the

Locklin Ranch house now." Bettiger motioned to a low scraggly copse of trees struggling to survive in a hollow some half mile ahead. "You boys rest there a mite. I'll ride on ahead and tell Mister Locklin we located his son and are bringin' him in. You give me about a half-hour head start to warn Locklin what Seth's been through and prepare him for what he's gonna see, then follow me in with him. He don't talk, that's not our affair . . . we're gettin' paid to fetch him home, that's all. What happens after that . . ." He shrugged and kicked his mount into a gallop across the plain. Northward.

Chapter Three

The house was two-story, spaciously elled, painted white, and surrounded by bunkhouses, barns, storage sheds, stables, corrals, and cattle pens. It sat beside an ample stream meandering among the hollows, in a sheltered dip in the gently rolling prairie, and was backed by a grove of trees all leaning slightly eastward as though buffeted by a continual west wind. The ranch was obviously settled and rich, but Ben looked at it and discovered that it meant nothing to him.

He had never seen the place before. Despite his companions' assertion that he was Seth Locklin, he knew he didn't belong here. He *was* Ben Hawthorne. Regardless of the events of the past weeks, in spite of the doubts raised in his mind, he had to be.

Those doubts and questions—and Murry Harding's death—were what had kept him quiet these last three days. He felt he would get no satisfactory answers from Reuben Bettiger, Al Hoffs, or Everett Ribble, so didn't ask. He had spent the time reviewing every memory he possessed, trying to settle in his own mind who he was, solidifying into iron his true identity. He had pictured a woman with snapping blue eyes and fine brown hair, a woman with a soft smile, a hearty laugh, and strong capable hands. Cora. Ben Hawthorne's mother—his mother, before she had been killed by the Comanches.

He saw a man with white-blond hair and black eyes. Galluses over underwear and bagging black pants. Worn boots. Not rich, but not poor, either. An honorable, Bible-reading, God-fearing, hard-working man. Eli Hawthorne. *Ben's* father, Eli. And the homestead. And the land around it as seen by a nine- or ten-year-old boy.

Then, the Indian attack, and his first months as Nighthorse's son. His life as a Comanche warrior. His decision to return to his own people. Working for Mr. Hosea Inman. Mrs. Inman, plump, her gray eyes as clear and bright as a winter morning while she refreshed in him how to read, write, and do numbers. It seemed he'd once known and just hadn't done it in many years, but had an easy time recapturing the skills.

These were all Ben Hawthorne memories, not Seth Locklin's past, and he had worked through them one by one until he had a good grip on every shade and detail.

Except for that Wanted poster. He knew—tried his best to know—that he had never, *ever,* held up a bank or slaughtered three women at any time in that recalled past. Yet, where had the broadsheet come from? Why did it carry his name?

The second item that had kept him quiet was Murry Harding's death. He knew the man had been murdered by one of his companions—it had been something Murry ate or drank. He kept waiting to see which one of the three bounty hunters left alive would go next. Forty thousand dollars divided by two rather than three was twenty thousand each. Forty thousand dollars not divided at all was forty thousand to the survivor. Many a man would do a lot of evil for that much money.

There must have been fifteen or twenty cowhands standing in curious clots in the yard before the big house, and every one of them stared silently at them when Ribble led Ben's horse in. Hawthorne's wrists were again bound to the saddle horn as though now that they were so close to winning their bounty, Ribble and Hoffs were afraid their charge would take it into his head to make a run for it.

Ev guided them up beside a readied buckboard at the hitching rail near the steps to the porch that girdled the house, dismounted, tethered his animal, then drew his knife and cut the leather from around Ben's saddle horn. He sheathed the blade and lifted hands to help Ben down, but Hawthorne threw a leg over, slid off the other side of the horse, and started immediately for the steps—he'd be damned if he was going to be dragged into the house like a naughty boy on his way to the woodshed—and left Ribble and Hoffs scrambling to catch up.

There was no feeling of anticipation in his heart, no hollow of fear in the pit of his stomach, merely a wanting to get this over with. He would present himself to the man who was supposed to be his father. Mr. Locklin would look at him, say that Bettiger and the others had brought in the wrong man, that he was someone other than Seth Locklin, then he could thank them kindly for rescuing him from the root cellar and go his way.

Still, he paused at the open front door to the big house, straightened his shoulders, gathered the dangling ends of the broken chains into each hand so their lengths passed across his body and they wouldn't clatter, and in that hesitation, Ribble and Hoffs caught up with him. He jerked his arms out of their grasp when they seized him. Casting each a glare that told them to keep their hands off, he moved on through the door and into the house.

He was in a vestibule carpeted in brown, black, white, and red oriental designs. Directly in front of him, the entry became a hallway passing the base of a staircase and vanishing on into the back of the house. The balustrade led upward to the second floor.

To his right, a large square archway opened into an expansive carpeted living room furnished with maroon velvet settees and occasional tables bearing kerosene lamps with painted glass globes. An ornate potbellied stove gleamed polished black iron and isinglass near the far wall beyond a crystal chandelier.

To his left, a smaller arch that could be sealed with sliding double doors led to what was obviously an office or study. The doors were pushed halfway back into their tracks, and he could see a group of people there. A young woman, light-haired and dressed for travel, sat in a chair at the left of a big mahogany desk, with a man in an Eastern suit standing beside her. In a chair on this side of the desk, Reuben Bettiger had turned to look back toward the hallway; on the business side of the desk, a man with dark eyes and whose hair was so fair that the white in it over the ears barely showed, leaned into his wingback chair and stared with alert expectation at Ben. Over all hung the scents of expensive cigars, fine whiskey, and lavender perfume.

Ben suspected that the man behind the desk was Mr. Locklin. He met the brown eyes and still felt nothing. There was no *Hello, Father,* no . . . Nothing. Yet the woman rose from her seat and held gloved hands toward him as she breathed: "Oh, Seth!"

Ribble and Hoffs shoved Ben forward. Still hanging onto the chains, he took a few steps farther into the room before he stopped again. He nodded to the man behind the desk, and said it: "I expect you're Mister Locklin?"

Again, the young woman gasped: "Oh! Oh, Seth!"

Locklin's eyes narrowed. The fingers he had wrapped around a pen whitened visibly before he asked: "Aren't you going to say hello to your sister, Seth? You owe her that much, at least . . . she was the only one who defended you when you brought that squaw home as your wife."

Ben's head jerked up. He said clearly: "I would be proud to say howdy to the lady if I knew her name, but I'm not your son, Mister Locklin. My name's Ben Hawthorne. I am twenty-five years old. I was born on a ranch outside of Nacogdoches, Texas. The Comanches killed my family when I was te- . . . te- . . ." His voice faltered under the vision of a cage in a root cellar, of whips and red-hot irons and hooded men shouting those same words at him over and over and over while he . . .

Reuben gestured at the Wanted poster unfolded and lying on the desk top between him and Locklin. "There, you see. It's like I said, sir." He turned back to order: "Seth, take off your shirt, Son."

Ben stiffened. "Not in front of the lady. 'T'ain't proper."

"That lady is your sister Priscilla, Seth," Locklin frowned. "She saw you shirtless when you were children together here on this ranch."

"I'm not a child anymore and neither is she," Ben shot back, "and I've never seen her or been here before."

"Al . . . Ev . . . help him with the shirt," Reuben said.

Ribble reached to unbutton the front, but Ben let go of the chains and fended the man away—if Locklin was determined to see his body, he'd let him. His fingers were abrupt on the buttons. He shrugged out of the shirt and let it hang from forearms and belt while he stood flushed under their scrutiny. There were various murmurs of horror at the half-healed burns over his chest, ribs, and belly, sharp curses from both Locklin and the unintroduced man beside Priscilla's chair when Ben turned to show them the whip cuts across his back.

Grimly, he completed his turn and pulled up the shirt, but left it unbuttoned. He said: "I apologize if I offended you, Miss Pris, but . . ."

Her face lighted to a relieved smile. She cried: "Oh, now I'm sure you're Seth! No one has called me that since you left!" She leaped at him, and he leaned away from her when she wrapped arms around his neck to hug him hard.

Bettiger growled: "Like I said, Mister Locklin, whoever them men were at the Wharton Ranch . . . why ever they wanted him to be this Ben Hawthorne . . . they did a real job on him. I don't know if he'll ever get his memory back, but . . ."

A flurry of hoof beats and shouts from outside cut the bounty hunter off. Locklin half rose from his chair to scowl toward the lace-curtained and velvet-draped front window, but before anyone could do more than turn toward the hallway, a young woman—hardly more than a girl—burst into the room. She was followed closely by two cowhands, one an older man whose narrowed pale-green eyes swept the room warily, the other a good-looking cowpuncher about Ben's own age. Both kept their hands near holstered but loosened sidearms.

The girl immediately began yelling: "This is the last time, Locklin! I warned you before, but you don't listen, do you! One would think twenty thousand acres would be more than enough for you, but evidently not! I'm telling you for the very last time, you keep your cattle and your men off my ranch, because if there is a next time, I'll order my hands to shoot down any trespasser . . . critter or cowpoke!"

"Miss Black," Locklin snapped, "I haven't the slightest idea what you're . . ."

"Like hell!" Her lip curled in her flushed face. "Your men don't shit 'less you say they can!"

"Caitlan!" Priscilla gasped from where she still stood beside Ben. "Really, Cat, such language!"

The girl turned to glare at her. "Oh, don't give me that, Priscilla! I've known you too . . ." Her mouth fell open when she noticed Ben. "Seth!" Now, her eyes swept him from head to toe, taking in the disheveled shoulder-length ash-blond hair, the many days' growth of beard, the unbuttoned shirt, the manacles, and her mouth curved to a grim smile. She stepped to him and reached to touch the links while she snapped: "Well, Locklin, it seems you had to have your eldest hauled home in chains! I don't doubt that after what you did to him and his wife and son, it's the *only* way he would ever come back to you!"

Seth had a wife and child? Ben tried for a memory of them, but located none. He looked at the angry girl who had just identified him as Seth. She had black hair, fine and floaty where it escaped the single braid down her back. Her blue eyes fairly crackled with fury. She was dressed in a man's shirt and britches, and bent-heel boots. A gun belt held a plain-handled pistol at her hip, and he would bet anything that she knew how to use it. Otherwise, she was pretty in an ordinary way, though she had little of Priscilla's elegance. Still, though she professed to know him, he felt he had never seen her before.

Locklin growled: "Our family affairs are our business and none of yours, Miss Black. As for the so-called trespassing, if either my men or my cattle were on your property, I'm sure it was inadvertent . . . or they merely came to get a drink of water from your spring."

"I already supply you with water, *Mister* Locklin. Where do you think Runoff Creek comes from? . . . my artesian spring, that's where!

40

You have pushed me and pushed me to either sell my spread to you or to marry you ever since my brother was killed. I know you don't need more land, so it's gotta be Bountiful Spring you want. I'm warning you, *Mister* Locklin, you keep this up and I'll build myself some fences . . . dam the creek, and then . . ." She whirled toward the door, saying in passing: "Now that you're here, Seth, maybe you can talk some decency into your father, if you're so inclined! You were always the only one with any sense of honor around here!" Followed closely by her unspeaking men, she left as abruptly as she had come.

"My," Priscilla murmured, "I've never seen the Black Cat so angry! I know she has a temper, but . . ." She shook her head.

The man by her chair spoke for the first time. "Priscilla, we have to leave now. It's a long drive to town, and if we are going to catch the stage east . . ."

She frowned. "Oh, Todd, now that Seth is home, I would really like to delay a few days to hear what he has been doing these last five or six years." She turned brown eyes to meet Ben's own. "Wouldn't you like that, Seth?"

Ben sighed. He said: "I don't mean to sound harsh, Miss Pris, but I ain't your brother and we got nothin' to talk about."

Todd put in: "No, we have to go now, Priscilla. My business is waiting, and I've been gone from it too long as it is." He stepped forward to extend a hand to Locklin. "Sorry to leave you with what might turn out to be merely another disappointment, Father, but we really have to go. Write us the end result of this . . ."—he lifted a brow at Ben as though Hawthorne was merely a range maverick brought in for identification rather than a possible brother-in-law—"if you would. Priscilla, we have to go now!"

Locklin rose. He said: "I'll see you off." To the three bounty hunters, he ordered: "Watch him and see that he is still here when I get back."

Priscilla touched Ben's cheek briefly. She whispered: "I'm so glad you're finally safe at home, Seth. I wish I could stay, but . . ." She shrugged before she followed her husband and father out.

Bettiger barely waited for them to pass through the front door before he was up and out of his chair and at Ben's throat. He seized the unbuttoned shirt in both hands, shoved his face close to Hawthorne's, and snarled: "Shut up with that I'm not Seth Locklin shit! We were real good to you on your way here, boy, but that can change damned fast! You cheat us out of our bounty money, and I tell you, you'll never be safe again. You try to run, you'll be dead before you make it to the property line, understand me?" He shook Ben. "Understand me? We tracked you seven months! Killed three men to rescue you!

Like it or not, you . . . are . . . Seth . . . Locklin!"

"Why?" Ben asked softly. "Your bounty money aside, why, after all these years, does Mister Locklin want Seth back bad enough to send the likes of you out lookin'? Somethin' had to change here for him to offer forty thousand dollars for a son he evidently drove away on his own. What changed? What?"

"I reckon you'll hear that soon enough, so you keep your mouth shut and stop arguin'." Bettiger released Ben and strode back toward the desk, snatched the Wanted poster from its top and shook the paper. "You convince your daddy he ain't your daddy and he don't pay us our bounden due, we'll just take you and this back to Texas, turn you in for hangin' and collect the reward up on you to keep it from bein' a total loss. Keep *that* in mind, boy!"

Bettiger was again sitting and smoking a cigarette by the time Locklin returned.

Chapter Four

"Can you make the stairs?"

Ben looked at the steep long series of risers leading to a shadowed hallway above, and nodded. "Yes, sir, I can. Why?"

"Because"—Locklin smiled grimly—"I'm going to show you why I had you brought back. Follow me, Seth." He turned and headed up the staircase.

Ben slid a sideways look at Bettiger, Ribble, and Hoffs. They lounged in a block by the front door, appearing merely eased and waiting, but he knew they were there to cut off any escape attempt. Slowly, he followed his host.

Locklin turned left at the top of the stairs and led down the hall to one of the bedrooms, and Ben took the opportunity to scrutinize the man who would be his "father." He saw that Arch Locklin was about his own height and build, middle-aged, but not getting paunchy. There was something lean and hard about the man that even the elegant Eastern-style gray suit, vest, silk tie, starched white shirt, and polished black town shoes couldn't soften. The man looked like a banker, or perhaps like his imagined version of a Mississippi riverboat gambler, but certainly not like the owner and manager of a vast cattle ranch. Ben didn't know whether Locklin had dressed this way in honor of his daughter and her obviously back-East husband, or whether it was his usual garb, but the duds seemed entirely out of place out here on the plains.

Arch pushed the door open at the end of the hallway, stepped inside the room beyond, and paused to beckon to Ben. Hawthorne followed warily—not only did he appear to have no choice, but he would have had to confess to curiosity, had he been asked. He saw a plump, matronly gray-haired woman dressed in a high-necked plain blue dress, a white bib apron, and tiny white starched cap, rise from her rocking chair over by the window where she had sat doing needlepoint in the sunlight.

"This is David's nurse, Missus McPhee," Locklin murmured. "How is he today, Annie?"

"Same as usual, Mister Locklin. Nothing has changed."

Ben looked toward the bed and shock slammed into him. It was himself lying there . . . or the ghost of himself. He stared at the long, wasted limbs, the swaddling diaper, the skeletal ribs and collar bones exposed to ugly view by shrunken muscles and vanished flesh. The hands curled like dry fall leaves, occasionally twitching to some nervous response. But the face was *his* face . . . or would have been if he lost about fifty pounds.

He looked from the bed to Locklin in horror, gasped: "Who . . . ?"

"David. Your twin brother. When Medicine Shield took you from me at spear point, he said I had no need for two identical sons. He would claim one and I could keep the other." Locklin laughed morosely. "He said that was only fair . . . that I should pay him a son for the land I had stolen from him.

"Years later, you returned bringing Blue Glass Bead and that baby with you. I didn't kill what you called your wife and son, Seth. Blue Glass Bead merely went back of her own free will to Medicine Shield's tribe where she belonged. I know you blame me for it, but it wasn't my fault the squaw evidently lost her way, got caught by the blizzard, and froze to death. Yes, I admit I was distraught at you marrying a Kiowa woman . . . I mean, to name your half-breed offspring Arch was . . . did you think I would be honored?" Locklin's voice was rising. He started to continue, but then obviously caught himself, finishing softly: "But I didn't kill her or her son . . . Seth.

"When you rode out into the storm to try to find Blue Glass Bead and the baby, but then never returned, I thought you had located them and gone back to live with Medicine Shield. I resigned myself again to having only one son. When I heard that she and the child were dead, for a while I had hope that you would come back to me, but you never did. Still, I had David."

He indicated the figure on the bed. "About a year ago, he was out at branding time, roping cattle with the hands. From what the men told me, he got his loop on a particularly wild steer that jerked his horse off balance. The horse fell, threw him, and somehow, the lariat wrapped his neck. The steer got up. The pony got up. The horse kept the rope tight as he'd been trained to do, and by the time the other men could get to David, cut the lariat and free him, he was like this.

"He didn't die. He should have died. It would have been better for everyone, especially for him, if he *had* died there and then. But his heart just keeps beating. Just keeps on and on, and . . ."

Locklin sighed. "Priscilla has married Todd Nichols whom she met when she went to finishing school back in New York. He is a successful businessman there with neither the interest in running a ranch this size nor the know-how to do it if he wanted to.

"And so . . ."—Locklin shrugged—"I sent men to find you. Somehow, Seth, we have to work out our differences. You have to understand that I wasn't the cause of Blue Glass Bead's death, that . . ."

Locklin's voice faded in Ben's ears as he stared at the tragedy on the bed, but it wasn't the shock

47

of a man seeing what had befallen his brother that stunned him. He thought: *Twins?* Two look-alike men in the world, yes, that was possible. But the odds against there being *three,* one of them totally unrelated, all favoring each other so closely that a father accepted a stranger as his own son, no, that was unthinkable. True, Seth Locklin had been gone for five or more years, yet he doubted that anyone changed *that* much in such a short time.

Perhaps when he got cleaned up, shaved his beard, had his hair cut, maybe the resemblance wouldn't be so . . .

He turned to say again that he wasn't Seth Locklin, but suddenly recalled Reuben Bettiger and his cronies waiting downstairs. If he convinced Mr. Locklin he wasn't Seth, the bounty hunters would see him hung for a hold-up man, yet if he let this go on, Mr. Locklin would pay forty thousand dollars for a sham.

In abrupt urgency, he whirled to Locklin and whispered: "Mister Locklin, you're bein' cheated! I'm *not* your son! I may look like him, but I swear to you, sir, I'm Ben Hawthorne, *not* Seth! I'm sorry! I'm so sorry for you, but . . . but you gotta help me! Them bounty hunters say if you don't claim me and they don't get their money, they'll turn me in to the law for the reward on the Wanted poster, only I never did what the broadsheet says I done, Mister Locklin!

They got both you and me between an anvil and a hammer, sir! Please, you gotta listen to me, sir!"

Locklin's eyes narrowed. He chewed his lower lip in silence for a moment, studying the young man almost crouched before him. Presently, his eyes slid to the wreckage on the bed, also scrutinizing David before he shook his head slightly and murmured: "I know we . . . don't know each other very well, Seth. All those years you spent with the Kiowas . . . then, you were back only two months before Blue Glass Bead died . . . then, you were gone again. . . . In the last fifteen years, Seth, we have seen each other only two months. I . . . want the chance to start over with you . . . the chance to get to know you, man to man . . . the chance for you to get to know me as your friend as well as your father. Mister Bettiger explained what those men did to you, how long it went on, and I've seen the results with my own eyes. I know your mind is . . . confused . . . right now. Give it some time, Seth. I think everything will work out."

That man is so desperate for a son, Ben thought, *for anybody's son to call his own, that he is willing to pay all that money for a lie! He is buying another man's son!*

Stunned and uncertain what to do next, or perhaps as importantly, what not to do, Ben cast one more look at David. His eyes lingered for a long moment before he followed Locklin back

49

down the stairs to where Bettiger, Ribble, and Hoffs waited.

In a daze, Ben sat on the bottom step, hands folded between his knees, chains dangling, and merely listened while the man who would be his father said to Reuben: "Obviously, I don't keep that much cash on hand here at the ranch. It will take me a week or ten days to get it here. You men can lodge in the main bunkhouse, eat with the hands, and rest up from your long search until you get paid. Is that all right with you? Yes? Then, please ask Ruffian Bullock to come see me and I'll get you set up."

Reuben nodded toward Ben. "What about him, Mister Locklin? He seems a mite skittish. Maybe one or two of us should stay here in the big house with you to keep an eye on him for you."

Locklin also turned to look back at Ben. "No, I don't think that's necessary, Mister Bettiger. I think he understands everything, now."

Yes, I think he's right, Ben thought. *I think I do understand.*

Ben stood by the window in his darkened upstairs room, but didn't really see the outside green-lighted by the fattening moon because he mulled over what he had learned and what had happened this afternoon and evening. It had been almost as strange as the last few weeks.

He had been taken to the blacksmith to have

50

his chains removed—had to wait until the man named Cory had finished nailing the hind left shoe on the bay gelding he was refreshing.

Then he'd been escorted into the back of the big house to where servants—yes, Mr. Locklin employed servants—had filled a porcelain tub with good hot water. He had taken a long, satisfying bath and had scrubbed his hair with strong soap, but he had about died of embarrassment when one of the hired help, a girl named Midge, came in to pour clear water over his head to rinse him even while he still sat in the tub.

Mrs. McPhee, David's nurse, had arrived to see to his wounds. Then he'd dressed in fresh clothing, clean underings, a light-blue shirt, and black pants. He'd heard they were David's items. Problem was, everything fit him like they'd been made just for him.

Regis Young, Arch Locklin's resident barber, had shaved his beard for him and cut his hair, and when it was all over and he looked in a mirror, he'd hardly recognized himself. Thence, he'd sort of been presented to Mr. Locklin. The man had studied him closely, front and back, had finally nodded, smiled, and had said: "Welcome home, Seth. Come with me to meet your cowhands."

By now, it was pushing suppertime, and what cowpunchers weren't out on the ranges were gathered at the cook house waiting for their food.

Mr. Locklin had called for attention and had said here was his eldest son, Seth Phillip Locklin, the prodigal returned home to stay. Most of the hands there had seen him and the condition he was in when he was brought to the ranch, and all were wary. A few were downright guardedly hostile from the looks he'd seen them slide his way when Mr. Locklin's head was turned. Only a couple seemed inclined to be friendly. Still, all of them had agreed when Locklin said they were to honor Seth's orders like the words had come from his own mouth.

And then there was that dinner served by two uniformed girls with just him and Mr. Locklin eating in what appeared to be a formal dining room. Lord, he'd never seen such fine china, cut-crystal glasses, monogrammed cloth napkins, and gleaming silver in his life—Mrs. Inman would have given her starched petticoat for some of that to bring out on special occasions. Mrs. Inman always made a big to-do over occasions. Since he didn't remember when his birthday was, she had picked a day for him, May 1st, because none of her own seven children had been born then. She and Mr. Inman always had him into the house for a party on May 1st. They all knew it wasn't real, but it was the thought that counted.

He suffered a chill. Could he lay that same idea on Mr. Locklin? Did the man *know* he wasn't really Seth, but it was the thought of a son that counted? Should he himself merely say: If the clothes fit, wear them?

The problem was, the damned clothes *did* fit when they shouldn't have. He did look like the picture Bettiger had showed him. He did resemble poor, pitiful David lying in the bedroom down the hall—or would have, possibly, had David been well. Everyone in sight recognized him immediately as Seth Locklin. For all of that, he *knew* he was Ben Hawthorne. Didn't he?

There were answers here, somewhere, and he was going to find them. Abruptly, he knew how to do it.

He glanced around the darkened room, at the dresser and mirror, at the chairs, one of them a comfortable wingback, at the closed camel-back trunk over against the wall, then at the big four-poster bed with the quilt turned back and crisp cotton sheets glimmering in the moonlight. Mr. Locklin had said this room and everything in it was to be his. He shook his head. Tomorrow he would see what was in those dresser drawers over there, what was in the trunk, if anything. Perhaps whatever they contained would help him with his plan.

Refining in his mind what he was going to do and how to do it, he undressed and fell onto the softest bed he'd ever had the pleasure of meeting. Regardless of all this comfort, sleep was a long time in coming.

Chapter Five

"You seem . . . different this morning, Seth," Arch said over breakfast.

Ben paused, a forkful of flapjacks and eggs poised in mid-air, and looked up at the man who would be his father. He smiled. "Oh? How so, sir?"

"I don't know. Older, perhaps. Surer of yourself. More . . . in command."

Ben nodded. He finished his plate, washed the last bite down with a swallow of coffee, and leaned back in his chair; subdued a wince when wood met the wounds across his back. "Well, sir, I just spent six days in a hole in the ground at the mercy of some *hombres* who seemed determined to addle my brains with the help of some hot irons and a bullwhip, then four or so days in the saddle comin' on here. I suppose it takes a while to get over something like that. But I've had a bath, some doctorin', a couple of good meals, and a good night's sleep, and I figger I'm about back to my old self.

"So . . ."—he shoved his chair from the table and rose stiffly—"if you'll kindly show me around the place, I'll start earnin' my keep."

Arch lifted brows at him. "I can tell by the way you move that you're still hurting. Best you take it easy for a few more days. We don't have to rush things. Yes, I'll give you a tour to refresh your memory, but as for work . . ." Footsteps out in the hallway cut him off. He smiled. "Ah! Ruff. Come in, men."

Ben turned to see a stocky orange-haired and mustached cowhand standing in the doorway. The redhead was backed by the three bounty hunters and four of Locklin's own punchers. He recalled that Ruffian Bullock was Locklin's ramrod, watched in silence when Arch threw down his napkin, rose, and headed toward the door.

The men parted to let Arch pass when he said: "Follow me, gentlemen."

Out of curiosity, Ben also followed. Locklin led them to his office in the room across the hall from the living room, stepped to the desk, and picked up a sealed envelope. As he handed it to Ruff, he ordered: "Give this to Jeff Yarboro in town, then get yourselves rooms at the boarding house or hotel, and wait until he sends for you. Then, you deliver the package he gives you back here to me, unopened, you understand, Ruff?"

The redhead nodded. "Yes, sir, I do."

"This will take a few days to complete. Here is expense money." Arch produced a key from his vest pocket, unlocked a desk drawer, and brought out a leather poke. He began counting coins into Bullock's hand. "A hundred ought to do it. You have to spend more, let me know when you get back and I'll settle with you. I'm trusting in you to do this right for me, Ruff."

"You can count on us, Mister Locklin," Bullock asserted strongly while he pocketed the money.

"Besides," Reuben Bettiger broke in, "me and Mister Hoffs are ridin' along to . . . protect our interests."

Arch's brows lifted. "As you wish, of course, Mister Bettiger. Understand, though, that the expense money I gave Ruffian is for my men's keep, not yours. Uh . . . and what is Mister Ribble going to do while you're gone?"

Bettiger turned to stare at Ribble. "Ev is . . . feelin' poorly. If it's all the same to you, he'll rest up here."

Bettiger is going to keep an eye on the money, Hoffs is keeping a look-out on Bettiger, and Ribble is here to ride herd on me. They still think I'm going to run at my first opportunity and they might lose the bounty. Ben subdued a morose smile. Good. It all played right in with his own plan.

Locklin nodded. "Yes, that's fine. Mister Ribble can stay in the bunkhouse. Ruff, you and your boys had better hit the trail. Who have you assigned to take your place while you're gone?"

"Dallas Youngstreet." The envelope rattled when Bullock flung up his hand to stifle Arch's protest. "I know! I know he's a hot-headed son-of-a-bitch, Mister Locklin, but he knows his business and the men respect him. He cain't do you too much harm in eight or ten days, and I'm hopin' a li'l responsibility will settle the kid down."

"Well, you handle the men, Ruff, it's your call. Have a safe ride and we'll see you when you get back. And Ruff . . ."—Arch reached to squeeze fingers strongly around Bullock's upper arm—"take *very* good care of the package you're bringing back, understand me?"

"Yes, sir." Ruff nodded to Locklin, to Ben, then turned toward the door. "Come on, men, let's get at it."

Locklin also turned away. He said to Ben: "Go pick yourself a horse that strikes you, Son. I'll put on some riding britches, meet you at the corral, and then we'll take a turn around the spread." He headed for the stairs.

Ben moved toward the front door, with Ribble hard on his heels—he could smell the whiskey the man breathed at his back; evidently, Everett had started the day with hair of last evening's dog. As he stepped off the porch and angled across the yard toward the stables and horse corrals, he turned to look at Ribble. "Sorry to hear you're under the weather."

"I don't feel that bad," Ribble snapped. "Just ain't up to a long ride."

"Uhn-huh." Ben kept walking, scrutinizing the area. Several cowhands were mounted preparatory to heading out onto the range. Over yonder, Ruffian Bullock and his men, followed closely by Reuben Bettiger and Al Hoffs, spurred their horses east. Far off to the west, a ridge of broken cliff faces preceded the range of low hills breaking vast expanses of rolling prairie, and from it coursed the tree-lined creek.

He hailed a lone man striding from the stables toward the bunkhouses, and said: "*Hola, amigo.* Hold up a minute. I'm lookin' for Dallas . . . uh . . . Youngstreet."

The man was perhaps an inch taller than he, and about his own age. He had dark brown hair flopped over his forehead from beneath his hat as though he purposely let the forelock hang to charm the ladies, but his boyish look was spoiled by the hard glitter in his hazel eyes and the double gun belt supporting a weapon on each hip. He halted and scowled at Ben. "You found him."

"I'm . . . Seth Locklin. . . ." Somehow, it was hard for Ben to say that.

Youngstreet said curtly: "I know who you are. What d'you want?"

"I need a horse. Would you . . ."

"I don't do no favors for no squawman." Youngstreet turned on his heel and walked on.

Ben and Ribble watched Dallas go.

Ev murmured: "Looks like you got a problem brewin', Son. What you gonna do about that?"

Ben gritted his teeth. He wasn't packing iron.

He was still slow and some weakened from what he'd suffered through the last few days, and he figured now was not yet the time to take issue with much of anything. He drew a deep breath and shook his head. "Nothin' . . . yet. I'll pick my own moment, and my own mount, I guess. I just didn't want to settle on somebody else's personal property." He continued toward the corral.

He selected a dark dappled gray mare with generous ears announcing a pleasing personality, and whose compact quarter horse frame promised strength and speed, picked a lariat from where it hung over a fence post, got his loop on the mare first throw, and knew from the general silence around him that everyone watched him. As he led the mare toward the corral gate, one of the cowhands opened it and grinned at him.

"Howdy, Mister Locklin. I'm Fred Perkins. If you don't recall, I can show you where the saddles and the like are."

So! Not all Locklin's hands resented him. That was a relief. Ben returned Perkins's grin and said: "Much obliged, Fred. And just call me . . . Seth. Uh . . . Mister Locklin'll be here shortly, if you need to rig his horse for him." He led the mare through the gate and had just turned toward the stable when hurrying footsteps barely warned him, someone rushed up behind him.

The lariat coils were yanked from his hands. The mare snorted and tossed her head when Ben whirled to see Dallas Youngstreet glowering at him.

Youngstreet snarled: "Violet is Mister David's mount, squawman. Git yourself a different horse."

Ben's eyes narrowed. He glanced around at the other punchers watching frankly, and knew if he backed down now . . . He said: "Mister David isn't usin' her at the moment, and it's . . . all in the family, Mister Youngstreet. I'll thank you kindly to hand her over." He reached for the lariat.

Youngstreet shoved him back. The heel of his palm hit one of the deep yet-unhealed burns on Hawthorne's chest, and the sudden pain of it almost sent Ben to his knees. Breathless for a moment, he clutched a hand over the wound, the other braced against his thigh, and waited until things eased.

None of the general punchers knew what his problem was, but Dallas curled his lip briefly before leading Violet back to the corral. He stopped abruptly when a voice snapped: "Halt right where you are, Dallas!"

Youngstreet jerked around to see Arch Locklin behind him.

Locklin scowled at Ben. "Seth, are you all right?"

Hawthorne straightened with an effort, and nodded. "Yes, sir. I'm . . . fine. Thank you."

Arch looked back at Youngstreet. "What's the problem here, Dallas?"

"He was fixin' to use Mister David's mare, Violet, Mister Locklin. I was just . . . gettin' him a different horse, that's all."

Locklin's brows rose. "You have some objection to Seth riding his brother's mount?"

"Yes, sir, I do!" Dallas said hotly. "Mister David raised Violet up from a filly, you know that, sir! Nobody but Mister David ever rode her. He'll be back in the saddle one of these days, and . . ."

"Dallas . . ."—Arch scowled—"David will never ride Violet again, I know that and you know that. I'm giving her to Seth."

"Mister Locklin, it takes a man to do right by this mare, not some faint-heart like him." Youngstreet indicated Ben. "I mean, I merely put my hand on him and he like to fainted! He could ruin Violet for Mister David, sir! Lemme get him a different . . ."

Abruptly, Ben witnessed another side to the man who appeared on the surface to be soft-spoken, well-educated, and Eastern-civilized. Arch's tone became icy when he snapped: "Silence!"

Youngstreet shut up in mid-sentence.

Locklin continued in the same glacial voice: "So you think Seth is a weakling? . . . that you merely touched him and he almost passed out?" Arch turned to look at Ben. There was a smudge of blood staining the front of the blue shirt. "Seth, open your shirt."

Ben glanced around at the cowpokes watching and listening curiously, slid a glance at Ribble merely leaning an elbow on a fence rail, and didn't want to do it. He began: "Uh . . . sir . . . I'm all right. There's no need to . . ."

"Yes, there is! I told you to open your shirt. Obey me!"

Ribble's lips pursed below round eyes when Ben stiffened and shook his head slightly.

Hawthorne looked equally narrow-eyed at the expression of cold unyielding command on Arch Locklin's face and thought: *No wonder Seth left rather than argue with him!* Mouth as grim as Locklin's, he finally nodded, unbuttoned the front of his shirt, and shoved the sides back. He stood with head up, and met Youngstreet's eyes when the man's mouth dropped open. The burn Dallas's palm had struck on Ben's chest showed a line of blood at the bottom where the blow had slipped the fragile scab from its seat.

Feeling like a Negro slave on an auction block, Ben asked coolly of Arch: "Enough, sir?"

"Yes, Seth, you can secure your shirt." Locklin again speared Youngstreet with dark eyes. "If you had been used like he has been used recently, you might also give the appearance of weakness. None of you . . . especially not you, Dallas . . . will touch Seth until he is ready to take you on, understand me? It'll be his call, not yours, do I make myself clear? Now, Dallas, saddle Violet for him."

"Yes, sir, Mister Locklin. Sorry, Mister Locklin, I didn't mean no offense here." Quickly, Youngstreet led the mare onward.

The other men went about their business hurriedly when Ben and Arch again headed for the stables. Grinning wryly, Ribble followed.

Locklin Ranch was twenty thousand acres of prime grassland grazing vast cattle herds. Ben didn't get to see all of it, but what he and Arch—and Ev Ribble—covered before noon was impressive enough. That Locklin was proud of his spread was more than evident; he spoke to Hawthorne of empires and bloodlines, both animal and human.

They had begun their ride eastward, had made a wide northwestern circle, and then had started following Runoff Creek back to the ranch house when a bullet sang past Ben's ear. He, Arch, and Ribble reined in to see a young woman, her smoking rifle in one hand, followed by four men as she rode out of the west toward them.

Ben asked: "Isn't that the hot-blooded filly that busted into your house yesterday, sir?"

"Yes. Caitlan Black. Let me handle this, Seth." Arch merely sat his bay gelding, Tomahawk, and scowled toward the riders until they were close enough that he didn't have to yell. When they reined in a few yards off, he asked: "Was that your way of inviting us to eat lunch with you, Cat, or had we strayed across your line?"

Her face was flushed, her hair unbraided this morning and blowing in all directions. Today, she wore a split riding skirt instead of men's pants, and a red shirt tucked into a wide, tooled leather belt, but no gun belt. She answered: "*You* haven't, Locklin, but two of your men did, and I sent them home with a couple of nicks to show them I was serious about their trespassing. I . . ."

"You shot two of my men? Today?"

"Yes, today! This morning! How come you don't know about it?"

"Seth and I have been touring the spread since right after breakfast. How badly are they hurt?"

"Not very. I merely grazed them. I made sure they were only pinked, but now maybe you'll accept that I'm serious when I say that . . ."

"Damn it, Caitlan, we're neighbors! Our families settled this area together! Your father was my best friend! Why won't you work with me to settle this amicably? I don't want things to fester into a feud that will only get a bunch of people killed!"

"I tried!" she flared. "You know I have tried, but you won't give an inch, Arch Locklin! Now, it's on your own head! Today, we just grazed your men. It happens again, they won't be so lucky! Remember that!" She whirled her mount and, followed by her hands, pounded back westward toward where Ben could see a low ranch house, barns, and corrals nestled at the foot of the brief cliff ridge perhaps a mile away.

He looked at Locklin when Arch breathed: "This whole thing will escalate into real bloodshed if that girl doesn't see reason, and soon!"

"What's the problem, sir?" Ben urged Violet after Locklin.

"The problem is water, Seth. You know that has always been the issue, even when the Black Cat's folks were still alive . . . even when her brother Frank ran their place."

"But, sir, you have water." Ben gestured toward Runoff Creek at their right as they headed east.

"Not enough. Some, yes, what with the creek and a few dug wells, but not enough. I have offered to buy, rent, lease, you name it, to gain greater access to Bountiful Spring, but she has always said no. Now, it may move from just a problem into outright war. God, but I don't want a war!" He spurred his gelding homeward.

Chapter Six

Ben sat in the chair beside the bed and studied David. Mrs. McPhee stood on the other side with a cool damp washcloth in her plump hands. Though all the windows were open, it was stiflingly hot in the room—the place stank of soiled diapers and wasting flesh. Even wearing nothing but the loincloth, David ran with sweat. So did the nurse. So did Ben.

He reached to take David's hand and discovered it wasn't limp, as he had expected, but frozen into a claw. It shocked him so, he almost dropped it.

He said softly: "David . . . David, can you hear me? It's your . . . brother Seth talkin' to you."

Nothing happened. There was no response. The eyes didn't even turn toward the sound of his voice.

He shook his head and rose, asked of Mrs. McPhee: "Will he always be like this? He'll never come out of it?"

"Mister Locklin brought famous doctors all the way from back East, Mister Seth. They said Mister David is . . . dead . . . only his heart just hasn't stopped yet. They said there was nothing to do for him but wait." Annie dabbed at David's brow with the cloth, mopped sweat from where it pooled in the livid scar marring the throat where—a year or more ago—rope had cut deeply into flesh.

Ben nodded. He bent closer over the bed, said: "David, Mister Locklin let me ride Violet today. If it's all the same to you, I'll cl-claim her as my own. I'll take real good care of her for you . . . won't let anybody else ride her. Won't let anybody abuse her. She'll be fine with me. The Injuns taught me how to gentle and respect a horse, David, so you know she'll be . . . in good hands."

There was still nothing from David. Ben put the hand back onto the collar bone where it seemed preferable to be and looked at the nurse. "Thank you, ma'am. Take good care of him, now."

"I always do, Mister Seth."

Ben sighed, turned toward the bedroom door, and was startled to see Arch Locklin standing there. "Oh! Sir! You surprised me!"

Arch smiled slightly. His eyes moved from Ben to David and back before he said: "That was . . . kind of you, Seth. We don't know whether he . . ."—his brow indicated David—"can hear and understand or not, but if he can, you have settled his mind about Violet. Thank you."

Ben cast a quick look back at the bed. "I hope so, sir. A man's horse is an important friend. She's safe with me. Uh . . . did the doctors say how long he would be like that?"

"No. But I doubt he will suffer much longer."
Locklin turned abruptly and walked away.

Ben picked a bottle of fine whiskey out of the
carved wood and etched-glass cabinet in Arch's
study, went out the front door of the big house,
across the porch, down the steps, and passed
onward toward the bunkhouses. It was evening,
late. A few hands lounged smoking and trading
stories in the hot twilight. He tipped a finger to
them, asked: "Any of you gents seen Everett
Ribble?"

"Don't know him," one answered.

"He's that leftover bounty hunter who brought
me in the other day."

"Oh. Last I seen him, he was at the cook
shack."

"Thank you." Ben angled toward the side
building.

"Hey, squawman, ain't you goin' to share some
of that booze you're carryin' with us?"

Ben stiffened at the squawman naming,
but forced a smile, turned, and said: "Later,
maybe. Thanks for the invitation." He turned
again and walked on. The squawman appellation
was beginning to rankle. One of these days . . .
But not tonight. He had other things to do
tonight.

He found Ribble sitting alone at the head of a
table in one corner of the dining room, drooped

over a ninety-percent empty bottle, his chin in a palm, eyes sad.

"Hey, Ev, you look like you lost your last friend, and you've nearly killed off that there bottle." Ben straddled the long bench, set the full flask he carried beside Ribble's, and leaned an elbow on the table top.

Everett cast a sour look at him. "I got another in my saddlebags. What you want, boy?"

"Just some company. Mister Locklin's men don't take to me yet. Mister Locklin himself is a mite . . . rich for my blood. . . ."

"Rich is right." Ribble's eyes settled on the fresh bottle. "Ain't decent to be that rich."

Ben nodded to the whiskey. "No reason why we shouldn't enjoy a little of his leftovers. I brought that from his personal supply. You seem to be a real discriminatin' man, try a swig and let me know what you think of it."

"Don't mind if I do." Ribble reached for the bottle, opened it, and tipped it. His eyes widened below raised brows. He wiped the back of his hand across his mouth before he gasped: "Oh, now, that's just about the finest reviver I ever laid lips on." He thrust the bottle at Ben.

Hawthorne grinned, nodded, took the whiskey, and tipped it. He sealed the opening with his tongue but worked his throat as though swallowing, before handing the bottle back to

Ev. He said: "Boy, you're right! That's real good stuff."

"Your daddy know you snagged this?" Ribble tipped the bottle.

Ben shrugged. "Don't know. Don't care, really. What's he gonna do, slap my little hand?"

Ev laughed and took another swallow.

" 'Cides," Ben went on, "you gotta have some reward for stayin' behind to keep an eye on me while ol' Reuben and ol' Al go off gettin' your money."

Everett nodded, and sipped.

"You know," Ben murmured, "this whole affair turned out real good, didn't it. I'm amazed at how good it has got."

"What d'ya mean by that?"

Ben spread his hands. "Well, look at what we have here, would you. You and Bettiger and Hoffs, you did your job and are gettin' paid enough to live like kings off the reward money for the rest of your borned days, so you're happy, right? Mister Locklin, he's got a healthy son back, so he's happy, right? I got a life of ease as the boy of some rich bugger, a ranch that goes on forever, and herds that won't quit, so I'm happy, right? Gimme another nip of that good booze, Ev, you're hoggin' it."

Ribble had gone narrow-eyed and wary, but he handed the bottle over. Ben tipped it, again only pretended to swallow. When he set the bottle down, Ev snagged it and asked: "You mean you finally got it through your head that you're Seth Locklin?"

Ben grinned. He cast a quick look around the shack before he leaned a little closer to Ribble and murmured: "Hell, I don't care if I am or I ain't. Now that I've seen what I got here, I'd be a damned fool to argue. I mean, like I said, everybody's happy . . . I ain't one to spit good fortune in the eye, I'll tell you. I ain't that stupid!"

Ribble pulled at the bottle. "So you're gonna just settle in here and say 'Yes, daddy' to ol' Locklin's 'Howdy, Son'?"

"You better believe it, Ev, ol' friend!" Ben leaned a little closer, lowered his voice to a whisper. "But tell me, Ev, how come you and Reuben and so on settled on me? I mean . . ."

Ribble tipped the bottle and humor sparkled in his blue eyes. He also glanced around the room before his breath nearly blasted Hawthorne off the bench when he chuckled. "Shit, I tell ya, we'd looked more'n six months, y'know? I mean, it was gettin' to be a lost cause. Hell, we even looked in a passel of redskin villages in case Seth'd gone back to the damned Injuns. Then, one day down in Texas, we seen you out ridin' herd, and ol' Reuben, he says . . . 'There he is! . . . and if it ain't him, it's good 'nough!'" He shrugged. "Didn't matter by this time you was or

71

wasn't, 'cuz, by damn, you look 'nough like that picture to pass."

"I know. Gives me gooseflesh. I don't understand that at all. Who were those men who had me in the . . ." Ben almost flinched under a flash of rusty bars, chains, smoldering irons, whips, and voices shouting the same words over and over . . . himself saying the same words over and over. He shuddered the vision away and finished: ". . . in the hole?"

At this, Everett laughed and slapped Hawthorne's arm. "Jus' three hands from the Wharton Ranch. Ol' Reuben hired 'em. Ol' Reuben, now, he's a smart one, he is!" Ribble tapped a forefinger against his right nostril; he was more than slightly drunk by now. "He says, O.K., we found the bastard. S'pose he knows he's somebody else? I mean, a man knows who he is, right?"

Not always, Ben thought.

Ev tipped the bottle—the whiskey inside was almost half gone by now, though Hawthorne hadn't drank any of it—swallowed, and again glanced around the room. "Ol' Rube, he says, what we gotta do is make that poor bastard think he's somebody else bein' made into himself, right? . . . so when we tell him he is somebody else, he'll take to it, right? So, he goes and has that Wanted poster printed up . . ."

"He did that?" Ben blurted.

"Yeah, he had the poster printed. Cost him a whole five dollahs for just one broadsheet! A whole five dollahs."

"Why?"

"He used it to convince them cowpokes they was convincin' you to be you so's we could collect on the reward money s'posedly up on you. Hee-hee!" Ev hit the table top with a fist, appreciating the ploy.

"I knew I never held up some bank or killed women." Ben heaved a sigh of relief. Actually, after all this, he hadn't been quite sure. "And there's only that one poster?"

"Yep. Only one. Ol' Rube, he showed it to them Wharton men and offered 'em a hundred dollahs each to make you think you was you and that you done it. Oh, they got paid, all right, didn't they. Yep, they got paid. Deader than a fence post.

"But we damned near waited too long to rescue you. We never expected them *hombres* to be so . . . I guess you could call it . . . enthusiastic in their work. They like to killed you."

Almost, but not quite. "Then, I'm really Ben Hawthorne?"

"Hell, who knows? You could be anybody! But who gives a shit, y'know?"

"Yeah." Ben slid a look out the open cook-shack door into the yard. It was getting dark outside. The evening of his first full day as Seth Locklin.

He turned back to Ribble. "How come, in all the time I was down in that root cellar, no one from the house came to get vittles and saw me in that cage?"

"Aw, hell, I tol' ya ol' Bettiger was a smart one. One of them *hombres* was the biscuit shooter, y'know? From what I hear, Miz Wharton, she's poorly. 'Course, Mister Wharton, he's got the ranch to occupy him . . . he don't never go into no root cellar. That left nobody but the cook and the other two, and they was in on it, y'know."

Ben nodded. "Makes sense to me. Well, we got a good thing goin' here, Ev. Let's be careful not to spoil it. Gimme that bottle . . . I want one for the trail. I guess I gotta get back to the big house, else my daddy take offense."

Ribble laughed in tipsy appreciation of that and handed over the bottle. This time, Ben truly swallowed, and the whiskey was smooth and hot against his throat. He set what was left in front of the bounty hunter and rose. "Keep it, Ev. The old man has got lots where that come from. And you don't have to ride herd on me fearin' I'm gonna ruin our good luck.

"Oh, by the way, how you feelin' tonight? Bettiger said you was ailin', and I thought for a while they'd poisoned you like they done Murry Harding."

Ev shook his head. "Naw, I feel fine. That was just so's I could keep eyes on . . ." The eyes in

74

question widened. "What d'ya mean, pizened me like they done Murry!"

Ben shot him a puzzled look. "You mean you didn't *know* Harding was poisoned?"

"No! No! What makes you think . . . he died of a heart seizure or somethin'! Din't he?"

"Hell, no! It was water hemlock in something he ate or drank, most likely in his coffee, since Hoffs conveniently lost the pot in the river!"

"No!" Ribble gasped. "H-How d'ya know that?"

"Aw, Ev, come on! I was raised by the Injuns! My people know all about roots and berries, nuts and plants, what's good to eat off the land and what'll kill you quick or slow. I recognized the symptoms when Harding passed on. Water hemlock, sure as shootin'."

"But why? Why?"

"My God, man, use your head! You said Bettiger hired those three Wharton men for a hundred bucks each, then paid 'em off in bullets. You and Reuben, Al and Murry come after me for forty thousand dollars. Now, there's only three of you to divide up that money. Or . . ."—he raised brows—"maybe only two? I wonder if that forty thousand will ever make it here from wherever it's comin' from. Forty thousand split two ways is twenty apiece for Reuben and Al . . . if ol' Al don't have some kind of accident between here and there. Well, I gotta get into the house. Gotta look after my own good fortune, don't I. G' night, Ev. See you tomorrow."

Ben walked out into the early night leaving Ribble clutching what was left of the bottle of fine whiskey, hurried toward the big house, and was satisfied that he had gained at least some answers to the many questions that harassed him.

He wasn't wanted for bank robbery and murder.

The hooded men had been hired by Bettiger to purposely addle his brains preparatory to palming him off onto Arch Locklin as his son.

Ev Ribble obviously hadn't known about the possible poison that killed Murry Harding, which meant either Bettiger or Hoffs had done it, most likely Hoffs, since he had dumped the coffee pot.

The bounty hunters had picked him at random out of desperation because they hadn't been able to find the real Seth Locklin, which meant he was Ben Hawthorne.

Still, he could accept the twins . . . Seth and David . . . being identical to each other, but that he, a total stranger, looked enough like those two that even their sister and a neighbor—never mind Arch, since he evidently had his own reason to accept him—took one look at him and welcomed him home as Seth . . . no, that was still too much. Too much. That was the primary question, and it had yet to be settled.

He found Arch sitting in a chair, his heels

76

propped on the porch railing, smoking in the dark, and hesitated beside him. "Good evening, sir."

"Good evening, Son. Been out?"

"Yes, sir. I had a drink in the cook shack with Mister Ribble. Took him a bottle from your fine whiskey cabinet . . . I'll work the price off, if you'd like, sir."

"Not necessary. Why were you drinking with him and not with the men?"

"The . . . hands . . . haven't gotten used to me yet, sir, and I don't want to push them. Let them come around to me. Besides, I was . . . thankin' Mister Ribble for his part in rescuin' me from those men who had me."

"Good of you, Seth. You like your liquor?"

"No, sir, I guess I never developed much of a taste for it. Oh, I will take a drink now and then . . . I ain't a teetotaler . . . but then, it's generally just one to be sociable."

"Wise. That's wise." Arch's cigar tip glowed brightly when he puffed. Finally, he said: "You know, your mother and I used to sit here many a summer evening just like this . . . before she died." He sighed heavily and rose. Turned toward the front door. "I still miss her. Do you remember your mother, Seth?"

Ben said: "No, sir. I'm really sorry, but I don't. What . . . what was her name?"

He went cold and had to grab at the porch post

for support when Arch answered softly: "Her name was Cora, Seth. Good night."

Ben Hawthorne's mother's name was Cora. Cora Hawthorne. Cora Locklin? No! NO!

Mind spinning, Ben also entered the house. He moved up the stairs and fell onto his bed, belly down, his face buried in the goose-down pillow.

Cora Locklin?

No!

Chapter Seven

Ben awoke feeling as hung over as he would have had he downed half the bottle of whiskey along with Ev Ribble—it wasn't what he'd drank or not that had ruined his night's sleep, it was Arch Locklin's parting words to him before he went to bed last night.

After his conversation with Ribble, and now that he knew what had happened to him and why, he'd almost settled on his real identity. Certainly, some questions still remained, but for the most part, he had begun to be more comfortable . . .

. . . until Arch had hit him with the name Cora.

He had to get out of here! . . . not run, but merely to be by himself for a while. No, come to think of it, he had been alone all night, and it hadn't helped.

Gritting his teeth, and in a near desperation to get his thoughts onto some other subject, he flung back the sheet, leaped out of bed, and slid into the pants he'd worn yesterday. Barefoot and shirtless, he stood for a moment staring at himself in the dressing table mirror. God, he was going to have some real ugly scars shortly—but his wounds seemed to be healing well.

He stepped to the dresser and opened a drawer. Empty. So was the next drawer, and the next. The closet was also barren of anything but a dowel and three unoccupied wooden hangers, but the camel-back chest was a different matter.

Neatly folded beneath a bib of white bones and porcupine quills lay a long, soft, leather loin-cloth, fringed and painted shirt, equally-fringed leggings, and moccasins—by their elegance, ceremonial clothing, the kind a warrior would wear to an important council or other meeting. A golden eagle feather was tucked along the right side of the trunk wall between the clothing and the wood. Slantwise from corner to corner, lay a lance, its haft broken into three pieces.

Ben gently fingered the trunk contents, knowing without being told that these had once belonged to Seth Locklin. Evidently, wherever Seth had gone, he had been wearing white man's clothes at the time.

He sighed, closed the trunk lid, and stepped to where his shirt hung over the back of a chair. He looked through the window out into the yard while he shrugged into the cloth—sight of the Indian garb had brought memories back of the freedom of merely wearing a loincloth and soft moccasins; the shirt, britches, underings, and boots seemed awkward and confining.

Oh, well. He finished dressing and ran fingers through his hair to comb it back. Another glance in the mirror showed pale morning stubble, the bane of his "hairy lips" heritage. No matter. He would . . .

Two sharp knocks preceded the door opening. "Good morning, Son."

Ben looked toward the hall door to see Arch Locklin standing there. Damn! Now, he supposed he would have to breakfast with Mr. Locklin. Make chit-chat. Smile, and . . . He swallowed, firmed his shoulders, and forced that smile. "Sir. I hope you slept well."

"As well as usual, or as poorly as ever, however you want to look at it. Come, eat with me."

Ben began: "Sir, I . . ."

"I said come eat with . . ." Arch shut teeth with an audible snap. He took a deep breath and grinned wryly. "I'm sorry. I promised myself I wouldn't do that to you this time. My . . . inflexibility was part of what drove you away before.

"Seth, it would pleasure me a great deal if you would share breakfast with me this morning. After all, we have a lot of lost time to make up. Now that you're recovering, I want to hear what you have been doing these past five years. All of it, so we can get to know each other. It's important that we accomplish that, isn't it?"

Resigned to it, Ben nodded. "Yes, sir, it is. It'd also be my pleasure, sir."

"For God's sake, stop calling me sir! I'm your father, Seth."

81

Ben nodded but made no comment, followed Locklin down the stairs and toward the dining room. He wondered what he could call Arch, if not sir. Mister Locklin probably wouldn't pass. They were definitely not on a first-name basis; therefore, Arch wouldn't do—and he wasn't yet ready to call the man father. Not even dad or pa. He decided he could work around it and just not call Locklin anything for a while until he settled things in his mind.

They had sat at the table and had been served hot corn pudding, eggs, and biscuits, when Dallas Youngstreet, hat in hand, appeared at the dining room door and cleared his throat.

Locklin said: "Come in, Dallas. Care for a cup of coffee?"

"Uh . . . no, sir, thank you kindly. Uh . . . I know it's real early in the mornin', Mistuh Locklin, but we got a problem brewin' that I'd like to clear with you before I take action."

Arch spooned corn pudding and nodded. "Out with it."

"It's about what happened at the west line yesterday, Mistuh Locklin." Youngstreet hawked his throat again, slid a look at Ben listening silently while he ate, then looked back at Arch and blurted hotly: "Them varmints over at the Black spread seem to have been given a free hand by that bit- . . . uh . . . by the Black Cat to blast away at anybody that even comes within a half mile of the border, Mistuh Locklin. You seen Buck and Harve yesterday! Yeah, I'll admit they was only grazed, not serious wounded, but that ain't the point! Point is, we got a critter meanderin' near the Cat's propity line, we can't even haze it back else we get shot at! We gotta go do something about it, Mistuh Locklin. The boys and me been talkin' it over. Let me take some of our men over there and teach them horse wranglers they can't fire on us and get away with it!"

Arch sipped coffee. "Blow them off the land?"

"Yes, sir, if it comes to that, yes, sir! It ain't right what that female is doin', Mistuh Locklin. She hoards Bountiful Spring water, we oughta just go on over there and take it! I mean . . ."

"Caitlan Black isn't hoarding water, Dallas, she just isn't letting us onto her land to use more than she already gives us."

"Yeah, and that ain't right! We need what we need, you know that, sir. She . . ."

"No, Dallas. You're not to go onto Miss Black's spread. However, from now on, if the Cat's punchers fire on you while you're still on my land, I give you permission to defend yourselves. All right? Good enough?"

"No, sir! By the time one of my men gets a bullet in his gizzard, it's too damned late to . . ."

"That's my decision for now, Dallas." Locklin's tone had grown cold and hard, brooking no argument. "If I change my mind, I'll let you know. Is there anything else?"

"Uh . . . no, sir. But I think you're makin' a mistake! Mistuh Locklin, the men are gonna start quittin' on us, if they can't do their work without gettin' plugged by somebody sittin' just on the other side of some imaginary line shootin' at them! You . . ."

"Mister Youngstreet." Arch pushed his plate aside, leaned back in his chair, produced a cigar, bit off the end, and fished the nub from his tongue. He lay the tobacco on his plate, and Ben's brows rose when Locklin asked, very quietly now: "Are you arguing with me?"

Better not, fella, Hawthorne thought. He slid a look between Arch and the puncher.

Dallas shifted from foot to foot. Red had crept up his neck into his jaws. He said: "No, of course not, Mistuh Locklin. It's just that . . ."

"Then, if you aren't arguing, why are you still standing there? You have work to do, don't you? . . . for which I pay you very well."

"Yeah, but the men . . ."

"One more word, and you can pack your gear, Dallas."

Youngstreet choked, shot a glare from Locklin to Ben, eyeing him frankly, swallowed, and muttered: "Yes, sir." He turned on his heel and left.

Arch shook his head, his expression now grim.

He muttered: "I don't want war! Caitlan Black's men shooting at mine . . . my men firing back . . . Damn!"

Ben heaved a heavy breath and flung down his napkin. He guessed it was time to get involved. Besides, if Arch agreed, it would give him that opportunity to get away for a while. He said: "If you'll excuse me, sir . . . uh . . . sorry . . . uh . . . I think I'll take a ride on over and visit Miss Black."

Arch's eyes narrowed. "No, you're not up to that yet."

"Yes, I am. Missus McPhee looked at me last evenin' and she says I'm comin' along fine. Everything is healin' up with no problem. 'Cides, the ride will do me good. It's only about three miles over there, right?"

"Yes, but what makes you think they won't shoot you as quick as any of my men?"

Ben shrugged. "Well, if I ride in unarmed and grabbin' sky, I doubt they'll do me serious damage. In any case, it seems I recall that when Miss Black came stormin' in here the other day, she said something about me bein' an . . ."—he grinned—"honorable man. We'll just see if her estimation of my character holds up or not."

"And what do you hope to accomplish while you're there?"

"I want to get a feel for the lay of the land. Find out what all this fuss is really about and see if we can figger a way to fix things before any real shootin' starts. That's all."

Arch sucked on the cigar for a long moment before he nodded. "We've tried everything else. I guess it can't hurt. Uh . . . you will come back home, won't you?"

Ben started to spout a heated retort, but stopped himself before the words left his mouth. He said evenly: "Yes . . . sir . . . I will. I'm not goin' to run off."

"Sorry, Son. I . . . had to ask. I'll get a couple of the men to go with you. In case you run into trouble, you may need backup."

"No, sir. I'll go alone or not at all."

"You're calling me sir again."

"You're askin' for it, sir. You treat me like a proper man, I'll treat you like a proper . . . father. Until then, it'll be sir, sir."

Arch's lips bent to a small smile. He studied Ben for a long, intense moment before he nodded. "You've made your point, Son. Have a nice ride and please report back to me when you return."

"I'll do that. I should be back by noon, unless Miss Black invites me to lunch with her . . . in which case, I will do it." Hawthorne rose and headed for the corral to get Violet.

Arch sat alone at the table and finished his cigar before he went out onto the porch and stood leaning against a post. It would be another hot, dry late-July afternoon, but the morning was clear and fresh.

When he saw Ben ride out, he stepped off the porch and walked toward the bunkhouse. He hailed two cowhands, ordered: "Saddle up and follow Seth. Stay far enough away that he won't notice you, but keep an eye on him. If he heads anywhere but to the Black spread or straight back here, stop him, and see to it he comes home."

Ben rode westward along Runoff Creek and studied the stream as he went. It had carved a permanent channel long enough ago that mature trees lined its banks. Occasionally, a barren, hoof-scarred bar showed where cattle drank and where fording to the south range was easy. Water seemed low in the creekbed now, but then, this was mid-July and in the heat of the summer. He was wondering how much lower it would be come August or September when he abruptly blinked with surprise.

The vision . . . memory . . . of children playing in a tree-shaded swimming hole, three boys and two girls, one tow-headed, the rest dark, had flashed so briefly behind his eyes that he hadn't been able to catch who they were, only hear the echoes of laughter. They had been having fun while his Indian mother, Gray Dove, sat on the bank and watched while she stitched a leather shirt for Nighthorse.

But that was a Comanche, not a Kiowa memory, he could tell by Gray Dove's dress and by the cinnabar face paint that bespoke her hope of warriors returning in victory from their present raid. Yet Gray Dove spoke two languages to the children. What . . . ?

He shook his head and glanced at his back trail. He was being followed. The men kept well arrears, but they were coming along.

So much for Arch taking him at his word. Well, let them waste their time; he wasn't going to head for parts unknown, at least not today. Things were too curious around here. If he left before he got the answers to all his questions, those questions would haunt him for the rest of his life.

He returned to studying the creek. Under him, Violet was strong and gentle; David had done a good job with her. He was briefly distracted by thoughts of David, wondering what kind of a brotherly relationship Seth and David had had before the Indians had taken off with Seth. Had they been inseparable twins or had there been such rivalry between them that David had been happy to see him . . . no, Seth . . . go? He would have to ask Mister Locklin about it someday when the time was ripe.

He didn't see any boundary markers, but because the house, barns, and all of the ranch seemed to be less than a mile or so on ahead of him, he figured he was probably trespassing on Caitlan Black's land by now. He glanced behind him again. Yes, the two Locklin hands who followed him had guided their mounts in close under creek trees and had halted. They'd obviously been told to stay on their own range.

His suspicion was confirmed when a bullet almost nicked Violet's ears. Immediately, Ben halted her and looked to his right to see three riders bearing down on him from out of the north. He wrapped reins around the saddle horn, lifted both hands high above his head, and waited tensely, hoping the punchers would talk first before shooting again, because he doubted they could miss him now.

Violet's muscles bunched preparatory to bolting when the riders neared. Ben didn't want to put his arms down; he spoke soothingly to the mare without touching the reins and sat frozen in the saddle when the men pulled their horses in around him, their weapons drawn and themselves looking like they barely restrained fingers from squeezing triggers.

One of the men he had seen the other day with Caitlan Black, a big man, clean-shaven but with graying brown hair shaggy on his neck and his hat so low it nearly hid his eyebrows, snarled: "Who are you and what are you doin' here?"

Ben answered: "My name is . . . Seth Locklin. I'm Arch Locklin's boy." Oddly, that was becoming easier to say. "I came to talk to Miss

Black, if it's all the same to you. Who are you?"

"Les Moody, head wrangler. What business you got with Miss Black?"

Still keeping his hands up, Ben grinned at the men and said mildly: "Well, now, sir, I believe that's between her and me, don't you? I come unarmed and lookin' to do nothin' but palaver."

"What?" Moody snapped. "You think your purty face and sweet talk is gonna make Miss Cat change her mind about anything? You got another think comin', boy."

Ben sighed. "Look, Mister Moody, my arms are gettin' tired, for one thing. For another, I been gone from these here environs for years. I'd just like to get acquainted with Miss Cat again . . . what she does about me is her business, right? I say again, I come harmless. No sidearms, no rifle, no derringer in my boot, no knife at my belt . . . let's go on and . . ."

"Search him, Ambrose," Moody ordered.

Ben continued to sit quietly with his hands high while the man called Ambrose dismounted and came to pull pants legs up above boot tops, feel that he didn't have a weapon hidden under his shirt or beneath the saddle apron, and finally muttered in what seemed to be surprise: "He's tellin' the truth, Les. Not so much as a hat pin."

"Humph," Moody growled. "All right, Mister Locklin, put your arms down and come with us."

90

Ben nodded, took up the reins, and, surrounded by Caitlan Black's wary and unfriendly men, urged Violet into a canter toward the cliff-backed ranch up ahead.

Chapter Eight

Ben got a reception from Caitlan Black the like of which he never dreamed would occur and that left her men staring round-eyed at each other. She was leaning on the corral fence watching one of her bronc peelers trying to stay on the mustang he was breaking when she saw her ramrod and his men ride in with Hawthorne. She gasped— "Seth!"—and dashed toward them.

He dismounted, Violet's reins in both hands while Caitlan Black flung herself at him, wrapped arms around his neck, and planted a quick but enthusiastic kiss on his mouth before she pressed her cheek to his and breathed: "Oh, Seth, welcome home! I'm so damned glad to see you!" She kissed him a second time.

Ben was completely taken aback. Except for Priscilla Locklin Nichols, no one had really welcomed "Seth" home. Even Arch treated him more like a lost possession found and returned than a beloved son back after a long absence.

Bemused, he gasped: "Well, if I'd known I was goin' to get this kind of a greeting, I'd have got here sooner, Miss Black."

She narrowed blue eyes at him. "Did you come on your own, Seth, or did your father send you?"

"I came on my own, ma'am. But . . ." He looked

quickly around the yard, seeing the low sprawling ranch house a far cry from the Locklin's big two-story near-mansion, the corrals and barns. The wrangler was tasting gravel; he had been thrown from the high roller he'd been trying to ride. A number of men stood here and there, glowering suspiciously at him. He had been going to say that for all the girl's apparent instant recognition of him, he wasn't Seth Locklin, changed his mind, and amended his words slightly.

"Uh . . . I gotta confess one thing to you straight off, Miss Black. I seem to have . . . lost my . . . memory somewhere along the trail. I don't rightly recall you or this place. I don't even remember Mister Locklin, though he says he's my daddy. If some bounty hunters he sent after . . . Seth . . . hadn't brought me here, I'd never have come. So if you speak of things you think I oughta know and I look . . . uh . . . blank, please bear with me."

Her expression had become tinged with—first, alarm—then, pity. She studied him closely for a long moment before her tone became crisp. "All right, Seth. I understand. After what Arch Locklin did to you, I don't doubt that you wiped him . . . us . . . all of it . . . out of your mind. Come into the house and have a cup of coffee with me."

"Miss Cat . . ."—Moody scowled—"do y'all think that's wise?"

"It's all right, Les." Caitlan lay a hand softly

on Ben's arm. "Mister Locklin and I were raised together. He and David and my brother Frank were best friends when we were all children. Priscilla and I played together. We were together until the Indians took Seth. There is no way he would ever harm me."

Ben handed Violet over to Moody and followed Caitlan toward the main house. He removed his hat as he stepped inside, and stood with the brim clutched in both hands, looking around.

There was a softness to the room. For all that this was a working ranch, the house seemed to be a woman's place, yet it wasn't frilly. There was the usual rifle hung over the fireplace to his right, and cowhide-upholstered chairs and such, but intermixed were lamps with painted glass bubble shades, and an occasional chair in red velvet. A rocker with carved arm rests, its seat and back covered with needlepoint, sat by the hearth. Rugs scattered here and there. In a large gilt oval frame at the left hung the charcoal drawing portrait of a man and a woman. Young, serious, pleasant. Obviously, Caitlan's folks' wedding picture.

Cat watched him study the room. Presently, she asked: "Look familiar to you?"

He laughed ruefully. "No, ma'am. S-Sorry."

"You used to call me Cat, Seth."

"You're . . . that sure . . . I'm Seth Locklin?"

Her head tipped as her frown grew. She

hesitated a long moment before she asked: "Who do *you* think you are, Seth?"

"I'm . . . I'm not sure. Every time I think I know I'm Ben . . . Ben Hawthorne, someone like you comes along who doesn't seem to have a doubt in the world that I'm Seth Locklin. But what memories I think I have seem to be Ben Hawthorne memories, not . . ." He shook his head. "But you see, what . . . I guess you could say . . . scares me is . . . I can accept Seth and David bein' twins, but I can't accept me . . . Ben . . . bein' a dead ringer for two other *hombres* I ain't even related to. Unless the Locklins had . . . what d'you call three babies born at the same time?"

"Triplets."

"Yeah. Unless they had triplets and just never told anybody."

Cat laughed, and Ben flushed. Miss Black wasn't what he would call overwhelmingly beautiful, but she was pretty, with her fine black hair and bright blue eyes, and her laugh was warm and real.

She said: "I doubt that. My brother Frank was older than any of us by a couple of years, and I'm sure he would have mentioned it. Besides, my mother helped midwife Cora Locklin when you were born, and I know that had triplets arrived in this world, she would have said something about it.

"All right, Seth . . ."—she turned, and he followed when she strode briskly into the kitchen and seized a coffee pot from the back of the stove—"let's just proceed here like you're a total stranger. What is it you want to know?" She poured two cups, then asked: "You doctor your coffee with anything?"

"No, ma'am." Ben shifted one hand from his hat brim to take a cup from her. "Thank you. Uh . . . I just sort of came by to say . . . howdy, and to . . . uh . . . see what all the uproar was about between you and F- . . . Mister Locklin. What the water problem is all about." He sat awkwardly when she waved him to a chair in the main room, dropped his hat onto its crown on the floor beside his feet, and leaned back with his cup.

Caitlan also sat. Eyes dark now, she sipped her own coffee before she said: "All right, like as if you're a total stranger. Ummm . . . what has Arch told you?"

"Not much. Just that while you do share spring water, it ain't enough."

She nodded. "Once, it was well enough. Runoff Creek has always supplied both this ranch and the Locklin spread. In the early days, there was an agreement between my father and yours that water was God's gift, never to be denied any by . . . golly, the source is on my land, not yours basis, or some such thing. But that was when

Arch Locklin only held about a thousand acres, and creek water was enough for his cattle.

"Over the years, Arch has expanded his holdings. Now, he owns twenty thousand acres, and the ranges out there . . ."—her cup made a wide eastward swoop—"are dry. Oh, he has looked for water in various places, has sunk wells and set up windmills to pump here and there, but he has mostly come up with dry holes. And there just isn't enough water in Runoff Creek to satisfy thousands and thousands of head of cattle.

"Now, I am more than happy to share the water from Bountiful Spring, except for one item. Bountiful is an artesian spring in the breaks back of us, here, with maybe plenty of water for everybody, rigged right. But for your daddy's herds to reach the spring itself, his men would have to drive cattle right through my front yard. There is only one way that we know of to reach the spring, and that's up the cut you see beyond the barn and stables out there. If I gave Arch permission to run his herds through here, it would destroy my home and also one of the loveliest places in this whole land."

She sighed heavily. "I have tried to work out some arrangement with Mister Locklin, even offering to sell him barreled water. Yes, I know the water itself is free, but the barrels and the men needed to fill and transport them aren't. Besides, we would then have to have a road running from

Bountiful to Arch's land, and what would begin as my property would shortly . . . if I know your father . . . become his property. Presently, maybe it would become some sort of public right of way.

"My parents worked their lives away building this ranch. My brother died for it. I . . . have to do my best to . . . keep it whole and well . . . for them. For me. For whatever children I may someday have. But . . ." She shook her head and stared at the floor, her coffee cup seemingly forgotten in her hands.

Silence fell over the room. Ben had sat and listened without speaking while the girl talked; now, he studied her, trying to find a memory of her somewhere in his brain, a picture of a place called Bountiful Spring, a thought of what this or the Locklin place looked like fifteen or more years ago, and couldn't. Yet he discovered he was strangely comfortable with Caitlan, almost as if they *had* been friends at some past time and were now renewing that acquaintance. Instinctively, he liked her. He found something honest and straightforward in the way she accepted his avowed lack of memory and desire to help.

Finally, he said: "I see you got a problem. You're sure there's no . . . umm . . . back way to the spring?"

"I've looked. Some of my men have looked

for me. So far, we've never been able to find anything but cliffs and impassable highlands back there."

"What about a flume?" Where had he come up with that idea? "H-Have you ever thought of something like that?"

"Yes, we discussed an aqueduct, or even a dam to create a water impoundment. The problem with the first is that if we piped all the water to Arch's lands, what would we do here? If we shunted enough to run this ranch and water my horses and stock, that wouldn't then give him enough. If we built a dam, it would cut water off from all of us until we could figure out how to pipe to both our places, the backup would destroy Bountiful Spring glade itself, and, most likely, Arch would still want to drive his cattle through here."

"The problem, then, ain't really the water," Ben mused, "or lack of it. If I'm hearin' you right, everything was fine between you, the Locklins, and the water supply, until Arch Locklin outgrew the available resources. And, I reckon, he's not fixin' to reduce his herds to fit."

"Not hardly," Caitlan said with asperity. "He will try to buy me out, drive me out, or marry his way to Bountiful before he'll do that. He won't even consider giving an inch, and I'm not going to let him destroy my ranch just to cater to his greed!"

Ben's head rose. "You run a horse ranch here, not cattle, right?"

"Both, though not on as grand a scale as your father. My father always said never put all your eggs in one basket. I do have about five hundred head of cattle, but I also have my horses to sell as backup." She smiled again. "The dappled gray mare you rode in on . . . Violet? . . . she's from my stable. David bought her from me a couple of years back before he had his accident. How is he?"

Ben shook his head. "A real sad case, Miss Cat. Would you show me Bountiful Spring, if you have the time and inclination? I'd like to see the place for myself."

"Of course." Caitlan set her cup onto the floor by her chair and stood. Ben copied her, grabbing his hat and following her out.

She said: "I'll ride double with you on Violet, if that's agreeable."

The mare was tethered to a corral post. Ben nodded, though commented: "That's fine with me, but I'm not that familiar with Violet yet. I don't know if it's all right with her."

"We'll soon find out, won't we." Cat waved to Les Moody and the other hands. "I'm taking Mister Locklin to look at Bountiful Spring. We'll be back shortly."

The men acknowledged the information. As Ben helped Caitlan into Violet's saddle, untied the reins, and handed them up to her, then grabbed the horn, put a foot in the stirrup and swung gently up behind her, Moody and another man headed for their own mounts tied to a nearby hitching rail. Neither Hawthorne nor Cat objected as the two punchers followed. Ben didn't know what Miss Cat thought, but the men's presence was fine with him—he didn't intend to do anything at all but look, so they weren't going to see anything dangerous.

Runoff Creek coursed near the south rise of the breaks backing the Black Ranch. Obvious care had been taken years ago when placing the buildings to keep barns, stables, corrals, bunkhouses, and the main house far enough from its banks that manure and outhouse contents wouldn't foul the stream. The cut that backed the ranch proper was barred by a fence—Ben dismounted to open the gate—before it widened into a grassy, rock-walled meadow green with moisture even in the heat of summer. A dozen or more brood mares accompanied by their growing spring colts, grazed there.

Still followed at a discreet distance by her silent, watchful men, Caitlan now guided Violet northward across the meadow toward where low tan cliff walls pinched inward at a stone-floored rise. The cleft's west side was deep-cut by the creek, its total narrow expanse softened by early morning shadows.

The girl reined Violet close to eastern walls; presently, the mare's metal shoes clattered against rock, and Ben studied their surroundings.

It was silent here but for bird calls, Violet's hoof falls, and the faint rush of water below and to his left. Clumps of some kind of low-growing bushes laden with small deep-purple berries lush among dark green leaves grew here and there, especially on the far side of the stream where traffic evidently never disturbed them.

Caitlan spoke for the first time since the fence. "Those are Indian Hawthornes. I hear that back East, they may grow to tree size, but here, they are bushes. In the spring, they have white or pink flowers. I don't know if they're natural to this area or if Mother planted them . . . I never thought to ask as a child, and now, of course, it's too late. Whatever, there have been hawthornes here ever since I can remember."

Ben suffered a jolt of shock at her phrasing. "There have been hawthornes . . ."

Been hawthornes . . .

Ben Hawthorne . . .

God, could it be that he . . .

They rounded a tall out-jutting stone, and what lay ahead cut his thoughts in mid-ponder.

It was a tree-bordered box cañon backed by more or less sheer medium-high cliff faces. At the far end, a perfect arch not quite a cave had been cut by Nature into pale beige stone. Reflections from the broad, deep pool at its base cast moving white patterns back into the arch above a fern- and moss-mantled split from which a glistening fountain of silver water spouted.

A pair of wild ducks waggled tails in aggrava- tion at the human invasion before they took off, circled the bowl once, and vanished over cliff tops, but a water dipper—what some called an ouzel—seemed unaffected by the newcomers and continued to flutter in and out of the pond in search of periwinkles.

The little box cañon was carpeted with grass and summer blossoms, the pond floored with painted pebbles nearly as bright, and edged by a stand of cat-tails. Over all hung a gentle moistness and the breath of peace and hidden serenity.

Caitlan continued to sit the saddle when Ben dismounted to walk slowly through the grass and flowers to the edge of the pool. He stared into crystalline depths for a long moment—noted schools of tiny fish and the occasional crawdad living there. He studied the foaming cascade spouting so abruptly from raw stone as to seem to be an artificial man-made fountain designed to please the eye, before he turned in a full circle to scrutinize cañon walls. He came to the conclusion that he had rarely seen any place so beautiful . . . and that there was no entrance other than the way they had come.

Caitlan nudged Violet nearer and eased the reins so the mare could lower her head and nip juicy grass. She murmured: "Now I think you see why I can't let your father run cattle here, Seth. Besides the fact that his herds would tromp right past my front door, the cut back there is too narrow. The cattle would get bottled-up in here, and . . ."—she shrugged—"secondly, to find a place like Bountiful Spring in this country is such a wonder . . . we have to do everything we can to preserve it. Arch can't dig a channel through the cliffs. Yes, this is the only stable, unfailing, year-round water source for a hundred miles, but . . ."

Ben scowled sharply at her. "Haven't you ever brought him back here to see this?"

"Of course! He knows this place well. Maybe you don't remember, Seth, but when we were children . . . before the Indians took you . . . your family and mine used to come here for picnics of an occasional Sunday." She sighed and shook her head. "But lately, since Frank died, it seems dollar profit outweighs this kind of treasure in your daddy's eyes, and I don't know how to . . ." Her voice trailed away for a minute before she finished. "I'm hoping, now that you're home, that you can talk Mister Locklin out of what seems to have become his obsession to use Bountiful Spring. He would destroy this, Seth. I don't have enough resources available to hold him off forever. I'm hoping you can think of some way to stop him."

Ben didn't have any idea at all how to do that, but, after seeing this, he sure as hell was going to try!

Chapter Nine

Ben had lunch with Caitlan. He stayed most of the afternoon, admiring her horses, hearing about his supposed past, and getting to know not only her and her wranglers and cowpunchers, but also Seth Locklin. He heard that when Seth had first returned from the Kiowas, he had brought his wife Blue Glass Bead and their son here to Caitlan rather than directly to meet his father, and that Blue Glass Bead and little Arch had stayed two weeks with the Blacks before Seth had chosen a time to introduce them to Mr. Locklin.

He asked Caitlan: "Tell me about Blue Glass Bead. What was she like?"

Cat looked uncomfortable for a moment before she said: "She was about seventeen or eighteen . . . very pretty for an Indian. Well, no, very pretty for any woman, I guess, white or Indian. And she just doted on her little boy." She laughed slightly. "So did I. In the two weeks you left them here with me before you took them to meet your father, I grew . . . very attached . . . to little Arch. I would have been happy to have cared for him when Blue Glass Bead's friend came calling, but she wouldn't hear of it. They . . . she and her friend . . . always took the baby with them when they went out to be . . . alone. I presume

106

they went to Bountiful Spring, but I don't know. I never followed them."

Ben frowned. "Blue Glass Bead's friend? What was she like? A girl friend? An older woman? Her mother, maybe?"

"Uh . . . oh, I don't know. Just a . . . friend." Cat frowned at the floor. "Maybe her . . . brother or . . . something. I don't know."

"A man?"

"Oh, well, they . . ."

He leaned toward her, and asked: "Her friend was a young warrior? You're sayin' Blue Glass Bead was bein' unfaithful to Seth . . . uh . . . to me, while . . ."

"No! No, I'm not saying that at all! I mean, here you are, visiting me, and nothing outlandish is going on, is there? No, just a friend."

"Who was he? What did he look like?"

"I don't know his name. You know Blue Glass Bead didn't speak English and I don't speak Kiowa. Besides, he just came to see her and toddle the baby. I'm sure it was merely an innocent friendship."

Ben let it go at that. Blue Glass Bead had been dead a long time and it was all water run by under the bridge more than five years ago. Still, he couldn't help wondering who Blue Glass Bead's guest had been and whether Seth had known his wife was being visited by another man during his absence.

He asked: "Why, after all those years of livin' as a Kiowa, did Seth . . . I . . . come back to the ranch then?"

"You said for the baby's sake. It was late September or early October. Little Arch was only six or seven months old. You were afraid of the upcoming winter . . . wanted him to live in the security of a white man's house during the cold months, at least until he was older."

"Not to bring Arch his grandson?"

"No. Only for the baby's safety. Everything you did was for the baby."

"Humph." Ben looked back at the yard outside Cat's front door. "And still, he died . . . in the snow."

It seemed, from what Caitlan related, that tragedy had struck all around. Arch Locklin had sent Blue Glass Bead and the baby back to the tribe and they had been caught by the first early blizzard of the year. After a terrible stand-off with his father, Seth had gone to try to find his wife and son and had never returned. Caitlan's own brother had died, gored to death by their seed bull, Romeo. Then, David Locklin suffered his near-fatal accident. All the while, those left alive tried to cope.

The maimings, mortalities, and disappearances had been spaced out over months or even years, though their pain lingered on. Nor, it seemed, was the series of events over.

● ● ●

Followed at a distance by his watchdogs, Ben arrived back at the Locklin place just before suppertime to see a group of cowhands gathered around a body laid out in the yard before the cook shack. It was Everett Ribble. He was dead.

Hawthorne reined Violet up to the group, dismounted, and shoved through to kneel beside Ribble. He asked: "What happened to him?"

"We dunno, Mistuh Locklin," one of the onlookers frowned. "He just come staggerin' out of the cook shack heavin' up his guts. Then, he fell down jerkin' and twitchin' like he was havin' some sort of fit, and presently . . ."—the puncher flung up his hands with finality—". . . daid."

Ben leaned closer to Ribble. Under the strong taint of whiskey and vomit, he could smell the odor of . . . "Parsnips."

"Parsnips?" The hands glanced at each other. "Parsnips don't kill a man."

"No." Ben stood and shook his head. "No, parsnips don't, but water hemlock does, and it and parsnips are kin. Water hemlock is sometimes called spotted cowbane or poison parsnip. There were originally four bounty hunters who found me. One of them by the name of Murry Harding died on the trail just like this. Now, poor ol' Ev. At first, I thought either Ribble, here, Reuben Bettiger, or Al Hoffs killed Murry, and maybe they did, but why Ev died, I sure don't know.

109

It's unlikely he would commit suicide, what with his reward money comin' to him in a few days."

"Uh . . . maybe one of his partners done it?"

"How? They been gone a couple of days, now."

"And how d'you know about such things as cowbane and parsnips, Mistuh Locklin? You kill him?"

Ben glanced around at the men frowning at him, and scowled back. "Every good cattleman knows about cowbane, don't you? Every housewife or Injun woman knows what water hemlock looks like, and I was raised by them. Besides, why would I kill him? I had no axe to grind with him. Sure, Bettiger and Hoffs left him here to keep an eye on me, but was he doing that? No, he just sat around here sloppin' up . . . ah! That's how they did it! He said he had an extra . . . where's the whiskey bottle he was suckin' on?"

"What whiskey bottle?" some of the men asked.

Ben turned toward the cook shack. "He came out of there?"

"Yeah, but he wasn't carryin' no bottle."

Hawthorne edged past men and strode to the dining room door. It took a moment for his eyes to adjust from brilliant sunlight to the relative dimness inside, then he walked up and down the three lines of wooden tables, benches, and stools. No bottle, empty or otherwise. That was a puzzle. He searched the room twice, located a puddle of

110

vomit on the floor in the far left corner, but that was all.

As he stepped back outside, he discovered Arch among the men standing around the body. He nodded greeting to "father" before he asked: "Any of you take Ev's whiskey bottle outta there?" His thumb jerked back over his shoulder to indicate the cook shack.

All the punchers shook their heads. Arch asked: "What is this about a whiskey bottle, Son?" Ben explained his supposition to Locklin. Arch made an expression of helplessness. "Well, there's nothing we can do about it now. Samuels . . . Rickey . . . get a shovel, pick a spot, and lay Mister Ribble to rest somewhere other than in my family plot, then go about your business. Seth, come with me, please. I want to hear what you found out at the Black spread."

Locklin's ranch-hand cook had seen Ev's half empty bottle—or, depending on how you looked at it, half full—sitting alone on the table. His motto was that possession was one hundred percent of the law and waste not, want not. He confiscated the whiskey, and by six o'clock that evening, he would never want again. The cowhands dug a grave for him beside Ribble. They buried the empty bottle with him.

"You can't run cattle through the Black Ranch and into Bountiful Spring, sir," Ben said over

111

coffee after dinner. He and Arch ate together in the formal dining room in the big house. "There's got to be another way around your water problem."

Locklin's eyes narrowed above his cigar. He puffed briefly and sent a blue cloud into the air around him before he murmured: "So, Caitlan Black got to you."

"No, sir, it wasn't Miss Black, it was the land itself." Ben sighed heavily and leaned back in his chair, absently running a forefinger around the rim of his coffee cup, not noticing the delicate gold design gracing fine china. "I've beheld some beautiful places in my time. The Hill Country down in Texas . . . farther on south near the Río Grande and the like . . . but I've never seen anything to match Bountiful Spring. To ruin that . . . no. You can't.

"Secondly, it's a box cañon. Miss Black said it, and there, she's right. You'd get the herd leaders trapped in there with no way out but back the way they came, and you'd end up with one hell of a mess on your hands. Drown trapped critters in the pool or in the creek itself. Injure 'em when they got crowded off rises. No, that's not the way to go at all, sir. There has to be another way."

Still staring hard at Ben, Arch breathed: "Do you have an alternative in mind?"

"Yes, sir. Tomorrow, if it's all the same to you,

I'd like to ride eastward a ways along Runoff Creek to see what I can see out there." He grinned suddenly. "You can tell those men you had doggin' me today that they can ride with me or quit wastin' their time . . . I'm not goin' to run off."

Arch's brows rose. "You knew they were following you?"

"Hell, yes! And it made me damned mad. I gave you my word . . . told you what I was goin' to do today . . . but you evidently didn't trust me. What did you tell those *hombres* to do had I took a turn . . . run me down, hog-tie me, and bring me back here in chains again?"

"No! Well, yes. Uh . . . maybe." Locklin smiled ruefully. "I apologize for that, Seth. I . . . think it is . . . fear on my part. I know you don't believe you're my son, Seth, but I also know you are, and I'm afraid . . . you might even say, terrified . . . of losing you again. Before, when David was . . . well . . . I missed you, yes, but I didn't need you, if you know what I mean. I still had a son to pass everything on to that I've worked a lifetime to build. To David. To his children and grandchildren. All this wouldn't . . . go to waste.

"But when David . . . died . . ." He ground his cigar butt out in the ashtray. "Do you still think you're . . . uh . . . Ben Hawthorne?"

"I don't know, sir," Ben said honestly. "Sometimes, I do, but at other times . . ." He shrugged.

"How long did you say those men held you captive?"

"I figger it was about six days . . . and . . . nights."

"Six days . . . and nights . . . of telling you you were Ben Hawthorne, of burning you and scourging you and making you say it . . ." Arch shook his head grimly. "It would seem to me any brain could be well-confused in half that time."

"Sir . . . sir, please don't talk about it! When you do, I see it all again . . . hear them yelling and feel the . . ." Ben grabbed at his cup and his hand shook when he gulped cold coffee. "The only thing I'm damned sure was a lie was the part about the bank hold-up and me killin' three women. I *know* I didn't do that, and Ev Ribble confessed to me that the Wanted poster Reuben Bettiger showed you is a fake. Ev said Bettiger had one printed up to . . . But . . ." He swallowed. Fell silent.

Arch said softly: "Where there is one lie, Seth, it's safe to bet there are others. You are Seth Locklin. My son. Home to stay. Home. And yes, you have my permission to go anywhere you want to go on your property. If you want men to go with you, that will be your choice. I will no longer send them after you, you can count on that. And I say again, welcome home, Seth!"

• • •

"Your name is Seth Locklin!" The hooded man slashed the whip across the naked back of the prisoner bound to a support post in the hole in the ground.

The captive flinched, jerked at his chains, and almost screamed: "Yes! Yes! My name is Seth Locklin! I told you that yesterday! I told you that the day before yesterday! My name's Seth Locklin!"

"You are twenty-five years old." The whip fell again.

The prisoner choked on pain, but finally got out: "Yes! My name is Seth . . . I'm twenty-five! I was born . . . born . . ." *This time, he twisted so desperately against the manacle chains tethering his wrists to the post that blood ran down his forearms. His voice rose.* "WHY DO YOU KEEP TELLIN' ME THINGS I ADMIT! . . . THINGS THAT ARE TRUE! I AM SETH LOCKLIN! YES!"

"There have always been hawthornes here." Blood was everywhere, on the whip, on the floor, on the dirt walls. Spotted with glittering crimson droplets, Caitlan Black's face floated in the smoky air in front of the prisoner's eyes. "Been hawthornes . . . been hawthornes . . ."

"Ben Hawthorne," the prisoner whispered. "Yes, Ben Hawthorne."

"I don't know whether my mother planted

115

you or not, but you are Ben Hawthorne. . . ."

"No! No, my name's Seth! Seth Locklin!"

The whip fell and fell while Arch, a pillow in his hands, looked back at him from beside David's bed, and smiled. Ben leaned against the bedroom door and smiled back. "When you do it, Father, do it quick and right so he doesn't suffer even more."

Arch murmured: "You're a good son, Seth. Welcome home, Seth, welcome home." Holding the pillow in both hands, he gently lowered it over David's face.

In the corner over by her own bed, Mrs. McPhee stood dressed in her blue dress and starched bonnet, her hands clasped across her white apron, nodding her approval.

Seth cautioned: "Do it right, Father. Don't . . ."

Ben sat bolt upright in bed and gasped: "Don't! Don't!" His heart pounded wildly. He was drenched in sweat. His hair dripped with it. His chest and thighs ran with it. His hands shook when he wiped both palms over his face before he stared wild-eyed around the room.

He was in bed, and alone here. Moonlight slanted through the open window, lighting a patch of rug and encroaching onto his pillow. He caught his breath and held it to listen into the night, but everything seemed quiet.

Had it been merely a nightmare? Or had it been

a medicine dream, as his other people would believe?

He didn't know. As silently as creaking springs allowed, he climbed out of bed and went to open the door that led to the hallway. There was no one there. Except for the faint stripe of light edging under the door to David's room that beamed from the lamp Mrs. McPhee always burned at night, the house was dark.

He shook his head and closed his door again. Praying the dream had been only a nightmare, not some sort of terrible prophecy, he went to the window to look out into the green-lighted yard for a moment to try to shake strong echoes shuddering in his mind. He couldn't do it. Though he slept undisturbed the remainder of the night, ghosts pursued him even into the dawn.

At least David still lived the next morning. Mrs. McPhee announced during breakfast that there was no change in his condition.

Chapter Ten

Ben had just finished saddling Violet and had tightened the cinch—he planned to take the ride out along Runoff Creek that he'd mentioned to Arch last evening—when a voice behind him asked: "You have any luck with a white woman yesterday, squawman, or did your dealin's with them Injun bitches spoil you for a Christian poke?"

Today, Ben was packing a six-shooter, though when something hot and red exploded behind his eyes, he didn't make a grab for it. He knew Dallas Youngstreet was the one who spoke, but couldn't have cared at this moment if it had been Santa Anna backed by four thousand Mexicans. He whirled, leaped, and flattened the unprepared Youngstreet with one hard, accurate uppercut to the chin.

Other cowhands readying to go to the ranges to relieve night guards paused and looked wide-eyed to where Dallas pushed himself up onto his elbows for a surprised moment before he breathed—"Oh, yeah!"—and sprang back to his feet. He crouched, fists raised.

Ben gritted: "Call me squawman if you want to, Youngstreet, but don't try to sully Miss Caitlan's person. She's a pure lady, and . . ."

"The Black Cat ain't no pure lady, Mistuh Locklin, any more than you're a pure white man. I think you oughta know I'm a Injun fighter from a way back."

Ben took a step forward. "Then you can call me your Injun of the day. I've had enough of you, Dallas. Let's see if you fight as good as you talk."

"Comes a time when talkin's done!" Youngstreet swung.

Hawthorne ducked, the fist slid past his shoulder, and he buried his own in Dallas's belly.

Youngstreet went down, but he was up instantly. Ben sidled around him out toward the open yard to gain maneuvering room, and met Dallas's next charge with a right to the cowhand's cheek bone and a left to the ribs, but Youngstreet's knuckles hit him solidly just below the left ear and knocked him off balance. Before he could recover, Dallas grappled with him, flung him to the dirt, and pursued his advantage.

The other cowboys had gathered around. They shouted more or less wordless emotion, few of them openly rooting for Youngstreet, none for Ben, because their own future well-being was also at stake here. Dallas was ramrod in Ruffian Bullock's place while Ruff was off on an errand for Mr. Locklin, and he could make life hell for them if they cheered Seth Locklin. On the other hand, Locklin was the boss's son—he could see them out of a job should they urge Youngstreet to victory. Though they couldn't keep quiet, they restricted themselves to unintelligible whoops, grunts, and sympathetic awwws.

Dallas hit Ben twice before Hawthorne could dislodge the man, roll free, and leap back to his feet. Ben dived immediately back at Youngstreet, landed a right that split Dallas's brow and blossomed an instant purple bruise under the eye, but Dallas's next blow sprang blood from Ben's nose.

Both of them went down again, and the ground-level battle continued until Youngstreet lurched upright and pulled Ben with him.

Hawthorne let the man drag him to his feet. Instead of standing there waiting to be hit, he abruptly grabbed Dallas's right wrist with his left hand, whirled, and rammed his elbow into Youngstreet's gut. When Dallas folded, he turned again and smashed his knee into the man's face. He let go of Youngstreet's arm when Dallas plunged backward and lay sprawled, arms and legs flung out, eyes closed, blood bubbling from his nose and mouth.

Ben wiped a sleeve under his own bleeding nose and panted heavily for a moment before he staggered to where Dallas lay, seized the man's shirt and arm, dragged him across the yard to the horse watering trough, and dunked him twice before dropping him into the mud beside the hollowed-out log. He bent to submerge his own head briefly before he straightened and glared at the cowpunchers and horse wranglers staring back at him.

He gasped: "All right, you call me a squawman. My wife was as beautiful and kind and generous and honest and virtuous and faithful and chastely as any white woman could ever be. She worked hard for me and bore me a strong, fine, healthy son that she loved and cared for like any mother would love and care for her boy . . . and I loved her like any man would love his wife! So you want to call me a squawman, go ahead. When you're wed to someone like Blue Glass Bead was, there ain't no shame in it.

"But you don't go besmirchin' Miss Caitlan Black's good name and good person. She's only tryin' to do her best with what she's got to work with, like anybody else would do.

"My name is Seth Locklin. My pa owns this spread. First, you obey him. Secondly, you obey me. You want to argue with me, fine. You want to see what I'm made of, fine. But you push me too damned far, and I'll fire you, and I can do it!"

"And if he doesn't, I will."

All of them jerked around to see Arch Locklin grinning broadly at them from where he leaned on the corral fence, his cigar smoking in one hand, the other palm resting on the grip of a pistol on his hip. It was the first time Ben had seen Arch armed and looking like a range hand,

121

and it startled him, because it flashed through his mind how much Locklin resembled another man at this moment. Eli Hawthorne. His father, who always carried a Bible instead of a gun.

At his feet, Dallas was beginning to come around. Ben blinked the vision of Eli Hawthorne back into the deep recesses of his mind, reached down, again grabbed the man's shirt, and hoisted him to sit him on the rim of the watering trough. When Youngstreet looked blearily up at him, he said: "That was one hell of a damned good fight, Dallas. You want to go at it some more, or you want to call it enough? I don't know about you, but I could do with a drink. If it's all right with my pa over there, I'll pour out of his supply, if you want to come on into the house with me."

Youngstreet looked astonished. "You'd drink with me?"

"Sure, why not? You had your say and I had mine. We fit a good fight here, and as far as I'm concerned, it's over and done with. You want that drink, or not?"

Dallas stared hard at Ben for a long moment before he whispered: "I don't drink with no squawman." Then he lurched upright and staggered toward the other hired hands.

"Your choice." Ben sighed, and passed fingers through his wet hair to comb it back before he, too, returned across the yard to where Violet stood eased and waiting. He touched his nose, then looked at his hand. Things had stopped bleeding, and he guessed he'd washed his face good enough at the trough to pass until lunch.

Still grinning, Arch met him. "Well done, Son. Uh . . . you're going for that ride you mentioned last night?"

Ben retrieved his hat from where it had fallen, slapped dust from it against his thigh, and settled it on his head. "Yes, sir, I am."

"Mind of I join you?"

Hawthorne shot him a sidelong glare. "I told you last night, you don't have to ride herd on me."

"I'm not. Is there any law that says a father and son can't go riding together? You didn't say what you were looking for. If you tell me, maybe I can help."

Ben untied Violet's reins from the post and swung astride. "I don't know what I'm lookin' for. I guess I'll know it when I see it . . . if I see it. But . . ."—he smiled suddenly—"yeah. I'd be proud to have your company."

Locklin rode his fine bay gelding, Tomahawk, taller and rangier than Violet's quarter horse configuration, pretty to look at but whose tiny pin-ears bespoke a basically evil nature. Arch seemed to take satisfaction in ruling the unruly without effort, but watching him and his mount, Ben decided he'd take Violet any day. She was much more of a comfort. You didn't have to be ready at every moment to cope with an unexpected shy from some fluttering leaf or vagary of whim.

He nodded eastward as they moved at a slow canter along the north bank of Runoff Creek, and asked: "What's out there?"

"Nothing but grazing land and Indians clear on to the Mississippi, I expect."

"No towns? No other ranches? Nobody else depending on the water in this creek?"

"Not that I know of. Towns are mostly north or far south of us, and where this creek ultimately goes, I haven't the slightest idea."

"But it flows onward past your eastern boundary?"

"Yes. Why?"

Ben shook his head. "I'll tell you that when I figger it out."

They rode onward in silence for quite some time, Hawthorne merely looking, Locklin's eyes sweeping his domain. The creek meandered with the slight rise and fall of the land, its banks heavy with fringe trees and low-growing water-hungry brush. Out to their left, the dark mass of one of Arch's herds blotted the landscape like a slow-moving cloud shadow. Otherwise, there was nothing but mile after mile of whispering prairie grass.

In the quiet, Ben pondered his recent bout with Youngstreet, Dallas calling him squawman, and the words in defense of Blue Glass Bead that had fallen from his lips so readily and seeming without guidance from his mind. He reined Violet a little closer to Tomahawk and asked: "Sir, tell me about Blue Glass Bead's last day at the ranch. What prompted her to take the baby and leave?"

Arch shot him a hard look. "You don't recall?"

"No sir, I don't."

Now it was Locklin's turn to study the landscape for a long moment before he said: "I'm not really sure. You and she . . . weren't getting along well, I think. Whether it was that she couldn't accept white man's ways or what, I don't know, but though you both always spoke in Kiowa to each other, even I could sense it. The day before she left . . ."

"She left on her own? You didn't throw her out? You didn't force her to leave?"

Arch looked pained. "I would never have done that, Seth. Much as I disapproved of you being wed to a squaw . . . having offspring by her . . . believe it or not, I understood. The day before she left, Priscilla tried to dress Blue Glass Bead in one of her dresses. That night, the squaw put your blanket outside your room into the hallway."

"She divorced me?"

"I guess so. Sometime in the night, she evidently took your son and left. When you awoke and found them gone, you went after

125

her. That was the last I saw of you for over five years."

"But you and I . . . had a row over it before I left?"

"No!" Now, Arch scowled at him. "Where'd you get that idea?"

Ben didn't want to say that Caitlan had told him that he and his father had "had a terrible row," as she'd put it. He merely answered: "I . . . heard that we'd fought over Blue Glass Bead . . . over her leavin'."

"No!" Arch repeated. "Oh, I yelled at you to come back, yes. I called for you to wait until I could get some of the men to go with you . . . the weather had turned, and I . . . but a row? . . . a fight? . . . no. And again, I didn't throw her out, Seth. I didn't cause her death. But I guess when the blizzard hit and killed them, you just . . . ran."

Ben pondered that. Though he expected that Arch told him the truth as he knew it, somehow he couldn't see himself fleeing because of an accident . . . he thought he would have at the least come back and told Arch where he was going.

He asked it. "If you never saw me again for all these years, how do you know how Blue Glass Bead and the baby died? Who told you?"

"Medicine Shield. He came here looking for you. He said one of his warriors had found the bodies in the snow and had taken them to camp, and Medicine Shield wanted to let you know what had happened to your wife and son. But that was a long time ago, Seth. I know I still miss your mother, though she's been gone some seven years now, so I understand if you still miss Blue Glass Bead. Comes a time when you have to go onward with life, Son. You can't run away forever."

That was true, Ben thought. Problem was, despite his recent words to the men—and he wondered where those words had come from— he didn't miss Blue Glass Bead or an infant son, couldn't even conjure a vision of them into his mind. Weighted by still one more unanswered question, he rode onward.

Perhaps an hour later, Hawthorne reined Violet in abruptly and sat merely scowling at what lay ahead. Arch fought his gelding to a standstill and turned back to look curiously at the man he called son. Presently, he asked: "What? What is it you see?"

"There it is." Ben nodded to a wide dip between two gentle land rises.

Arch also looked. Ahead, lay rolling prairie with Runoff Creek crossing a shallow gully. On the far side of the dip, the stream had made a sharp cut into the low hill instead of running around the rise before vanishing on eastward. Again, he asked: "What?"

Ben pointed at the dip, indicated the cut. "You build a dam across that outflow channel over there, and, presently, you'll have a fine lake. Plenty of water for your herds far enough from the house and barns that, come spring storms and the like, it won't swamp out the ranch. You been thinkin' all along to grab the source of the creek to water your cattle. This oughta do better. Hell . . ."—he grinned abruptly at Locklin—"put a few catfish in the pond and you might even go fishin' in a couple of years."

Arch frowned. His brows lifted. Ben followed when Locklin urged the gelding on down the side of the near hill and into the dip. They discovered that the north end of the gully debouched into flatter plain, considered the profitability or not of a second dam at its mouth. On the south side of Runoff Creek, they found a natural rise. That end of the proposed lake had been taken care of for them by Nature.

Back on their side of the stream, Arch again sat his nervous bay and studied the project. Finally, he said: "We have enough trees handy along the creek for construction of both dam walls. We might even content ourselves with just one barrier over there . . ."—he nodded at the eastern cut—"let the lake fill, then let its natural runoff create a new creek running north so cattle won't have to come so far." He smiled at Ben. "I like it. I wonder why I didn't think of this years ago."

Ben shrugged. "I figger you been so fixed on Bountiful Spring, you didn't see anything else."

"I think perhaps you're right. The only problem, now, is getting my hands to build what we have in mind."

Ben scowled. "They work for you. What's the . . ."

"They're cowpunchers and horse wranglers, not dirt diggers or lumbermen. I expect they'll think that cutting trees and the like is beneath them."

"So hire yourself a herd of Irishmen from back East. If you can throw away forty thousand dollars locating me, you oughta be able to afford that. Besides, buildin' a dam and the like ain't beneath me. Mister and Missus Inman taught us boys that honest work was honest work, no matter what you did for your pay, and if you got dirty along the way, you could always take a bath." He waved a hand at the gully. "But you've decided? You're gonna quit houndin' Miss Cat for Bountiful Spring and build your own lake here?"

Again, Arch studied the land for a long moment before he nodded. "Yes. We'll try it. We don't have a thing to lose but a few acres of grassland, and we have plenty of that." He sighed heavily. "Amazing."

"What's amazing?"

"A man . . . gets so used to looking at something that . . . I guess . . . he just doesn't see it anymore. It takes a fresh eye, a different way of thinking, to find an easy . . . obvious solution to a long-standing problem. I'm proud of you, Seth. Thank you."

Ben tipped his head. "Don't thank me yet, sir. We don't know whether it'll really work or not. Seems good, but we'll have to wait and see."

"You're calling me *sir* again. You named me father to the men earlier this morning."

"Yeah, well, that was in the . . . heat of the moment, I guess."

"You took Youngstreet right and proper, Seth. Where'd you learn to fight like that?"

Now Ben's expression became grim. "I've had to fight for myself all my life, sir." He wheeled Violet and kicked her into a gallop back toward the ranch house. Regardless of his last words to Locklin, he was excited about the dam project. He could hardly wait to tell Caitlan that he had saved Bountiful Spring glade for her.

Chapter Eleven

They were only about two miles from the ranch when Ben hauled Violet in sharply. A band of eight or ten red men had urged their ponies out from among the trees lining Runoff Creek and halted in a crescent to bar his and Arch's path. The Indians didn't make any hostile moves, merely sat their mounts and waited as though they had something to say, but Hawthorne looked aside at Arch and asked softly: "You know them?"

"Yes," Locklin frowned. "And so do you. That one on the red and white pinto is Medicine Shield, the man who took you from me."

Ben squinted against noontime glare at the one Arch indicated. He saw a strong middle-aged Indian with lips full beneath a straight hawk-nostriled nose, his dark eyes hard and watchful under hairless brow ridges. Medicine Shield wore a single black-tipped white eagle feather upstanding behind the flounced ruff of a black horsehair roach attached to his scalp lock. Part of his own hair was plaited into many tiny braids, their ends and the rest caught with furred bindings at the jawline. In deference to the summer heat, the man was shirtless; he wore only a chest plate of hollow white bones sewn into a chevron pattern, long-fringed leather leggings under his blue loincloth, and moccasins. Surprisingly, though his men were well armed, he carried only a knife.

"Let me talk," Arch murmured. He urged his bay ahead of Violet, lifted both hands, palms outward, and said: "Greetings, Medicine Shield. What brings you here?"

Medicine Shield almost ignored him; his eyes were on Ben. In English, he noted: "I had heard that the son left to you had suffered a great wound and was all but dead. It is good to see he has been returned to you, This World Stealer."

Arch smiled grimly. "You're mistaken, Chief. David is still not repaired. This is Seth, the one you named Snow Fox, the son you took from me who has returned to me after many years of being gone."

Medicine Shield's eyes narrowed. He urged his pinto a few steps closer and scowled at Ben, studying him from head to toe. Hawthorne met the Kiowa's look openly; as far as he could tell, he'd never seen the man before, but . . .

In his own language, Medicine Shield asked: "Why have you returned to This World Stealer instead of to me, Snow Fox? I am your father."

Before he thought or even considered the implications of what he did, Ben answered: "Despite what This World Stealer says, I didn't come by choice, Father. I was brought back as a prisoner. I . . . he . . ." Abruptly, his mind spun to shock. He, Ben, had been raised by the Comanches. This was a Kiowa talking to him. They didn't necessarily speak the same language, yet he understood and talked back to Medicine Shield. The word *father* had slipped easily and naturally from his tongue, but Medicine Shield wasn't his Indian father, Nighthorse, chief among the Comanches, was!

Both Arch and the Kiowas saw all the blood drain from the younger man's face. The warriors with Medicine Shield frowned. One asked something, the chief replied, and now it was the young Kiowa whose face turned a shade of sickly yellow-green.

The warrior flung up his hands—he held a war club in his right—gasped something in what seemed to be a horror-strangled voice before he cast the weapon at Ben, wheeled his pony, and headed northward at a dead run.

The other Indians steadied their mounts while they muttered puzzlement to each other. Locklin made a grab for Seth but missed when the one he called son toppled from the saddle, for though wildly thrown, the club had struck Hawthorne a glancing blow at the temple; it knocked him unconscious and out of the saddle. His left foot slid through the stirrup loop; had Violet been less gentle and taken the opportunity to bolt, Ben could have been dragged by the trapped ankle.

As it was, both Arch and Medicine Shield leaped from their horses' backs; the Kiowa seized the mare's bridle to hold her while Locklin disentangled Ben's leg.

Then, with Medicine Shield's remaining men still mounted in a closed circle around them, Arch and Medicine Shield knelt to turn Ben over onto his back.

The Kiowa studied the bruises, blue now, on Ben's face. In English, he said to Arch: "I see you beat him to your will."

"No, I didn't." Locklin brushed fair hair back from Ben's forehead. "He had a fight with one of my men earlier today. Those bruises and cuts are the result. I would never force him to me."

"A fight?" Medicine Shield's hairless brows rose. "Who was victorious?"

"He won."

"Good. Why the fight?"

"For honor. Seth . . . Snow Fox . . . defended Blue Glass Bead's name." Arch tilted his head northward toward where the one fleeing Kiowa warrior was still visible in his hasty retreat. "But why did that one attack him?"

Medicine Shield also glanced northward. "Crow Runs loved Blue Glass Bead. He wooed her also, but she chose Snow Fox. When she died, Crow Runs vowed that should Snow Fox ever return to our camp, he would kill him."

"But this is my land . . . his land . . ."—Arch

indicated Ben still motionless on the grass—"not your camp."

"Crow Runs's blood is hot. It burns for vengeance." Medicine Shield shrugged. "Perhaps seeing Snow Fox, so unexpectedly, crazed him for the moment. When I return to camp, I will tell him that though he can meet my son there, he cannot attack him here."

Arch nodded and sighed. He studied both Ben and Medicine Shield for a moment before he said: "Chief, we, you and I, both claim this man as son. You took him from me in payment for the land. I have bought him back from you by never denying your people use of what is now mine. My land . . . my son." He indicated the welt the club had raised above Ben's ear, the other bruises and cuts from Hawthorne's battle with Youngstreet. "These wounds are minor compared to what we . . . you and I . . . have done to his mind. We have done a terrible thing to him, Medicine Shield. He is neither white nor Kiowa, now neither your son nor mine. He doesn't know who he is, and to meet you again . . . to talk to you . . ." He shook his head.

Ben was beginning to come around. He opened his eyes and looked at those surrounding him when both Arch and Medicine Shield helped him to sit up. He wiped a palm over his face before he gasped: "What the hell happened? How'd I get down here?"

"You were hit in the head with a war club, Seth," Locklin said. "Can you stand?"

"Yeah. Sure." With Arch's help, Ben stumbled upright, but his eyes were on Medicine Shield. He asked of Locklin: "He speaks English, right?"

"Very well," Arch nodded.

Still looking at the Kiowa warrior, Hawthorne asked: "What . . . tongue . . . did I sp-speak when I answered your question?"

"Ours, of course, Snow Fox."

"Kiowa?"

"If you want to call it that."

"Not . . . not . . . Comanche?" Ben made the hand signs for Snake Indian.

"Don't you know?"

"N-No. No, I . . ."

Medicine Shield leaned close, and said in his own language: "Now that you have returned, we can do one of two things. Regardless of Crow Runs's vow of vengeance against you, you can come home with me where you belong, or you can be This World Stealer's son . . . we will kill him for you so you will inherit the lands, and you can then return to the people the paths he has taken so that things will once again be as they always were since the beginning of This World. Your choice, Snow Fox."

Ben hardly heard the proposal. He looked from the warriors to Locklin, and back before he asked

136

breathlessly: "Medicine Shield, how . . . how is it I speak your language?"

Medicine Shield made a low, moaning sound. Scowling, he stepped to his pinto. To Arch, he growled: "You are right, This World Stealer. Contraries have stolen his mind. Send him home with me so our shaman can make strong medicine to drive them away and heal him."

Arch shook his head. "He is now a man, not a child, Medicine Shield. I can no longer send him anywhere, and neither can you. Wherever he goes . . . whatever he does is now his decision."

"But the Contraries rule him. How can he choose?"

"I . . . think . . . he will have to do battle with the spirits on his own."

Desperately, as Medicine Shield vaulted aboard the pony, Ben yelled again, this time in what was evidently the Kiowa language: "Medicine Shield, how is it I speak your language? It's not the same as what we Comanche talk, is it?"

The Indian looked down at him with great sadness in his eyes. His companions murmured among themselves and backed off—it was dangerous to be too close to someone seized by evil Contraries, because they might also attract the spirits' attention. As he reined his pinto northward, Medicine Shield said: "No." He kicked his pony into an instant gallop, also headed home.

Ben made a choked gasp of frustrated confusion. Under an urgency to escape the unexplainable, he lunged for Violet, flung himself into the saddle, and bent low over the horn, shouted her into a run toward the ranch.

He caught Arch by surprise. Still afoot, Locklin yelled: "Seth! Seth!"

Ben didn't stop, didn't even slow Violet's headlong run. Swearing passionately, Arch remounted and followed, but at a slower pace—no sense in killing two good horses today—but when he reached the ranch, Seth wasn't there.

Fred Perkins said: "Yeah, Mister Locklin, your boy come ridin' by here like his tail was on fire and kept goin' straight on west. Looked like he was headin' for the Black place. You want me to gather some of the men and go after him?"

Arch gritted teeth for a moment, thinking about that. Finally, he shook his head and dismounted. "No. I guess Seth will come home . . . when he comes home. Take care of Tomahawk for me, please, Fred." He turned and strode toward the house, vanished inside, leaving Perkins holding Tomahawk's bridle and wondering what the hell was going on.

One of Caitlan's horse wranglers yelled to Moody: "Rider comin', Les! I wonder how he got past the border guards?"

Moody squinted from beneath his eyebrow-hugging hat brim. "I dunno, but he's sure comin' on hell-bent for leather, ain't he. Git some of the men together in case this is trouble on the hoof."

"Yes, suh, Mistuh Moody." Ambrose headed toward the stables, leaving Les alone in the yard.

Presently, Moody recognized the rider. He yelled: "Miss Cat! Miss Cat, I think you oughta come out here! I think you got company!"

Caitlan appeared at the front door to the house, a dish towel in one hand, the other shading her eyes from sun. She, too, recognized Violet more than Ben, and started to smile, but her pleased expression faded under puzzlement when— looking neither right nor left—Seth Locklin guided the lathered and heaving mare through their yard and onward without slackening their pace.

"What the hell?" Les growled. He glanced at Caitlan who stepped off the porch, her mouth open, and hurried up beside him. "Wasn't that Arch Locklin's boy, Miss Cat? Where he think he's goin', fer gawd's sake!"

"Yes, it is . . . and I think I know." She whirled to head back toward the house. "Bridle Picket Fence for me, Les . . . never mind a saddle! We don't have time for that!"

"But he didn't look like he wanted no company, Miss Cat. You . . ."

She hesitated long enough to snap: "I don't care whether Mister Locklin wants company or

139

not! This is my ranch, and I want to know what his rush is all about!"

"I'll go with you."

"No!" Caitlan vanished back inside the house. By the time she returned wearing britches in place of her skirt, and strapping a gun belt around her waist, Moody had brought a sorrel with four white stockings out of the stable. He held the horse's head while Caitlan grabbed mane and flung herself astride.

Moody tried: "Miss Cat, it ain't safe for you to go alone. That buckaroo looked half crazy. At least . . ."

"Hush, Les. I'm armed. You keep an eye on the place for me while I'm gone. Seth was headed for Bountiful Spring. I'm not back in an hour, then come after me." She kicked the sorrel into a quick trot, also headed for the glade.

Ben had had to halt Violet long enough to open the gate to the foaling meadow—the quarter horse wasn't a jumper, and, besides, both the fence and gate that sealed the area were built high enough to prevent exuberant horses from clearing them. His own instincts told him never to leave a gate open so someone's stock could roam; he shut and locked it behind him, but once again in the saddle, urged Violet back into a gallop toward the stone-buttressed cut leading to the artesian spring.

He had to slow the mare while traversing the slippery uneven rocks there, but when he reached the box cañon, he raced Violet across it and didn't halt her until he'd nearly run her into the pool itself.

He leaped from the mare's back. In a frenzy he ripped off the saddle, blanket, and bridle and flung them aside. His hat followed. He tore off his boots, shirt, pants, and underings, dropped it all in a heap on the grass, and, naked, fell into the pool.

Depth eased gently down to some eight or ten feet near the cliff face; though he could have waded, Ben started swimming immediately. The water was cold but not icy, fresh and invigorating, but he wasn't here for a pleasure swim. When he reached the far wall, he grabbed out-jutting rocks for support and ducked under the waterfall where he let water beat down onto his head for a long time, trying to use its force as a barrier against thinking, hoping the battering would cool what he felt was an overheated brain, but without much success. The inside of his head swam with pictures, images of past things he was no longer sure were real people, and happenings that may have never actually occurred.

How could a man spend a lifetime being someone and then suddenly discover he was somebody else? How could he keep knowing he was Ben Hawthorne when so many people . . . all other people . . . good people, not those men in the root cellar . . . were sure he was Seth Locklin? Yet, where were his Seth memories? Had the men in the hole on the Wharton Ranch done a more complete job on his mind than he'd ever dreamed they had?

He pulled back from under the waterfall and glanced at the dappled gray standing spraddle-legged and still heaving for breath beside the pool. Even after promising David he would care for Violet, he had nearly killed the mare, fleeing questions without answers and answers that only brought more questions.

Under another surge of emotion, he flung back his head and his wordless scream of frustration rang against sheer walls, was loud over even the waterfall's own voice. The sound of it froze Caitlan in the narrow pass, for the cry reeked of pain. Rather than riding Picket Fence into the glade, she slid to the ground and led the horse the rest of the way.

Ben had swam back across the pool by the time Cat arrived, had pulled himself up onto dry land, and now sat staring at the fountain. He was still as naked as the day he was born; his back was to the glade entrance, his legs sprawled, hands clasped between his knees. Either he was mired so deeply in thought that he didn't hear her footsteps, or was so bogged-down in misery that he hoped someone would shoot him in his

142

unprotected back; whichever, he didn't move when the girl came up behind him.

Caitlan was horrified at sight of the wounds she saw marring his skin. When she gasped— "Oh, Seth, I had no idea you'd been so terribly hurt!"—and he leaped to his feet in surprise and whirled to face her, she got to see the rest of him.

All the rest of him.

Chapter Twelve

"I never saw anybody blush all over before," Cat grinned. "I mean, I've seen people get red in the face, yes, but all over? That was quite a feat, Seth."

Too slowly, and far too late for modesty, she had turned her back to allow Ben to at least pull on his underings and britches.

On the other side of the pool, Picket Fence drank from the clear water while Violet—recovering from her miles-long run—rolled luxuriously in green grass. Sipping at hidden reservoirs, bright yellow butterflies clustered on moist gravel. Birds hopped from branch to branch in the bordering trees, their twittering a barely heard background chorus. Some small aquatic animal rustled briefly in the little stand of cat-tails at the northern pool edge. It would have been a perfect setting, but for Ben's words.

Caitlan sat Indian-fashion in the sun while Seth Locklin—or Ben Hawthorne—lay propped on an elbow beside her. The last time they had been together, she had done most of the talking, he the listening. This time, she listened in silence while he told her everything—all about his Ben Hawthorne life and the memories that seemed to be at least partly false, about the men in the

144

root cellar, about the bounty hunters, and, the latest, that he somehow spoke and understood the Kiowa tongue, and that even Medicine Shield claimed him as son.

She finally nodded, then said: "Some men take a half dozen or more names for themselves in their lives, but I reckon they always recall who they started out as. That must be a pure pain, not to know . . . not to be sure. And I agree with you that the likelihood of you being Ben but looking so like Seth and David is . . . preposterous, so . . ."

"So I must be Seth, despite my other . . . memories."

"Yes."

"Then, where'd those Ben memories come from? Sure, the men in the cellar kept tellin' me I was Ben Hawthorne. They kept sayin' the same things over and over, but that's all they said. They never mentioned the rest of it or talked about my Comanche father, Nighthorse, or his chief wife, Gray Dove . . . Cora and Eli Hawthorne . . . Mister and Missus Inman . . . none of the rest of it!"

"Are you sure? Are you real sure?"

He shook his head. "No. Now that you ask, no." He lifted his eyes to look around the glade. "What peace, here. If I could just stay here for the rest of my life . . ."

"Yes. After my father died, Mama and I came here often. After she died, Frank and I came here.

145

After Frank was killed, I came here. Somehow, we have to save this, Seth. Somehow . . ."

"Oh! In all this stampede, I forgot! We can save Bountiful Spring!" He told her about the dam and the lake with a new runoff creek he and Arch Locklin contemplated creating.

"Oh, Seth, thank you! Thank you!" She leaned to him suddenly, flung arms around him, and pressed her cheek to his. "Whether it works or not, thank you for trying!"

The hour deadline she had given Les Moody was well past. The ramrod had gathered three of his wranglers, and they arrived at the glade in time to see Miss Cat in what appeared to be an intimate embrace with a half-naked man.

Moody halted his companions. They scowled toward the couple by the pool for a long grim moment before one muttered: "That son-of-a-bitch, Arch Locklin! Couldn't get Miss Cat's ranch and the spring any other way, so he sent his kid to woo it out of her. By damn, we gotta stop that!"

"You're right, Ambrose," Moody agreed. "But don't discredit Miss Cat . . . we'll wait to see what she does about it herself. In the meantime, we'll tighten our boundary guard and just keep a closer eye on things."

They waited, semi-hidden and silent, until they saw Seth Locklin rise, put on his shirt, socks, boots, hat, and gun belt, then catch his mare and begin to saddle her, before they retreated to the ranch yard. They didn't want Miss Cat to know they'd been spying on what might be her personal affairs.

Still, they were never too far away, in case she needed them to protect her person.

"Les, I'm going to ride to the property line with Mister Locklin to make sure no one accidentally shoots him, then I want you and all the hands not out on range duty to meet with me in the main house. I have some good news to tell you." Caitlan slid a quick glance at Ben sitting silently astride Violet a small distance aside, and smiled.

Moody and his men had made it back to the ranch far enough ahead of Ben and Cat to hide that they'd been into Bountiful Spring; the ramrod stood with a palm resting on Picket Fence's shoulder while he looked out from under his hat brim. "Well, if you want to tell me, I can pass it along to the men, Miss Cat."

"No, thanks anyway, Les. I want the pleasure of breaking the news, myself. I'll be back shortly." To Ben, she said: "I'm ready if you are, Seth."

Hawthorne nodded. He touched his hat brim to the men around them—none of them returned the gesture—and kneed Violet up beside Picket Fence. Together, he and Caitlan guided their mounts eastward.

Presently, he commented: "Your men don't

147

trust me any farther than they can fling a barn."

"Yes, well, you're a Locklin. Once, we all worked together out here, the Blacks and the Locklins . . . it was us against the Indians and the land and the weather. But lately . . ." She sighed heavily. "Maybe after I tell them about the dam and the lake, things will change back to the way they should be. If it's not too late."

"A lot of resentment on both sides now, I expect."

"Yes. And it didn't just happen overnight. It has grown through these last years, sort of along with your father's holdings, you know. The bigger Arch Locklin's spread got, the worse my men hated him for it. Now, the anger has settled in deep. Just like it took a while to build, it will take a while for it to die. At least, the dam will be a start. When they hear about the lake and all . . ."

But her wranglers had their own ideas of what their lady boss was going to tell them when she returned. One of the men who had accompanied Les Moody to Bountiful Spring glade, and had seen Miss Cat and Seth Locklin in what appeared to be a loving embrace, growled to the ramrod: "You don't s'pose Miss Cat's gonna tell us she's fixin' to wed that there Locklin boy, do you, Les?"

"I dunno," Moody returned gloomily. "We'll just have to wait and hear her out."

The wrangler persisted. "She marries that boy, that'd make this, at the worst, part of Arch Locklin's spread . . . at the best, a Locklin son's ranch. I ain't workin' for no Locklin, I'll tell ya that!"

"Yup," Les scowled. "Whichever, we'll just see that don't happen. We may have to protect Miss Cat from herself, comes to that. She may own this place and be our boss, but she's only a li'l girl. Sometimes, females don't quite know what's good for 'em. Takes us men to look out for 'em.

"You, Ambrose, go tell the others to gather 'round, here. I think we'll have a meetin' of our own before Miss Cat gets back."

"What about the line riders what just left? They won't be in till tomorrow."

Les shrugged. "We'll just have to wait and tell 'em then. Go on, now, Ambrose, collect the men. I got words to say to 'em, soonest."

Ben had had what amounted to a bath in Bountiful Spring pool; he merely changed into clean clothes for what was evolving into a ritual—dinner alone with Arch Locklin.

It started out in strained silence, and the lack of conversation held until Arch suddenly commented: "That meeting with Medicine Shield today really stampeded you, didn't it."

"Yes, sir, it did."

"Why?"

149

Ben gnawed the fried chicken leg for a moment, chewed thoughtfully, and swallowed before he answered: "Because I didn't know him. Because I shouldn't have understood his lingo, but I did. Not recognizin' him is one thing, but that other . . ." He shook his head. "Sir . . . sir, how far off is Medicine Shield's regular camp?"

"Well, it depends on the day you're speaking of, I suppose. They move around regularly, following the hunt."

"I know, but ain't . . . isn't there one spot where they lite more often than not?"

"Umm . . . yes, I believe so. It's about ten miles north of here. Why?"

"Didn't Seth . . . uh . . . I ever come back here to visit when . . . I . . . got older? When I was no longer a tad? I mean, seems like it's not all that far."

Arch wiped his mouth and hands on a cloth napkin and leaned on forearms braced at either side of his plate before he studied Ben from beneath fair brows drawn into a half frown. "Yes, you did. Once. Only once, before . . . years later . . . you brought Blue Glass Bead and the baby here to live. That was one of the strangest days of David's and my lives."

"Really!" Ben also propped elbows on the table top, the chicken leg forgotten in his fingers. "Why?"

"You don't recall it?"

"No. What happened?"

Arch flopped back in his chair, his chin on his chest, his eyes opaque with remembering. "David . . . David and I were having breakfast here in this very room, when Ruff Bullock came charging in yelling that we had to come outside to see something. Of course, we went." He laughed slightly. "There you were in the middle of the yard, seeming almost . . . posed, you know? You were fourteen, then, I believe. Yes, you and David were fourteen.

"You had long hair done in braids. You were wearing a fringed leather shirt and leggings . . . a red loincloth. You carried a bow and rawhide quiver, had a painted shield on your left arm and held a lance in your right hand. You sat your spotted pony and didn't move a hair. You just looked at us. After four years of separation, there was no hello, no . . ." Arch shook his head.

"David yelled . . . 'It's Seth! Seth has come home!' . . . and ran out to greet you. He was so happy . . . ecstatic to have you back. But you merely turned your head to look down at him and your expression was about the same, I'd say, as a man would hold had he been bucked off his horse and landed face-first into a rotten carcass. You didn't say anything at all until David put a hand on your knee, and then you lowered your lance, touched his chest with the point, and snapped some Kiowa words in what sounded like total disgust before you wheeled your pony and just . . . left. We never knew why you had come. We never saw you again until now."

Ben's own expression had become as closed as he expected Snow Fox's had been then. He recalled his—Ben Hawthorne's—own decision to leave the Comanches. He could remember riding into Hosea Inman's yard, his own long hair hanging in fur-wrapped braids down the front of his leather shirt. Otherwise, like Seth, he wore loincloth, leggings, and moccasins; unlike Snow Fox, he had carried no weapons but a knife.

He remembered most of the Inman children surrounding him at a safe distance—Jacob had been about seventeen, then; Matthew his own age—fifteen. Arnie would have been about thirteen, Lucy ten, Harve maybe seven, and Karen almost five. Little Josephine, clinging to her mother's skirt, was all of two. In his mind's eye, he saw Hosea, sturdy, a staunch Christian, a man of cattle and soil, asking—"Who are you?"—and how hard it had been to bring the words of a language neither spoken nor heard for so many years back to his mind and tongue well enough to answer.

At first, all he could get out was: "Know . . . my name . . . is Ben." But he had been lucky. Mr. and Mrs. Inman had welcomed him as a lost white child escaped from the heathen, a boy come home to his own. They had been patient with him while he tried to recall a life that was now only a shadowy dream world, and a language he had suppressed while desperately trying to learn both Comanche and Kiowa well enough that he could ask to go home. They . . .

"Ah!" His eyes lighted. That was how he had learned the Kiowa tongue! Nighthorse's wife was a Kiowa woman. She had taught it to him along with Comanche words because she missed her own language and took pleasure in teaching it to someone else!

"What!" Arch scowled. "You just remembered something! What is it?"

Not wanting to go into the real answer, at least not yet, Ben evaded the question by merely saying: "When you haven't heard or spoken . . . a language in years . . . especially if you only knew that tongue as a child, hearing it again sort of . . . addles your brain. I think the reason S-S-S . . . uh . . . I didn't answer David back then was probably because hearing English brought back too many . . . hard emotions. It was maybe a sense of . . . loss that kept h- . . . me from speakin', and a fear I wouldn't do it right. A warrior has to do it right or not at all."

"But why did you come in the first place? Why?"

"I don't know." Ben shook his head. Like so many other things, he had no answer to that, maybe wouldn't have been able to tell, had Arch asked why Ben Hawthorne had gone to the Inmans.

Answers! God, how he needed some answers!

PART TWO

Chapter Thirteen

Ben awoke well before dawn, and in the dimness of pre-light, eased out of bed and to the camel-back trunk. He lifted the top and braced it gently back against the wall before he took out the loincloth and its belt, the leggings, moccasins, bone-and-quill bib, and the beaded knife belt. Slowly, one by one, he donned each item to discover they fit him well. The only things he didn't take were the broken spear and the feather—the latter was Seth's trophy won by a brave deed he wasn't sure he could claim, and, if not, it would be a travesty to wear it.

The house was silent, all occupants but himself still sleeping when he slipped out his bedroom door and down the stairs to the ground floor.

The air held the cool freshness of night not yet become a new day when he stepped through the front door, off the porch, and hurried toward the corral where Violet rested with other horses. Carrying a bridle he picked off a corral post, and moving easily so not to spook the animals, he located the mare, slid the bit into her mouth, adjusted straps and led her out into the yard. Flinging himself astride her bare back, he nudged her northwest toward where the barest hint of light limned the crests of the broken hills just north of the cliffs enclosing Bountiful Spring.

Out on the prairie, he nudged Violet into an easy trot and merely sat her back, savoring his surroundings. The light wind was scented with a brief dew moistening untold miles of grass, the quiet broken only by the mare's legs swishing through the blades, her hoofs soft on thick underlying root masses. Most of the night predators had already returned to their daytime dens; the day hunters had not yet ventured out. The prairie was a vast empty landscape of momentary peace that would hold its serenity until the rising sun lighted the first kill of the day.

By the time Ben reached the abrupt up-jut of the small rocky ridge north of Caitlan Black's place, there was enough light to show him rock faces and hand- and toe-holds. He left Violet ground-tethered there at the foot of the bluffs, picked his target, and began to climb. It took him perhaps ten minutes to make it to the top of the cliff, but when he rose at the crest of the drop off and turned to face east, the sun showed its first bead above the horizon.

He stood with feet together, back straight, lifted his arms and face to it, watched the eerie phenomenon of light racing across the prairie toward him like phosphorescence poured from a pitcher, and said aloud: "Dear God . . . Supreme Spirit . . . Great Mysterious Power . . . *Wakan Tanka* . . . whoever you are . . . by whatever name

you like . . . here I am. I need your help. Help . . .
help! Nighthorse, he says you are part of every
livin' thing, that you manifest yourself in every
bird and tree and critter roamin' the land. Missus
Inman, she also says you look after all things
livin' here. Well, I'm alive . . . at the moment . . .
so I guess you also look after me.

"My name is Ben Hawthorne . . . I think.
But everybody else in sight tells me I'm Seth
Locklin. I . . . don't recall ever bein' Seth, God
. . . Great Mysterious Power . . . and this whole
thing is drivin' me crazy, Lord . . . Great One . . .
and I come lookin' for some answers, if you're so
inclined. A spirit vision, maybe? I ain't askin' for
much, you see, just . . . just maybe a hint of who
I really am, because except for a couple of people
. . . and I don't mind discountin' them at all . . .
everybody has been real good to me. I don't want
to hurt anyone, Lord. I ain't interested in power
or riches or ownin' huge hunks of land. My Injun
folks taught me a man lives with your lands and
your critters, never owning it because This World
is a gift from you to be cherished, not . . . not . . ."

He took a deeper breath and closed his eyes.
The sun was now a half round casting the sky
above it into gold and pale blue, driving the night
at his back farther and farther away. He felt the
life-warmth on his bare chest and lifted arms. It
seemed to pulse on his throat in time with the
beat of his heart. Eyes still closed, he emptied

his mind, waiting for some voice other than his own to fill the spaces there even while his lips whispered: "Help . . . help . . . help. . . ."

Mrs. Inman's words flashed through him: *Sometimes God's great love is best shown by the prayers He never answers.* He fought that idea away and kept waiting, though he continued to call for help. He was so deep in prayer, he neither heard nor saw the small band of riders approaching from out of the south.

Les Moody led PeeWee Moore, Roy Harkins, and Ambrose Clair out for their morning check on Caitlan Black's cattle herd. They were in no hurry, merely letting their breakfast settle and their horses walk until PeeWee pointed and said: "Glory be, look up there, wouldja!"

The others turned eyes in the direction he indicated; they saw a lone figure motionless at the edge of the cliff, arms and face lifted to the sun.

PeeWee laughed and went on. "I think I'll start my day off right and rid the world of one more Injun." He yanked his rifle from its saddle scabbard and threw a shell into the chamber.

Moody reached over and batted the rifle barrel down.

"Hold it, PeeWee! That ain't no Injun. Look at the color of his skin. Look at his hair. Shit, that's that tow-headed Locklin boy . . . uh . . . Seth!"

"What in tarnation is he doin' up there lookin' like that?" Ambrose frowned.

"Hell, y'know he was raised by them Kiowas," PeeWee scowled. "Bein' raised up by redskins addles a white's brains. They never git over it."

Roy Harkins nodded. "Ain't that the truth. I recall a li'l gal took by the Dakotas up north. Plumb loony by the time her people got her back. Seemed to think her total purpose in life was tannin' hides. You couldn't skin a gawd-damned rabbit for dinner else the gal would be out tannin' the critter's hide. Finally had to ship her off to some bedlam back East. And now, what's he doin'?"

"Looks like he's prayin' or somethin'," PeeWee put in. "Some heathen ritual, mebby."

"Whatever," Moody grinned mirthlessly, "I think we got us a stroke of good fortune here. Let's catch us a white Injun, men! I got some words I need to say to that Locklin bastard!"

Without any answers, Ben sighed, lowered his arms, bowed his head in gloomy thought for a second, and in that moment saw four horsemen waiting around Violet at the foot of the cliff. He'd known he was on Caitlan's land, but in his need for help, hadn't given it much thought. The feeling that maybe he had been dangerously stupid to come here alone and essentially unarmed bounced his heart briefly, but he shoved that

161

aside. Those were Cat's men; he had probably met them and they him the day he'd come to visit, so if he merely climbed down the cliff, said good morning to them, got on Violet, and went home, there should be no trouble.

They continued to wait while Hawthorne made his way down the side of the rock face. Ben negotiated the broken rip-rap at the base of the cliff, walked easily toward them, sidled between horses, and reached for Violet's reins. He said: "Howdy, men. Fine mornin', isn't it?"

"Is that," Moody returned. "Locklin, we want a word with you."

"Oh?" Ben vaulted astride the mare, but tightened reins to hold Violet steady. "Well, shout it out."

"First off, you're on Miss Cat's property. We could have shot you for trespassin'."

Ben turned to look from man to man, noted hard eyes and unfriendly expressions. His gaze ended up on Les who he recognized as Caitlan's ramrod. "Well, sir, Mister Moody, I expect you could have, though I'm grateful you didn't. I came unarmed and merely to make my peace with the Supreme Spirit."

"I'll ask you to take your heathen ways elsewhere, Locklin. Don't go sullyin' up Miss Cat's land with pagan doin's. And while I'm mentionin' Miss Cat, you keep your makeshift Injun hands off her, understand me?"

Ben's open expression hardened. He noted the men's hands resting near their sidearms, that one held the stock of a sheathed rifle, knew all he had with him was a Kiowa hunting knife, and again felt that he'd been a damned fool coming here. He had prayed for answers but had gotten none. Now, he was faced by four armed men who didn't like him one bit. Still, while it behooved him not to be prideful, he wasn't going to fling up his hands and cry *please don't shoot me, I'll never rile you again!*

He said: "What goes on between Miss Cat and me is my business and hers. You got concerns, you go talk to her about them. When she tells me to stay off her land, then I'll listen." He reined Violet around and nudged her into a slow walk back toward Arch's spread. He took it easy so not to give the impression of flight. Neither did he want a burst of speed to spook the wranglers into some dangerous action. He was prepared to duck a bullet; he wasn't ready for the lariat loop that settled down over his head and shoulders, cinched tight around his chest, pinned his arms to his body, and jerked him off Violet's back.

He almost landed on his feet, but the wrangler kept backing his horse and tipped him off balance; he hit the ground hard but not violently enough to break anything. He found himself sliding across the slick grass when the cow pony kept the lariat tight as it had been trained to do, tried to bend elbows, grab at the loop around him, and push it up to free himself, but two men were there, one on either side of him. They seized his wrists and forced his arms down. While Roy Harkins kept the rope taut and Ambrose Clair and PeeWee Moore held their prisoner secure, Moody walked up, knelt to drop a knee onto Ben's chest, grabbed a handful of fair hair to hold Hawthorne still, and drew his six-shooter.

Ben would have fought them, but he knew he couldn't escape at the moment and squirming like a worm on a hook would not only cause himself damage but would probably goad these men into serious violence. He set his teeth, met Moody's narrowed green eyes, and merely waited while the man said: "Now, listen up, Locklin, or whoever you are, I seen you at Bountiful Spring with Miss Cat yesterday, you half nekkid and holdin' her in your arms like she belonged to you. She ain't your woman, and if yer daddy thinks to send you over here to confuse her head with your sweet talk, know you gotta git through us men, first."

Ben gritted: "What went on at the spring was purely innocent, Moody, just a friend comfortin' a fr- . . ." His words cut off sharply when Les jammed the pistol barrel up under his nose.

Moody snarled: "Ain't nothin' innocent where a Locklin is concerned, boy. The likes of you don't do nothin' 'cept it's for more land and more

164

power and more money. I tell you, you ain't gettin' Bountiful, this ranch, or Miss Cat, you hear me?"

"Take that damned hogleg out of my face, Moody. Yes, I hear you. Didn't Caitlan tell you men about the dam we're goin' to build? That'll solve the water problem for everybody."

"Speakin' of bodies, the dam's one thing, it's Miss Cat's body we're most concerned with here!"

Now Ben did try to wrench free. It was a failed effort and his first assessment of his situation proved to be correct. Moody didn't shoot him, but he did shift his weight to ram his knee into Hawthorne's belly and drive the breath out of him.

Ben gasped a choked cry. He panted heavily for a moment before he got out: "Caitlan is a grown woman and who she sees or not is . . ."

"Miss Cat's a li'l girl all by herself out here but for us men to look out fer her, and, by gawd, boy, we *will* look out after her. You hear me?" Moody's fingers tightened painfully in Ben's hair, emphasizing his words. "You hear me, boy?"

"Y-Yeah, I hear you. If you're so mortally concerned about Miss Cat's safety, wh-why don't one of you marry her to protect her person?"

"Some of us have tried, but . . ."

"No luck, eh?" Ben forced a grin. "Well, at

least Miss Cat's got good . . ." Moody's knee had driven into him again.

"Whut goes on 'tween us and Miss Cat's our business, boy. But you take note here and now. We're watchin' over Miss Cat, so you keep yer Locklin hands off her. You have to talk to her, you make damned sure it's Yes, Miss Cat, ma'am . . . no, Miss Cat, ma'am, and I'll stand way over here by the doorway with my hat in my hand, Miss Cat, ma'am, 'cuz next time we see you with a arm aroun' her, that arm comes off at the shoulder, get my drift?" The knee gouged into Ben's midriff a third time before Moody rose and stood back. He said to his men: "Gawd damned Locklin stray shoulda stayed with the Injuns where he belonged. Let him up, boys, and haze him on outta here."

Harkins nodded and urged his horse forward a few steps to slacken the rope; he began to pull it in when PeeWee yanked the loop from around Ben and tossed the business end of the lariat back at him. Moore and Ambrose let go of their captive and stood back, scowling, their palms pointedly on their pistol grips while they watched Hawthorne roll over onto his belly before he thrust himself upright. The mounted man finished coiling his rope, draped it temporarily over his saddle horn, and drew his rifle from its scabbard. Ben had been going to say that he had never intended anything but honest friendship toward Caitlan Black, but he looked at the four men glowering at him, clenched teeth, and made his way more or less unsteadily to where Violet waited a short distance off. He moved slowly, torn by the need to get the hell out of here before one or more of those wranglers lost hold on restraint and started shooting, and, again, the need not to appear to be in full retreat.

He mounted, nudged Violet into motion, but held her to a trot for a few minutes. He didn't look back. Finally, when he felt everyone, including himself, had calmed down sufficiently, he allowed the mare to canter. Only when he was well out of rifle range did he relax enough to shake his head sadly.

This whole operation had been an exercise in futility. He had prayed to God—both the Indians' and the white man's, if they were different—though somehow he felt the Supreme Power was one and the same despite names and popular opinion—but he got no answers. He had professed innocent friendship to Cat Black and her men and was met with open mistrust.

He glanced southward. He could merely head that way, go back to Texas, and to the Inmans and forget this whole thing.

No. Maybe one day, but not yet. He had to find the answers, and maybe God or whoever would supply them, in His own time, not his . . . Ben's . . . or Seth's . . . regardless of his urgent need.

• • •

What appeared to be the preponderance of the Locklin cowpunchers were gathered in quiet, murmuring clots in the front yard before the big house when Ben guided Violet toward the stables. He reined in, frowning and abruptly wary—something had happened here, but . . . Was it something he had done?

Reluctant to dismount in case he had to make a fast get-away, he nudged Violet toward the nearest group of men.

"What's goin' on?"

Most of the men eyed him with scowls and aside comments to each other about the way he was dressed. Only Fred Perkins answered him. "Glad you're back, Mister Locklin. Best you hurry on into the house. I expect your Pa needs you bad about now."

"All right." Ben dismounted and handed the reins over. "Would you take care of Violet for me, please, Fred? She's ate up a long hard trail this mornin'."

"Sure, Mister Locklin." Under silent looks from the others, Perkins led the mare away.

Ben glanced again at those around him, thought: *No love lost here.* Nevertheless, he nodded. "Men."

A few nodded back. Some merely glared. Others turned their backs.

All right. Ben started for the big house.

Wringing her hands, the hired girl, Midge, stood in the front doorway. There were tears on her cheeks. She gasped: "Oh, I'm so glad you're home, Mister Seth. You go on upstairs, now, please. Hurry, please."

"Why? What is it?"

She burst into outright bawling. "Your poor, poor brother, Mister David. Hurry on, please, Mister Seth."

A kind of cold gray premonition swept through Ben. He patted Midge's arm, said: "You go set in the kitchen and compose yourself, girl. I'm goin'." He headed for the stairs. He knew what he would see even before he reached David's room, because that nightmare or medicine dream the other night had prepared him. But then, his chill deepened. He had prayed for help from the Great Mysterious . . . was this God's answer? No! No, not possible!

David didn't look any different to Ben than he had the last time he'd seen him—still white and skeletal, the hands still curled over the stark collar bones. Except that the eyes were closed, the only other differences were that the limbs no longer twitched spasmodically and the chest didn't rise and fall to breathing.

Arch sat in a chair beside the bed, his own hands folded, his expression sad. At the window, Mrs. McPhee rocked in her chair, her gaze fixed on the floor. Today, she wasn't sewing.

Ben stepped up behind Arch and lay a hand on his shoulder.

Arch looked up. "I'm glad you're back, Seth." He resumed staring at David's corpse.

Ben asked: "When did it happen?"

"A little while ago. Missus McPhee came to . . . change his . . . his diaper, and . . . She'd been here all the time. He evidently went so quietly . . . so without struggle . . . she never even knew it had happened until . . ." He sighed softly. "It seems that David decided to live until you returned, Seth. Now that you're back, he felt . . . free to go."

Part of Ben's mind cried: *No! No, don't put that on me!* Another part searched for something decent to say. Finally, he came up with: "It's a blessing . . . for him. He maybe should have gone a year ago."

"Yes." Arch's shoulders shuddered. "If I'd been more of a man, maybe I could have . . . helped him along, but I still had hope." He breathed a bitter half laugh. "Hope. That's the most obscene word in any language, Seth. Even after the Eastern physicians I brought here told me there was none, I still had hope . . . hope that maybe one day David would come out of it, would heal on his own, would be David again.

"Hope can kill your soul, Seth. You hang onto it and hang onto it, partly because you want to, partly because everyone around you keeps telling

170

you that you mustn't lose hope . . . you have to have hope . . . until, when you finally have to face the fact that there is no hope and never was, it makes the hurt cut twice as deep. Damn hope to hell!"

Ben's fingers tightened on Arch's shoulder. Otherwise, he said nothing to that, merely asked: "Will there be a wake?" Mrs. Inman had been big on wakes.

"No. We have actually held a wake over David for a year and a half. That's long enough, don't you think? Uh . . . his coffin is in the attic. I h-had it made . . ." Arch's voice roughened briefly; he swallowed hard before continuing. "Shortly after the accident. I never expected him to survive so long. We have to get the coffin down and send a couple of men to town to bring Reverend Mason here for the burial."

Ben patted the shoulder. "You set, sir. I'll see to it." With Arch staring at the corpse and Mrs. McPhee still rocking, he left hurriedly to do what was necessary.

Chapter Fourteen

"Where exactly is Medicine Shield's camp from here?"

Ben's question brought Arch up sharply from over his plate. It was the day after David's death. They ate a somber breakfast together in the dining room, neither speaking of David—it was as though Seth Locklin's younger twin had been deceased for years.

Locklin snapped: "You already asked me that once and I told you. The way you were dressed yesterday, I thought you'd already gone there. Why do you ask again?"

Ben sighed and sipped coffee before he answered: "I was awake a long time last night."

"I know. I heard you pacing your floor. What troubled you?"

What troubled Ben was a feeling of being trapped, of being in a place where he shouldn't be, of being named as someone he still didn't believe he was, of being used. As long as David Locklin was alive, he'd felt he still had a partial out; if worse came to worst, he could merely saddle Violet and vanish one day into the vast wilderness to the south or west—he doubted that, rich though Arch Locklin was, he would spend another forty thousand dollars running him down again—and he would still be able to say he'd left

Arch with at least one son. But now that David was dead . . . To leave a father in his sorrow . . . Whether he was Seth Locklin or not, he couldn't do that.

What he needed to do was to see the Kiowas' camp for himself, to discover if it brought back any memories. He had tried to think of a woman named Blue Glass Bead last night, struggling to conjure a picture of her in his mind. There were visions of plenty of young Indian women there, yes, and he could attach names to each . . . Pretty Chipmunk, Deer Stands on Hill, Swallow . . . but their facial paint and the decorations on their dresses told him they were all Comanche, not Kiowa. He needed to go talk with tongue or sign to Medicine Shield and try to either recapture Blue Glass Bead in his memory or settle that he had never known her as wife and the mother of a son he also couldn't recall.

He knew Arch would never go for that and devised a lie. "I was thinkin' about the dam, the lake, and maybe the new runoff creek. You said there are no white settlements yonder that would be harmed by us shuttin' off their water, but what about the Injuns? I think we should at least tell 'em what we're gonna do, and why, so if need be, they can be prepared for it. You got enough trouble without gettin' the Kiowas ruffled at you, too."

"You want to warn Medicine Shield?"

"Yes, sir, I do. Let him and his people know that even if they see Runoff Creek dryin' up downstream that there'll most likely be a new stream runnin' a different way shortly, and that they can water their folks and horses and the like from the new lake and so on."

Arch flung down his napkin. "You seem to assume I will allow that."

Ben was surprised. "Uh . . . won't you?"

"I don't know." Locklin scowled at his plate for a long hard moment. "You build a lake for our own use, give the savages permission to use it, and presently they set up camp on its shores. Pretty soon, they consider it to be their lake . . . their shores. They object to cattle coming through to water . . . either kill or claim the animals as their own. No, I've spent years securing this spread. . . ." His voice faltered when Hawthorne abruptly laughed; he asked: "What do you find humorous here, Seth?"

"Those reasons you're givin' for not lettin' the Kiowas use water from your lake are damned near the exact same reasons I heard from Caitlan Black for not lettin' your critters use her spring. Shit!" He flung aside his own napkin, shoved his chair back, and stood. "Can't win no matter how hard you try! Where's Medicine Shield's camp from here?"

Arch looked bemused. He raised brows at Ben. "You really don't remember?"

174

"No, I don't. Where is it?"

"Go about seven or eight miles straight north of here. But, Seth . . ."

"No, I'm goin' to go tell 'em about it all, now, before it gets started. We don't need a water war with the Kiowas, too. And yes, before you ask, I'll be back. I give you my bounden word, I'll . . . be back." He headed for the door.

Arch called after him: "Seth, don't go alone! Take some of the men with you."

Ben hesitated to comment. "The only one of your men that can stand the sight of me is Fred Perkins, and I sent him in yesterday to gather the minister to perform buryin' rites for David. Given the way the rest feel about me, I'll be safer goin' alone."

"Then, if you'll wait a minute, I'll go with you."

"No. It wouldn't look right, you and me goin' ridin' while David's still lyin' dead in the house. You have to do right by your son's memory. Seven or so miles there . . . an hour palaver . . . seven or so miles back . . . I'll have lunch with you." Ben proceeded on through the house and out toward the stables.

At the corral, bridle in hand, Ben called Violet to him. As he grasped the mare's chin, she nuzzled him, and he led her through the open gate. Shots—merely the faint tail ends of echoes—seemed borne toward him on the wings of a bird flying overhead. He hesitated and frowned westward, waiting for more gunfire, but nothing happened. Finally, he shrugged and slipped the bridle into place.

While he was saddling Violet, Dallas Young-street sauntered over and looked him up and down. The man's nose was still slightly swollen, his left eye still darkened with a bruise, but he seemed to have regained his self-confidence.

He asked: "Where you goin', squawman?"

Ben slid a cool look toward the ramrod. "On an errand for Mister Locklin, if it's any of your business. Why aren't you out on the range lookin' after your own job?"

"My business is to see to the ranch for Arch while Ruff's gone, and I take my job serious."

"I didn't know you and Mister Locklin were on a first name basis." Ben tightened the cinch and let the stirrup down from where he'd hung it over the saddle horn. He wore a pistol on his hip. Briefly he considered taking Dallas out just to be rid of the man but, instead, swung astride the mare.

Youngstreet's lip curled. "What I call Mistuh Locklin is between him and me, squawman, and none of your affair. You got my permission to go about your business for him . . . if it's for him."

Reins in one hand, Ben folded forearms and leaned on the saddle horn to look down at the

176

man. "You're really pushin' for a rematch, aren't you."

Dallas grinned. "You bet."

"All right, you got yourself a deal. But it's gonna have to wait a decent time after my brother's funeral. Let's say three days. That ought to give you time to heal up from the damage I done to you last time."

Youngstreet hooked thumbs in his gun belt, asked: "Shoot-out or fists?"

"Ah, hell"—Ben grinned coldly—"let's make it fists again. Bullets are expensive, and I sure ain't gonna waste money on the likes of you." He whirled Violet and kicked her into a canter northward. Regardless of his smile, he was tense until he was out of pistol range—to deliberately turn his back on Dallas invited a bullet in the spine. Since he was alone, he let himself heave a loud breath of relief when nothing happened.

He reined Violet into an easy, mile-eating running-trot and settled into the saddle to merely use up the distance between here and Medicine Shield's present camp, wondering if he could actually locate it. The prairie ran on and on for what seemed to be forever. Over to his left, one of Locklin's vast herds grazed placidly. Ahead, a coyote loped by, head up and ears alert, a mouse in its jaws. Once, Violet shied to avoid a rattlesnake's strike—what the varmint was doing out here in the growing heat was beyond Ben, for the reptile should have finished its night hunt and returned to its hole or to the shade of some likely bush to rest out the day.

An hour later, he frowned, pulled Violet down to a walk, and squinted through rising heat shimmers at what approached from the north. When he made out that the wavering vision was not a mirage but instead a band of Indians riding toward him, he gritted teeth before he halted the mare, looped reins over the saddle horn, and, when the Kiowas were close enough, lifted both hands into the air, palms outward.

The Indians didn't hurry. When they were some twenty feet from him, all but Medicine Shield and an old man whose white hair was nearly hidden by trophy feathers, came to meet him.

Medicine Shield halted his red and white pinto beside Violet and nodded to Ben. He said: "Snow Fox, my son, Talking Buffalo told me you approached. It looks as if your wounds have healed well. I'm glad. The last time we met, you were sick."

Ben's eyes slid to the old warrior accompanying Medicine Shield. A shaman. A medicine man who knew such things, who could predict the future, heal illnesses, and who was one with the spirits.

He looked back at Medicine Shield and spoke in what he wasn't sure was the Kiowa or Comanche tongue. "Does the shaman also tell you why I have come?"

"He says it has something to do with water."

"Yes." Rapidly, Ben explained about the proposed dam, the lake it would create, and the possible new runoff creek, why they contemplated the project, and finished with the question: "Does this create a problem for the people?"

Medicine Shield turned to look at Talking Buffalo. The old man, in turn, scrutinized the prairie for a long, silent moment before he said: "No, it does not. The new creek will run there . . ."—his hand swept from southeast to a point directly east of them—"then form a second lake there before moving onward. This World Stealer can have his first lake. We claim the other. Unless This World Stealer thinks to build a second barrier to stop the new creek from birthing its lake, there will be no trouble for any of us." His black eyes became sharp and narrow in his ancient, weather-seamed face as he impaled Ben on their hard gaze; Hawthorne felt as though he had been pierced by arrows. Talking Buffalo said: "Trouble. You are deeply troubled, Snow Fox. I see your soul has been seized upon by a desperate spirit. You must return to This World Stealer now . . . a different trouble gathers as does a spring storm . . . but I will make fire magic to free you so you will know who you are."

Ben felt a flash of hope. He had no doubts the old medicine man could do what he proposed. He said: "Thank you, holy one, I appreciate that. Uh

179

". . . but I can tell my . . . Arch Locklin . . . you have no objections to the dam?"

"None, unless there are two barriers, two lakes," Talking Buffalo agreed.

"Thank you." Ben looked back at Medicine Shield. "Why did you come to meet me instead of letting me come to you at your camp, Father?"

Medicine Shield turned to call toward the group of warriors waiting quietly behind him. "Crow Runs, come here."

Obediently, a young Kiowa about Ben's own age, urged his black pony forward. The man was tall, lithe, very dark-skinned, and obviously held a grudge against Snow Fox.

Medicine Shield watched his borrowed son meet the warrior's glare and nod in greeting. He stated: "I can tell by your expression that you don't recall Crow Runs, Snow Fox."

Ben shook his head. "No. I'm sorry, but . . . no, I don't. Should I?"

"Yes, you should. Crow Runs is your brother. You grew up together. Trained for war together. He loved you as his birth brother until you killed Blue Glass Bead. Now, he has sworn to take revenge upon you should you ever return to camp. This place is not camp. His vow does not hold out here. That is why we came to meet you."

"But I didn't kill Blue Glass Bead. She . . . she was . . . Snow Fox's beloved wife! She bore him a son! She went with him to his other father's camp as was . . . I didn't . . ." Ben's mind had begun to swirl again. He barely noticed Crow Runs when the young man scowled and urged his pony closer.

The young Kiowa reached a finger to tentatively touch Ben's arm. Presently, he squeezed flesh before he jerked his hand back. "He is real. I thought he was perhaps a spirit returned to haunt me, but he is real. But why does he speak of himself as though he is someone else?"

Talking Buffalo snapped: "I see a hole in his mind and spirit that calls to be filled. But not today. Today, he must return to This World Stealer's camp, and he must hurry or there will be a worse tribulation than what is already written on the wind. Go, Snow Fox! We say the water barrier is agreeable as long as there is only one . . . but you must go now! And I must return to camp and prepare to make rain." Without further delay, the old medicine man reined his pony around and into a trot northward. With a lingering glare at Ben, Crow Runs followed.

Medicine Shield held out a hand. As Hawthorne reached across to clasp the Kiowa's wrist, Medicine Shield ordered: "Take care of This World Stealer's lands first, then come to me and let Talking Buffalo heal you. Will you do that, Snow Fox?"

"Yes, Father. If I can, I will. But . . ."

Medicine Shield released him and kicked his pinto to join the others. Immediately, the band urged their mounts into a trot. Their passage northward was relentless; no one looked back.

Ben watched them go for only a moment before he sighed and turned Violet to retrace his own trail toward the ranch. Over the next hour, he pondered what had just happened.

The word "father" fell readily from his lips when he spoke to Medicine Shield, as easily as though their lives had once been bound. Yet why didn't he know Crow Runs by sight if, as Medicine Shield had claimed—and he felt the man had no reason to lie—he and Crow Runs had been brothers? It was as old Talking Buffalo said. The medicine man had seen truly; there was a hole in his mind that needed filling.

One day, after this was all over—he frowned to himself; after *what* was over?—he would, in fact, go to the Kiowa camp, let Talking Buffalo perform fire magic for him, and see if the hole could be filled. Providing Crow Runs didn't kill him first. No, he assumed the young man was honorable. There was no honor in slaughtering a brother who didn't recall you, and was— hopefully—innocent of any offense.

He hadn't killed Blue Glass Bead, he was sure of that. If anyone could be blamed, it was Arch Locklin, and even then, he thought that the worst Arch had done was to send the woman and her child back to her people. The blizzard had been a fluke. But . . .

Again, he sighed. But . . . but . . . but! Searching for words, or pictures, or memories to fill the hole, none of which came to him, he rode onward. During his pondering, Talking Buffalo's final words popped into his head. Had the old man said he was going to make it rain? He cast a quick eye at the hot clear blue sky. Not a cloud in sight. And why would the shaman want to make rain now?

Huh!

He arrived back at the Locklin Ranch just before noon, and discovered that at least one of the problems Talking Buffalo had predicted was in full flower.

Chapter Fifteen

A bony, weary-appearing mare still hitched to a buckboard was tied to the rail in front of the big house. Fred Perkins's bay gelding lazed beside her. Otherwise, there was no activity in the yard.

Frowning as he looked around, Ben led Violet to the watering trough for a drink, then on to the corral, unsaddled her, and let her in through the gate before he headed for the house. He found no one there, not Arch, not the visitor, only Midge.

He asked: "Where is everybody?"

"Out in the east bunkhouse, Mister Seth, tending Billy Lee."

He frowned at her. "Tendin' Billy Lee! Why?"

"Miss Black's cowpokes shot him. Missus McPhee, bein' a nurse and all, dug the bullets out of him, and Mister Arch, the Reverend Mason, and others, are there helpin' see to him, but I hear he's real bad off."

Even as Ben said absently: "Thank you, Midge," his mind thought: *Shit! Why now?* He had told Caitlan about the planned dam and the lake and all, had expected that to solve the problem between the Locklin and Black spreads, yet . . . Hadn't she passed the information along to her hands and told them the controversy was over?

Scowling, he turned on his heel and headed back outside toward the east bunkhouse.

The inside of the building was crowded with Locklin men but as quiet as a church during prayers. On one of the bunks at the far end, Billy Lee lay white and rasping for breath. His chest was swathed in bandages. Mrs. McPhee sat on a rickety three-legged milking stool beside the cot. Arch, arms folded and face grim, stood nearby. On his knees beside the cot, his Bible open, knelt a florid-faced youngish man, his worn black suit smudged with dust and his black string tie askew beneath his wilted white shirt collar. Eyes closed and expression taut, he prayed earnestly in a soft Georgia drawl.

The cowhands glowered but stepped aside to let Ben through when he entered and sidled past toward Arch. Locklin looked at him as he approached and took off his hat; Arch's brown eyes were the darker under concern. He shook his head when Hawthorne asked softly: "Is he gonna make it?"

"I . . . think Reverend Mason will have two funerals to conduct while he's here."

"How'd it happen?"

Arch shrugged, murmured: "From what I hear from Dallas, he says Billy Lee, Ralph Morton, and Gaston Washington were retrieving cattle that had strayed onto the Black property when her hands shot at them. Billy Lee got two slugs

185

in the chest, and . . ." He sighed heavily. "It's a wonder he made it back here at all, much less survived this long."

Billy Lee had begun to pant. Eyes still closed, his pale face turned the whiter. His throat made a bubbling sound. Both Mrs. McPhee and the minister leaned closer. Presently, Reverend Mason reached to close the puncher's eyes and then took the man's limp hand in his, clutched the Bible to his chest, and shut his own eyes. As he began the Lord's Prayer, those in the room who still wore their own hats removed them—they all knew death when they saw it.

When the minister finished the prayer, he pulled the light blanket up over Billy Lee's face, rose, and turned to look at Arch. "Y'all want to bury this boy before or after your son's rites, Mistuh Locklin?"

Arch chewed his lower lip briefly, thinking about that. Presently, he said: "Billy Lee died in my service. I want to do right by him. David's grave is already dug in the family plot. Dallas . . ."

"Yes, sir, Mistuh Locklin?" Youngstreet, eyes hot and angry in a face frozen into what appeared to be barely restrained fury, stepped forward from among the clot of men by the door.

"Assign two men to dig a proper grave. Pick a good spot, Dallas, one you'd choose for yourself, and we'll put Billy Lee down right after David's funeral. Agreeable?"

"Yes, sir, Mistuh Locklin. But what we gonna do about the Black Cat? We can't let this go by without . . ."

"One thing at a time, Dallas," Arch said sternly. "Let's get the funerals over with first, and then . . ."

"But, Mistuh Locklin, we ain't gonna let them horse wranglers get away with shootin' Billy Lee over nothin' at all! We . . ."

"I said after the funerals, Youngstreet!" Arch's tone had become sharp and hard.

Glowering, Dallas moved back and nodded. He led the others out the door and into the yard.

Mrs. McPhee rose from the stool. There were tears in her eyes; her hands were still stained with Billy Lee's blood. She said: "I'm sorry, Mister Arch, I did my best. I'm not a doctor, as you know, but I did my best."

"You did all anyone could, Annie." Arch's voice had softened. He patted the nurse's shoulder. "Go rest, now. You earned it." He turned to Mason. "Reverend, this is my eldest son Seth. Seth, Reverend Feetfirst Mason. He will be conducting the funerals this afternoon, will stay the night, then head back to town after breakfast tomorrow morning."

"Reverend." Ben shook Mason's hand.

"Mistuh Locklin." As they headed for the door, Mason looked Ben up and down. "You're the one taken by the Indians as a child, aren't you? I'm gratified that you escaped the heathen redskin.

187

I trust the Lord preserved your immortal soul, even though you were a boy surrounded by pagan sorcery and other devilish practices."

Ben shot back: "Reverend, in their own ways, the Injuns are a hell of a lot more pious and God-fearin' than any white man ever thought of bein'. They worship the Supreme Being and honor all His creatures, land, water, and sky, and . . ."

"But they don't know the one true God! They . . ."

"Reverend, I ain't gonna argue religion with you." Out of sudden perversity, Ben grinned. "Right now, Talkin' Buffalo is preparin' to rescue my spirit from Contraries that he sees have seized it and is fixin' to make it rain, so . . ."

The minister looked horrified. He cried: "Oh, God in Heaven, I'll pray for your release from heathen heresies!"

"I don't need your help, I got lots. And, sir . . ."—Ben turned to Arch—"Talkin' Buffalo sees a second lake formin' out there. Medicine Shield says the dam, lake, and new runoff creek are fine with the Kiowas. We can have the first pond. They'll take the second, and then everybody will . . ." The minister had grabbed his arm. He turned to look at the man, found the Bible thrust into his face.

Mason gasped: "You choose to put your immortal soul in the hands of some redskin sorcerer called Talking Buffalo instead of mine? I represent God! I . . ."

"Reverend Mason," Ben cut the man off, "can you make it rain, or not, whenever you need to?"

"Wh-Why would I want to do that?"

"To end a drought. To stop a flood. To keep a cloudburst from spoilin' an important ceremony. I've seen medicine men do just that. Now, I don't know why Talkin' Buffalo is plannin' on makin' rain shortly, but he's obviously got his good reasons . . . and when you can come up with a healthy storm when you need it, or stop one, then I'll come talk to you."

Mason glanced around at the sky. It was clear, blue, and hot, holding not the slightest shred of cloud. He muttered: "If that heathen plans to make it rain today, I also would like to see him try. You put your faith in precarious places, young man. Faith in the godless is doomed from the start."

"Uhn-huh." Ben turned back to Arch. "Sir, unless there's something you need me to do, I'll go get cleaned up to be presentable for David's burial."

The funerals were over. Dinner was done with. Arch and Reverend Mason sat in the living room chatting over brandy and cigars—both furnished by Locklin—but Ben perched on the porch step in the early evening, alone because he preferred it that way.

Instead of settling the issue, his defense of Indian shamans today had only seemed to rouse the minister to greater efforts to rescue his soul from what the man interpreted to be heathen clutches. All during dinner, Mason had expounded on the fires of Hell that waited for the unconverted sinner. While he ate or puffed his cigar, Arch's eyes had shuttled back and forth between Ben and Preacher Mason; he didn't interrupt the minister or try to defend Seth and the Indians, but neither had he seemed to cleave to either side.

Ben had tried his best to be polite, but when the minister all but fell out of his chair, lifted both hands toward Heaven, and asked Ben to join him down there and be saved, Hawthorne decided he'd had enough hellfire and brimstone, excused himself, and walked out.

Now, he shook his head. He could hear Reverend Mason still carrying on in there, and silently congratulated Arch on his long-suffering. He hadn't known Locklin possessed that much patience. Presently, a different sound caught his attention, that of far-off thunder. He rose from the porch step and walked around the house to look out over the plain. Bank after bank of dark-bellied silver-tipped thunderheads burdened the northern horizon, and he grinned, stifled the perverse inclination to go get the preacher and ask him what he thought about that, the past day being so clear and the like. No, that would be a young 'un's trick. Just let it go.

"Looks like it's gonna rain, don't it, Mistuh Seth?"

Ben turned to see that Fred Perkins had come to retrieve his horse—and about time, Hawthorne thought. The animal had been tethered to the hitching rail beside the reverend's scrawny mare ever since he'd returned to the ranch bringing the preacher. He started to note that some people ought to take better care of their mounts, but then changed his mind. Fred was about the only puncher here who would even talk to him; he wanted to stay on the man's good side.

He said instead: "You're right. Sure does look like a good storm is brewin'. Uh . . . Fred . . ."— he kept staring at the approaching clouds— "could you tell me something?"

Perkins led his bay up beside Ben. "Sure, Mistuh Seth. What about?"

Ben waved a hand around. "Why do most of the men seem to resent me so much? What is it they got against me?"

Fred looked at the clouds, at the ground, shuffled his feet for a moment, fiddled with the reins. He was a pleasant-appearing man about thirty or thirty-five, with brown hair and blue eyes, merely an ordinary cowpuncher who looked

191

like he ought to be running a general store instead of riding the range. Finally, he said: "It ain't you they don't like, Mistuh Seth, it's Mistuh David they honored. Gawd rest his soul, Mistuh David was one of the finest, kindest, best *hombres* to be found in this here land. I mean, he made a man feel like he was workin' with, 'stead of for him, y'know? Then, he's hurt like he was and laid up so long, and then you come here, and . . ."

"And the men think I'm tryin' to just walk in and take David's place?"

"Well . . . uh . . . yeah."

Ben nodded. "I can understand that problem. I'm not tryin' to take David's place. Hell, I didn't even come here on my own. Those bounty hunters hadn't hauled me in by force, I'd still be down in Texas."

"I know it," Fred agreed. " 'Course, Dallas and his squawman business ain't helpin' you much, either. And now that Mistuh David's gone, you . . ."

Ben cut Perkins off. "What is it with Youngstreet and his squawman business, anyway, Fred? Can you tell me that?"

"Oh, yeah. I hear Dallas's dam was a Missouri Osage woman. His pa was some kind of Mississippi river-runner who never done her or her kids no good . . . he rented her out to any passers-by who needed a poke and could pay for it. Ol' Dallas, he's got it in for anyone . . .

man or woman . . . who has any dealin's with Injuns of any kind. And since you was raised up by the Kiowas . . . married your li'l squaw and what-not . . ." Fred shrugged as if that explained it all.

Ben guessed it did. He thanked Perkins and returned to studying the clouds. Presently, he realized that Violet was still in the corral, out in the open. The least he could do was put her in a stall in the stable to keep her out of any possible rain, should that far storm advance and produce.

He strolled to the corral, picked a lariat off a post, opened the gate, and stepped through. He called the mare to him, and while she nuzzled him, stood for a moment stroking her cheek and neck, thinking of David and of Seth, not of *David and me*. Strange that though no one else seemed to hold any doubts that he was, in fact, Seth Locklin—not Cat Black, not any of the hands and wranglers, not even the Kiowas—deep down, he knew he was Ben Hawthorne. He would have thought that by this time, under the weight of popular opinion, he would at least have a stronger twinge of doubt. Even though he had gone to ask the Great Mysterious for help in deciding who he was, when he considered himself, he always thought Ben, never Seth. Was this God's answer to him?

He shook his head, passed a loose loop around Violet's neck, led her out of the corral and toward the stable. Because of the double funerals held today, only a token crew tended the range herds; Arch Locklin employed almost thirty men, and at least twenty had come to the ranch to pay their final respects, therefore, spacious though the stable was, nearly all the stalls were full.

He found an opening at the far end of the alleyway near the northern door, jockeyed Violet into it, slipped a halter on her, picked up a nearby brush, and began to smooth her back. The mare's skin rippled appreciation under the hog bristles. Ears perked, she turned her head to look at him, and he grinned when she nickered softly.

"Yeah," he answered. "You and me, girl. I'm gonna take real good care of you."

He was down working on her left foreleg when voices caught his attention. He couldn't see who was there without rising from his crouch, but something told him not to do that. Instead of standing, he eased onto his heel, the brush still in one hand, braced his back against the stall wall, and heard a voice he knew belonged to Youngstreet, speaking hotly.

"No, it's past time! This ain't a Arch Locklin against the Black Cat issue any more, or even who owns Bountiful Spring or who don't, it's us men against them men. Us against them, I tell you!"

A different voice put in: "But, Dallas, we work

for Mister Locklin. I think we oughta at least let him know what . . ."

"No! He put his son in the ground today. The preacher is still visitin' . . . he's got company. He's got other things on his mind right now. Are we men?" Youngstreet's voice took on a sarcastic tone. "Or are we young 'uns that we got to get Mistuh Locklin's permission to wipe our noses, or ask politely whether or not we can take care of our own? We ask Locklin and he says no, then what do we do?

"Them Black hands winged you, Buck, and did Locklin do anything about it? No. You was grazed at that same time, Harvey . . . did Locklin care enough to take issue with anybody about it? No! Billy Lee was a *compadre*! Are we gonna just sit back and let him lay six-foot under and forget him? I say no! I say we had enough of them Black wranglers shootin' at us and us doin' nothin' about it 'cause Mistuh Locklin says not yet, not now, maybe never. I say we go over there and burn 'em out, now! Are you content to just be handy targets for the Black Cat's boundary riders to practice on, or are you with me like men?"

Ben heard: "Yeah, you're right," and "We're with you, Dallas." He started to stand and show himself, and opened his mouth to tell them that Billy Lee had evidently been plugged by one of Caitlan Black's men who had not yet heard about the solution to the whole water situation,

195

but stopped himself. However many Locklin cowhands were out there, only Fred Perkins was even semi-friendly to him. The mood those men were in, they would be more likely to shoot him down than to listen to him. Even if he told Arch what was going on, he doubted that from the snarled curses and vows of vengeance he heard growing in intensity out there, not even Locklin could stop the men now.

Fingers white around the brush, he stared hard at straw softening the stall floor for a moment, gritted his teeth, and pondered what he could do, should do, or not do. Was this really any of his business? He could just let matters proceed to their natural finish.

Let these men catch Caitlan's wranglers by surprise. . . . Let unsuspecting men be slaughtered while they ate dinner. . . .

Let Caitlan's house and barns burn. . . .

Let Cat's horses die in their stalls. . . .

No, that wouldn't be right. He had to warn Cat; at least give her and her men a fighting chance.

He had come to stable Violet directly from his own dinner, wasn't packing iron, was defenseless. But he couldn't just sit around and do nothing.

Cautiously, still without standing and betraying himself, he set the brush aside, reached for the halter rope, and jerked the slipknot free. The mare began backing out of the stall when he looped the loose end of the rope around her neck, grasped her mane, and lifted himself as quietly as possible onto her back. Lying flat along her spine, and using the halter rope as a neck rein, he got her completely out of the cubicle and into the alley.

Just as he turned Violet toward the open back door, Dallas shouted: "Jesus! It's the Injun lover! He must have heard us! Stop him! Not with guns, you idjits. . . . Catch him!"

Thunderheads around the edges of the horizon had piled higher and seemed closer. Ben abandoned all efforts at stealth, forked Violet's back, leaned low over her neck, and shouted urgency. The quarter horse's muscles responded; the mare put on a burst of speed, and guided only by knee pressure and the halter rope around her neck, wheeled westward.

Behind, still in the stable, Locklin cowhands who had missed stopping Ben scrambled to saddle their own mounts, and pursued.

Chapter Sixteen

Far-off lightning cut through thickening air and thunder grumbled from out of the north. Still leaning low over Violet's neck, her flying mane whipping his face, Ben urged the mare onward toward Caitlan Black's spread at the feet of the western hills. Had Violet been Arch's unruly gelding, Tomahawk, he might not make the ride without a saddle, but Violet was sweet and obedient. And he was accustomed to riding bareback.

All during his growing-up years, he had practiced horsemanship daily with the other Comanche youths, practiced until he could pick a fallen comrade from the ground at full gallop, practiced until he and his chosen horse had become one. The skills stood him in good stead now. It didn't matter to him whether he rode a saddle or not; during this westward race, he and this present mount would also become one.

When he thought he had enough of a head start over Dallas and the other Locklin wranglers, Ben slowed Violet from the flat-out run to a steady gallop, and still leaned over her neck but not so tightly, scowled around at the land ahead.

He felt he must be close to Miss Cat's property line, because far off to his right, he could see two riders pull in their horses and an arm point his way before the men urged their mounts toward him. He again shouted Violet into a hard run. She had rested some from her initial burst of speed, and responded strongly. Eye-measuring the distance between himself and the oncoming punchers, Ben knew he could make it past the point where they would meet before they could intercept him—unless, of course, seeing that they couldn't catch him, they tried to shoot either him or his mount.

He cast a quick look back toward the Locklin Ranch. A faint plume of dust announced his pursuers coming on fast now, but he thought he was at least five minutes ahead of them, and if he could just hold that lead . . .

A bullet sang past him before the sound of a firing gun reached him. Grimly and cursing to himself, Ben took a stronger hold with his right hand on the ends of the bridle rope around Violet's neck, braced his left elbow in the resulting loop, and slid down the mare's side until only his left arm, and his right heel hooked over the horse's spine, kept him with her. This was the position warriors used in battle to make their mount a shield while—braced by neck loop and heel but with their hands free—they shot arrows at the enemy.

Violet wasn't a Comanche war pony; she wasn't accustomed to the altered weight, and faltered briefly. Ben began talking softly to reassure her until she regained her stride and raced onward. Since he was now mostly hidden by the mare's body, he figured that unless those Black wranglers had exceptionally good eyesight, it would appear to them that their one warning shot had downed the man and a panicked riderless horse continued its westward run alone.

It seemed the ruse worked. The two outriders pulled in their mounts and merely sat to watch the dappled gray gallop past. Ben maintained his hidden, side-hanging position until well by the wranglers before he pulled himself back upright, straddled the mare, and again urged her to more speed. Caitlan's punchers didn't see him. They had noticed other riders carrying lighted torches far behind the first but coming on hard, and, guns again drawn, turned their horses to intercept.

The yard between Caitlan's house and where the bunkhouse and cook shack sat beyond the corrals and stables was mostly vacant—only a few men on the front steps lounged, smoking and telling tales. Ben barely slackened Violet before he leaped to the ground and slapped her on toward the fence to the foal pen; he wanted her well out of harm's way. Some of the men started up, scowling, when he shouted at them: "The Locklin ranch hands are headin' here to burn you out! Call all the men you got! We have to set up defenses. You, get me a weapon . . . I came here unarmed. You and you, pull that wagon over here to use as . . ."

"Whoa, boy!" Les Moody strode toward Ben, his eyes fierce beneath his low hat brim. "Ain't you never gonna learn? We tol' you t'other day to stay away from here! What are you tryin' to pull?"

"Nothing! And you're wastin' time! There are fifteen or twenty men carryin' torches, and . . ."

"Why should we believe that Arch Locklin's son has got our best interests at heart in any . . ."

"Dammit, listen to me!" Ben shouted. "You only got about five minutes to barricade yourselves. They're gonna burn you out if you don't get ready!" He again indicated the wagon fitted fore and aft with upstanding racks and burdened by a half load of straw. "Get that wagon away from the side of the stable and out into the middle of the yard! You can use it as shelter, and if the hay catches fire, it won't be so likely to take buildings with it!"

The heel of Moody's left palm hit Ben hard on the shoulder, staggering him briefly. The ramrod snarled: "We don't take no orders from the likes of you, Locklin! You can't come bustin' in here and just take over. You . . ."

In frustration, Ben yelled: "You damned fool, ain't you listenin' to me? You got a war on your hands! You're all gonna just stand here and be slaughtered if you don't . . . Where's Cat!

Where's Caitlan?" Maybe she could shove a stick of dynamite under these men who were doing nothing but glowering at him.

"I told you it's Miss Caitlan or Miss Black to you, boy!" Moody snapped. "I expect Miss Cat's in the house downin' a peaceful dinner, and . . . hold it! Where you think you're goin'?"

Ben had turned toward the main house. Les grabbed his arm to stop him, but Hawthorne spun around and his fist in Moody's teeth jolted the ramrod loose. Les stumbled back and sat down hard in the dirt. Ben whirled again and, shouting Caitlan's name, bolted for the house.

Expression puzzled beneath a frown, she met him at the front door. He grabbed at her, shoved her back into the main room, and indicated the rifle over the fireplace. "That loaded and workin'?"

"Yes! Seth, what . . . ?"

Swiftly, as he lunged to yank the weapon from its stanchions and checked the magazine, he explained, then finished with: "Go to the stable and let your stock out so if the buildings go, your critters won't go up with them. If they run out into the range, we can always catch 'em later. And get yourself a gun. You may need it."

Flushed with outrage, she gasped: "I never thought Arch would do this to me! I never thought your father would go so far as to . . ."

"It ain't Arch. He don't know anything about

202

this. It's the men. They've gone hog wild and are takin' matters into their own hands. Don't just stand there, girl, go turn your animals loose!" Ben levered a cartridge into the chamber of the fine repeating rifle he now held and leaped back outside again to try to get Cat's wranglers to set up defenses.

Gunfire sharp from out of the east had done the job for Hawthorne; evidently, the oncoming Locklin men had met the two outriders who had shot at Ben. Finally convinced that young Seth Locklin wasn't joshing him, Les Moody, a pistol in his right hand and a dribble of blood on his lip, began to shout orders.

"PeeWee! Lister! Ambrose! Move that there hay wagon out here in the middle of the yard, then take up a position behind it! Hurry it up! Reno, you take the watering trough! Lewis, you and Pettigrew, over there by the corral! Conley, take the corner of the house! Brent and Lacy, find yourselves a good spot! Miss Cat, where the hell you think you're goin'!"

Without slackening her headlong run, Caitlan yelled back: "To let the stock out!" She disappeared into the stable.

Ben skidded to a halt beside Moody. "You believe me now?"

Les eyed him quizzically. "Yeah. Why you doin' this, goin' against your own daddy?"

"Mister Locklin's got nothin' to do with this.

Your men killed Billy Lee, and that's what riled the hands. They've come after you without askin' Arch."

Moody's brows vanished up under his hat. "Some of my men shot one of his men . . . today?"

"Yeah. You didn't know?"

What Moody said next turned the air blue beneath the steadily advancing, ever-growing storm overhead. He ended with: "No! I tol' 'em . . . When I get my hands on . . ."

"You may not get the chance! Here they come!"

Led by Dallas Youngstreet, nearly twenty riders thundered up the slight grade toward the Black Ranch.

Over half of the men carried flame-sputtering torches bright in the growing darkness as evening and storm steadily dimmed the light. Their hoped-for element of surprise had been spoiled by Ben's warning; still, they were a formidable force to be dealt with.

Moody bellowed: "Keep them torches away from the buildings, men!" He fired at the oncoming riders before he took up his own position behind a buckboard.

Ben joined him. He shouldered the rifle and had drawn a bead on Dallas when Youngstreet hauled his mount to a skidding halt and, gun drawn, flung himself from the saddle. His followers copied him just as mares led by Caitlan's stallion,

Ready Boy, began streaming out of the stable and galloped toward the plain. The stud and unsaddled mares met riderless saddled Locklin mounts in a swirl of bucking, kicking horseflesh before—driven by Ready Boy—what suddenly became a herd of more than forty animals headed unhindered down the hill. Under cover of tossing manes and flashing hoofs, Dallas took the opportunity to get his men spread out and situated.

Hair flying like the manes of her horses, Caitlan dashed from the stable door, back across the yard, and flung herself down beside Ben. She panted: "The stock is out. The brood mares with colts are back in the pasture. The cattle are on the range. The only one still penned is . . ."

A burst of gunfire cut her off. One of the Locklin hands had tried to carry a torch toward the house; Conley had taken the man out.

Ben grinned mirthlessly. "Problem with holdin' a light at this time of the evenin' is that it makes you a damned good target. You got a gun, Cat?"

"No. I didn't have time. Cover me while I go back to the house and get one. And I'll bring more shells for your rifle."

"Good." Ben eased around the edge of the buckboard and sighted on a flame out there. His rapid fire took the heads off three torches. He missed the fourth, but it gave Caitlan the time she needed to run from the buckboard to the house.

His fire also brought a hail of response. Another Locklin hand tried to rush a torch toward the barns and was brought down. What had begun as a tumultuous lightning raid settled into a game of cat and mouse, Youngstreet's men making sporadic and fruitless attempts to slip fire past Moody's lesser forces, the Black wranglers attempting to whittle the Locklin two-to-one advantage down to a more manageable size.

Caitlan ducked a hail of bullets on her way back to the buckboard. She now had a gun belt strapped over her heavy split riding skirt, a big Bowie knife at her belt, and carried a box of rifle shells. She flung herself to the ground between Ben and Les and thrust the box at Hawthorne.

"Ammunition, but that's all there is. The box isn't even half full. Make good use of it, Seth."

"You bet," he said, and rose onto one knee.

Another Locklin man, a torch in one hand, his pistol belching fire but its sound nearly drowned by a blast of thunder from overhead, was making a run for the nearest bunkhouse.

Ben's rifle barked. The man flung up his arms. The pistol flew in one direction, the torch the other. There was a spark and a sputter, and the grass began to burn.

"Oh, shit," Ben whispered when he realized what was happening. The prairie out there was summer dry, its grass baked golden under the July heat. If that fire spread and got out of hand . . .

He half stood and eased around the rear of the buckboard to yell: "Dallas, it's Seth Locklin here! You got a big problem! That torch caught the grass, and . . ."

Youngstreet's bullet stopped his words. Caitlan gasped—"Seth!"—when the rifle dropped from Ben's nerveless hand and he plunged to the dirt. She fell to her knees to bend over him, saw the long gouge the bullet had cut through hair above his left ear, and knew he was dead. Still, she shook him and cried: "Seth! Seth!"

A hand on her arm jerked her around. Les Moody snapped: "Leave him and git back into the house where you belong, girl."

She flared, "I can shoot as well as any . . ."

"You're only a little girl! This is man's work! Now, do like I tell ya!"

Her mouth fell open. Her eyes widened before they narrowed to anger. More gunfire behind her made her draw her own weapon even as she said: "I own this ranch, Mister Moody, and you don't give me orders! I'll help defend . . ."

"I and some of the other men worked for your daddy! Most of us worked for your brother!" Moody sent two shots at a Locklin puncher scrambling hastily from where the growing grass fire edged toward him, before he grabbed the pistol from Cat's hand and finished: "We keep workin' here outta respect for their memories even though you're just a woman! Now, I tol' ya to git into the house where you belong, girl! Do it! This is men's business, not yours!"

On the ground beside Caitlan, Ben groaned and lifted a shaky hand toward the wound matting his fair hair and masking his face with blood. Her voice vibrant with relief, Cat breathed: "Seth, you're alive!"

Moody sucked his teeth thoughtfully for a second before he shoved Caitlan aside, seized Ben's shirt, and rolled him over onto his stomach.

Only half conscious, Ben tried to raise his head, but something pounded his already aching skull.

"Lay still, you Locklin bastard." Moody holstered his pistol, stuffed Cat's weapon under his belt, and pulled a leather pigging string from his back pocket. As he yanked Hawthorne's left arm up and wrapped a loop around the wrist, he yelled: "PeeWee . . . Reno . . . come help me here! Bring a rope! The rest of you, cover us!"

The two men left their strategic positions and zig-zagged across the yard to join Moody.

Caitlan cried: "Les, what are you doing?"

Moody hoisted Ben to his feet. Hawthorne was groggy and weak-kneed. Supporting him, Moody snarled: "Them Locklin hands want to see somethin' burn, we'll show 'em burnin', all right." PeeWee and Reno had arrived. Les flung Ben at them. "Take this bastard to the hay wagon and bring some matches!"

Chapter Seventeen

Using Ben as a shield, the three horse wranglers moved out from behind the buckboard. Moody pressed his gun barrel hard against the prisoner's bloody temple and bellowed: "Hold your fire! Lissen up, you out there . . . this here's Seth Locklin, your boss's son. Look at him so's you'll know I ain't lyin'!" He jammed the pistol back into its holster, then reached around Reno holding Hawthorne's right arm. With one hand, the lariat PeeWee had brought coiled in the other, he grasped hair and jerked Ben's head up. Even in the nearing darkness, a flare of lightning showed everyone that the wranglers had who they said they had.

Les continued: "You wanna go back to Locklin and tell him you kilt his son, eh?" To those holding Ben, he said urgently: "Take him over there, tie him to the hay wagon, pile straw around his feet and make ready to light it. We go up in flame, *he* goes up in flame." He shouted again at the attackers: "You hear that? You shoot at us while we're gettin' Seth situated, we shoot him! You burn us out, we burn him! You think about that, now, and consider that I ain't foolin'. I think that maybe you oughta give it up and go on home!"

They were at the hay wagon. Ben tried to resist when the men raised the wagon tongue and backed him up to it, but he was still seeing double and they outnumbered him. The men yanked his arms back around the tongue and finished binding his wrists with the piggin' string. They wound the lariat around him and the wood, wrapping him tightly from chest to knees before they tied the rope off and stepped back.

Moody ordered: "PeeWee, take that pitchfork and pile hay around him."

As the wrangler yanked the fork from where its tines were stuck into the mound of straw on the wagon bed, and Moody again kept Hawthorne covered, Reno climbed the rack at the front of the wagon, grabbed the end of the tongue, and bound it securely to the hayrack to make sure it stayed upright.

Caitlan had been frozen with surprise at Les Moody's words. She still crouched behind the buckboard, but when she saw Reno twist a handful of straw into a makeshift branch, jump down from the wagon, and swipe a match head against pants' material tightened by a raised knee to ignite the torch, she leaped forward and tried to shove the men away from Ben.

"Stop it! You can't do that! Seth warned us! He came to try to help us!"

Moody grabbed her arm and she fell when he flung her aside. "I tol' you to git to the house!"

She was up immediately, made a grab for his gun. This time, he hit her across the face and she again fell. He yelled: "I ain't gonna argue with you, girl! Git in the gawd-damned house!"

The torch was now lighted. Caitlan started to rise, but ducked down with her arms braided over her head when a bullet sang over her and struck Reno in the chest. He dropped the torch and stumbled back just as Dallas Youngstreet's voice called from out of what was now darkness.

"You picked the wrong man to hold up against us, Moody! We don't have no love for that white Injun whether he's Arch Locklin's son or not! We been waitin' to see what you was gonna do with him, but far as we care, let him burn!"

A refreshed hail of bullets made Les and PeeWee lunge for cover. Still on hands and knees, her nose bleeding from Moody's knuckles, Caitlan scrambled under the wagon.

Ben had regathered enough wit now to discover his predicament. He looked at the hay piled around his feet and legs to the knees, saw flames spreading toward him from the burning twist that had fallen into the mound when Reno went down, and choked back a cry of horror. Desperately, he struggled against the ropes that bound him to the wagon tongue, but they held—what wrapped him was so tight that, though he could shake the spar, he couldn't slip free.

He kept struggling even as he looked up at

the heavy black storm clouds now lying low in the sky, at the slash of lightning far out in the prairie behind where he knew the Locklin Ranch sat, then back down at flames gaining vigor as they rose around him, and something shifted inside his head. There was a sick fascination about watching those flames; once he looked back at them, he didn't seem to be able to turn his eyes away. Perhaps it was the after-effects of the bullet that had creased his skull, or maybe it was a mind rejecting the terror of being burned to death; nevertheless, part of what fixed his eyes to the flames was the picture he saw there.

He was naked but for a loincloth as he sat cross-legged close beside a fire. His long hair was decorated with a single eagle feather.

He cried a harsh sound of pain and renewed his struggle to free himself when flames bit at his knees. Still, the pictures drew his eyes.

Talking Buffalo sat in front of him. The old shaman rolled a live coal easily in one palm. Its heat seemed to have no effect on the medicine man while he brushed an owl feather over both Snow Fox and the flames to cleanse all before putting the live coal into his mouth. He blew a stream of sparks at Snow Fox.

Ben flinched when wind swirled burning chaff around him. He could feel their searing touch, knew they were igniting his shirt and hair, and ground his teeth against an agonized scream. Again, he jerked at the wagon tongue.

The sparks entered his nostrils, his ears, and heated his eyes until Talking Buffalo leaned to him, placed lips against his brow, and sucked hard. The medicine man sat back and stuck out his tongue—a fat white larva wriggled there. Talking Buffalo nodded sagely and spat the worm into the fire.

Ben said to no one in particular: "My name is Seth Locklin. I am twenty-five years old. I have a twin brother, David, who is three minutes younger, but David is dead, now. Dead . . . dead . . ." He took a deeper breath and choked on smoke and heat. His voice rose. "I was taken by the Kiowas when I was ten! My Kiowa father's name is . . ."

Something touched his hands and though they were nearly numb from the tightness of the leather binding his wrists, he felt it. Shortly, he heard an urgent: "Grab the tongue when I cut the thongs so you don't fall into the fire when the rest of the ropes come loose!"

It was Caitlan. She had crawled out from under the wagon behind him and was freeing him, but there was fire all around him now, hot and hurting, fire climbing his legs . . .

One by one, the ropes sagged. He flung them aside, leaped through flame out onto hoof-bared yard soil, and fell. His pants legs were burning.

Caitlan, the knife clenched in her teeth, used the wadded hem of her heavy riding skirt in her hands like a hot pad to beat at the flames. Together, they killed the fire—though he was well-singed, the tops of his boots had protected much of him—and in that moment, he got his mind to thinking again.

He scrambled up and grasped Cat's arm to shove at her. "Wait for me around back of the hay wagon. I'll meet you there in a minute."

She didn't argue, didn't ask him what he planned to do. Crouched, she disappeared toward the rear of the wagon.

Ben glanced quickly at what went on around him. Gunfire was still fierce out there—weren't they ever going to run out of bullets? He spotted the pitchfork where the wrangler named PeeWee had left it with tines stuck into the ground, lunged toward it, wrenched it loose, and forked burning straw from the mound at the wagon tongue up onto the mass loaded on the bed. Flaming chaff stung his face and hands again when he added the second forkful. The dry grass on the wagon burst immediately into a greater blaze. Ben dropped the fork and leaped around to the rear to join Caitlan. He braced his shoulder against the rack. "Help me! Push!"

She also shoved at the wagon. Above them, flames began to roar. The wagon wheels turned slowly at first, but when it picked up momentum on the slight downgrade, Ben wrapped fingers tight around Caitlan's wrist and the two dashed for what cover the watering trough provided.

The tongue guided the wagon's front wheels and it was still securely bound to the hayrack. Unable to turn, and scattering fiery dèbris to all sides, it plunged straight toward what remained of the Locklin group.

Men yelled in alarm. Abandoning cover, they fled to each side to escape what had become a fountain of fire. In fury, Youngstreet shouted his men back into some semblance of control and ordered a full attack, but, abruptly, a heavy rifle boomed. It was a weapon none of them had heard here before, and its sound overrode other gunfire.

Three of Dallas's men went down, each with a bullet in the back.

Les Moody yelled: *"Yaa-hah!"* He leaped up and also pumped lead at the Locklin men, but the rifle boomed again and blew Moody's hat off and took his brains with it. Two more Locklin men and a Black wrangler went to the Great Hereafter before it dawned on everyone that whoever the interloper was, he was taking out anyone who essayed to shoot, regardless of which side they were on.

The wagon had run up against a boulder and its sudden halt dumped burning straw onto already burning grass. The slope quickly became a sheet of fire. By that light, everyone saw a lone rider on a rangy bay. The man wore total black, like some dime novel road agent. There was something lean and menacing about him besides his clothing, and there was no doubt he would shoot the next man who moved. When the newcomer ordered harshly—"Everyone lay down your weapons and get out here or you're all dead."—Caitlan whispered: "It's Arch! Arch Locklin! But . . ."

Ben nodded. It was indeed Arch, but not the Arch Locklin any of them had ever seen before. The dark eyes were hard and narrow, the look of a man who killed without hesitation. The tone was of one who expected his order to be obeyed *now*. He sat the nervous bay gelding easily, not even holding the reins, as though even the horse was wise enough not to fight him. The Sharps buffalo gun was ready in his hands; he watched for the next man to so much as hold his mouth the wrong way.

Arch continued: "This is settled! It's over." Lightning flared above and around him for a moment, but didn't touch him—Ben got the ridiculous impression that the elements knew better than to try it. The scent of ozone mixed with that of burning grass and gunpowder was whisked away by a suddenly heightened wind that pushed the fire ahead of it out into the prairie in a flash flood of flame racing to meet the storm.

Expressions stunned, nine Locklin cow-punchers—all that was left of the nineteen who had come—holstered their weapons, put their hands up, and stepped forward. Caitlan's six surviving men likewise muttered among themselves, but came out of hiding. Ben and Cat rose from behind the watering trough to join the others.

"How come you're shootin' your own men, Mistuh Locklin?"

The Big Fifty still at the ready, Arch turned to look at the man and said somberly: "When two boys fight, it doesn't matter which one started it, you whop them both. What's your name?"

"Levi Lacy, suh. You . . ."

"We ain't children," Dallas snarled. He grabbed for the sidearm he had just leathered.

Ben saw that Locklin was looking the other way. He shouted: "Watch your back, Father!" He sprang at Youngstreet.

Arch jerked around to see Ben hit Dallas full on. Hawthorne seized Youngstreet's gun hand and shoved the arm up just as the weapon discharged; the bullet nicked Locklin's hat brim before it passed harmlessly on. Arch leveled the Sharps, but couldn't shoot because Seth had Youngstreet down on the ground, both struggling for the pistol, and if he fired, he might hit his son instead of Dallas.

Preceded by a sharp, brilliant gash of lightning and a soil-shuddering blast of thunder, the first raindrops fell. Fat, hot from warmth of the past day, and glossed into silver spears by more lightning, the drops thickened, abruptly became a deluge that killed the prairie fires and doused what blaze remained on the hay wagon.

An absolute darkness crashed down over the yard. Except for one additional gunshot, the storm masked any sounds the two men on the ground might be making. Arch yelled: "Somebody get a lantern, quick! Someone bring a light! Hurry! Hurry!"

"I'll get one from the house," Caitlan cried.

Blinded by downpour and storm-night, she stumbled toward where the golden rectangle of the open living room door glimmered faintly.

Stabbing a spurt of fire into the darkness, a gun again went off from near ground level. Nearby, an unseen man yelped before he gritted: "My laig! Gawd-damn! Got me in the laig!"

Caitlan was back with two lighted barn lanterns swinging from their bails, their solid glass sides and metal caps protecting flames from wind and rain. Light showed that she had also gotten another pistol from inside the house; its grip glimmered steel and carved brown hardwood in her holster as she thrust a lantern at one of the men and ordered—"Hold this!"—before she rushed around the impromptu arena to lift the second lantern high beside Arch. The light revealed a no-holds-barred battle in what was now a sea of mud in the middle of her yard.

Chapter Eighteen

Both Ben and Dallas were on their feet. When he moved, Hawthorne's burned-through pants legs flapped and flung water droplets back at the rain. With that last shot, Youngstreet's pistol had disappeared somewhere.

Ben ducked a straight right jab from Dallas, dropped to the ground, and jammed his feet hard at Youngstreet's ankles. Dallas nearly went down, but caught himself with a hand. Both bounced upright; there was a flurry of fists, each man landing punches on the other, body and head, neither backing off until Ben turned half sideways and drove his boot heel into Dallas's belly. Youngstreet staggered, whirled away to keep his balance and rebounded, but was met by Hawthorne's rapid-fire fists to the face and midsection.

Lightning far brighter than Caitlan's lanterns showed that this time Dallas went all the way down. Ignoring burns that glared red through the charred pants at knees and thighs, Ben danced in front of Youngstreet, his fists cocked, his eyes fixed on his opponent until Dallas drove his own foot against the blisters flames had raised on Ben's right leg above the boot top. Thunder, the roar of the downpour, and the onlookers' involuntary curses nearly drowned out Hawthorne's cry of pain; even the Locklin hands scowled to each other that a man didn't do things like that in the midst of a good brawl.

Shock of it made Ben stumble back, and it gave Dallas time to get to his feet. Ben gritted teeth and recovered quickly, but when he lunged to strike, Youngstreet bent, thrust an arm between his adversary's legs, flung the other over Ben's shoulder, heaved Hawthorne into the air, and slammed him to the mud. Before Ben could get up, Dallas pursued his advantage.

Again, onlookers howled when, as Ben tried to roll away from the attack, Dallas drove his boot toe into Hawthorne's side. The impact flipped Ben over onto his belly. Dallas took a step forward and repeated the kick. Ben drew up his knees, to block it, and when Youngstreet kicked at him once more, grabbed the ankle, jerked hard, and Youngstreet sprawled on his back on the ground. Ben leaped upright before Dallas made it back to his feet.

Beside Locklin, Caitlan reached to grab at Arch's arm. "Stop them, Mister Locklin, they're killing each other. Do something! Stop them!"

Eyes narrow and black in his grim expression, Locklin shook his head.

"But you've already buried one son this week! You can stop them! If you don't, Seth might die, and then . . ."

"If I interfere now, in the men's opinion, Seth will become daddy's little boy, never Mister Locklin, boss of the spread. It would follow him for the rest of his life. This is his fight. We have to let him finish it himself. Ah! See?"

Cautiously now, Ben and Dallas circled each other until, in another storm of blows, Ben staggered Youngstreet. As the cowboy spun away from him, Ben drove knuckles and knees into Dallas's back, pounding kidneys.

Both were bleeding from nose and mouth. Though the bullet gouge through Ben's hair had begun to clot, it again poured fresh blood around his ear and down his cheek to drip a rainwater-thinned stream from the point of his chin. When Dallas's fist caught him square on the jaw and he went over backward, Youngstreet howled in triumph: "Gotcha, you Injun-lovin' bastard!" Hands clawed to clutch and hold, he made a dive for Ben, but Hawthorne jerked up his legs and boot soles in Dallas's belly hoisted the man over him.

The watchers shouted encouragement and advice when Youngstreet landed face-first in a puddle. Ben got to his knees, shoved feet again, and flung himself onto Dallas's back, but now there was a knife in the cowboy's hand.

Caitlan yelled—"Seth!"—and tossed her big Bowie knife toward Ben. He would have caught it in mid-air, but his own blade flashing, Dallas lunged at him. Hawthorne had to evade the cut and he missed snagging Cat's weapon. He ducked three slashes in a row before he could seize Dallas's wrist with his left, and then he put everything he had into a backhanded right across Youngstreet's face.

Dallas dropped the blade and fell. He lurched upright, but Ben was ready; with another hard right, Hawthorne flattened Youngstreet again. Caitlan's horse wranglers and Locklin's cowpunchers pressed forward, jockeying for a better position to see the fight; the man with the lantern lifted it higher to widen the pool of light as Dallas got up. Water splattered from Youngstreet's face and shirt sleeves when Ben's left again sent him to the ground.

Amazingly, seeming so enraged that he felt little or nothing, Dallas got up once more. Ben pursued him, staggering him with each blow, but Hawthorne was also tiring and his punches were losing their power. Still he drove Dallas back into the buckboard, and for a moment it appeared Youngstreet was trapped there. But when Ben tried to take advantage of Dallas's lack of maneuvering room, Youngstreet again wrapped arms around him, and this time flung him onto the buckboard.

Springs bounced and nearly threw him off balance when Dallas leaped up onto the wagon after Hawthorne. Using the buckboard's rebound to add force to his own movement, Ben rolled off the far side of the wagon and landed on his feet. He reached up, grabbed Youngstreet's rain-soaked shirt, yanked the man off the rig, drove Dallas face-down into the mud, braced his knee against the back of the cowboy's neck, wound fingers in Dallas's hair, and water splashed when he shoved Youngstreet's face deep into the semi-liquid ooze.

This time, it was Cat who cried: "Now you've got him, Seth! Good, Seth, good!"

Dallas clawed back over his shoulders at Ben, but couldn't dislodge him. Ben held until he felt the strength leach out of the man, then—himself gasping and weak—rose and staggered back. He leaned an elbow against the buckboard for a moment because his knees had gone wobbly, but presently recovered enough to move toward where—limned by a double circle of light—some men cheered him and some were warily silent. He saw Locklin and Cat coming toward him, wiped blood and rain from his face with what felt like a broken hand before he really went to his knees this time, his head hanging between arms braced wrist-deep in collected rain. Both Cat and Arch leaped to bend over him.

Behind them, coughing up muddy water, Dallas lifted his head. He spotted bits of metal glinting in the lantern light, got himself onto his feet and almost fell over them, but came up with Caitlan's

Bowie knife in one hand and his own hunting knife in the other. Roaring fury, he lunged at Ben's unprotected back.

Arch whirled and jerked up his Sharps. Cat grabbed her pistol from its holster, but a surge of desperation made Ben shove them both aside, fling himself to where the pitchfork lay, seize it in both hands, whirl, and lift the business end. Steel tines caught Dallas in the chest just before two bullets slammed into him, one from Locklin's buffalo gun, the other from Cat Black's pistol.

Supported by the fork handle his weight rammed into the mud, Dallas stood for a moment looking at Ben. Just before he toppled sideways and plunged to the ground, his lips whispered: "You gawd-damned Injun lover!"

Panting, Ben fell back to his knees. He lurched upright, but his legs wouldn't hold him for long; he collapsed again, this time against Caitlan. Trying to keep himself upright with both arms wrapped around her, he failed and slid down her body back to the mud.

Arch cast a quick glance at Seth sitting within the circle of Caitlan's arms before he looked back at the men standing around them and growled: "This is over. Let's get inside out of the rain. Over there to the cook shack, all of you." He twitched the Sharps. "Move."

Without argument in the face of obvious

authority, their belligerence killed by expended violence, those hands still alive headed toward the building.

Caitlan tugged at Ben. "Come on, Seth . . . can you make it or should I get someone to help you?"

"No!" He forced himself to his feet, staggered briefly, then steadied himself with an arm over her shoulders. "If you will walk with me . . ."

The lantern in one hand, the other arm around Ben's waist, she led him after Locklin and the men. Inside the building, she sat Hawthorne on the end of one of the benches at a table before she used fire from her lantern to quickly flame other lights hanging about the room.

Arch himself removed his dripping hat and lay it on a table before he cradled the big gun in both arms and, for a silent moment, studied the men who had automatically formed two groups— horse wranglers at his left, cowpunchers to the right. All were muddy, soaked to the skin, some fire-singed, and all wary of him.

He waited until Caitlan, her hair stringing in rain-slick tendrils and as mud-smeared as the rest, returned to stand grimly beside him and wiped a drip of water from her nose with the back of a hand before she folded her own arms and spread her feet to cast a look equal to his in disgust at the men.

Finally, Arch nodded to the man with the

bleeding bullet hole in his thigh. "All right, Cornelius, who started this?"

The puncher waved a hand toward Caitlan's men. "Them, Mister Locklin. They shot Billy Lee down for no good reason a'tall, just like he was a dawg, and we . . ."

"Ain't so!" PeeWee snapped from the other side. "If you're talkin' about that two-legged skunk what winged Phil Creasy, I was there, and ain't so that Phil shot that bastard down for no good reason, Mister Locklin. Miss Caitlan, she told us y'all are fixin' to build yourselfs a dam downstream, that the fuss over Bountiful Spring was solved and over, and ever'thin' was hunky-dory. Then comes this wrangler chasin' some of your critters that's on Miss Cat's propity. Phil and me, we go to help. Your men says, keep your rustlin' hands off Locklin cattle. We says we ain't rustlin', we're only tryin' to round 'em up for ya. One thing leads to 'nother, and your hand swipes Phil acrost the face with the ends of his reins.

"Ol' Phil, he goes for his gun. Your man outdraws him, but he ain't such a good shot . . . he damned near misses, even at that close range. Ol' Phil, he don't miss. He din't start it, but he surely finished it. That's what happened, and that's the truth."

"You're saying Billy Lee brought it on himself," Arch noted.

"Yes, sir, I am."

Arch looked at what was left of his men. "Any of you see that?" He caught one of them shifting eyes guiltily to the floor. "Wayne? You were there?"

"Uh . . . well, maybe, Mister Locklin."

"Yes or no, Wayne!" Arch's tone was so sharp that at the table, his head supported in both hands, even Ben jumped.

"Uh . . . y-yes, Mister Locklin."

"He telling the truth?"

"Uh . . . well . . . I guess so, yes, Mister Locklin."

"Why the hell didn't you come to me instead of . . ."

His face screwed into pleading, Wayne waved both arms. "Well, Dallas, he said . . . uh . . . watchin' Billy Lee die . . . uh . . . the funerals and all . . . uh . . . in the heat of the moment . . ."

"Hah!" Ben spoke for the first time. He lifted his face out of his palms and his eyes swept both groups.

"Don't talk to me about the heat of the moment. They were fixin' to burn me at the stake like some god-damned Salem witch when all I did was try to warn 'em you were comin' on, and you were fixin' to let 'em! There's the heat of the moment, I'll tell you!"

Arch grinned mirthlessly at Ben's equally mirthless humor before he looked back at his men. "How many of you began this venture?"

The cowpunchers glanced among themselves before Cornelius mumbled: "Oh . . . eighteen or twenty, I expect, Mister Locklin."

"And there are . . ."—Arch counted quickly— "eight of you left standing. Ten or twelve men dead, for nothing. For nothing!

"Now"—he looked briefly down at Caitlan still standing beside him—"whatever Miss Black chooses to do from her end, I'll tell you this. Under some misguided feeling of revenge, you came to destroy someone else's home and property. You nearly killed my son . . . were willing to see him die horribly to satisfy your egos. I give you your choice. Either you're fired . . . all of you . . . or, you work for me and for Miss Black without pay for three months to help repair the damage you've done here tonight. Your choice, but I'll hear your decision *now*."

Cornelius limped closer, his expression outraged. "Three months without pay. I ain't gonna work no three months without no pay!"

"Then, get out now!" Arch repeated.

"But it's a downpour out there!"

"No." Locklin shook his head. "The main storm has moved on south. It is merely raining now."

"But . . . but all the horses have run off."

Caitlan's lips quirked to a smile when Arch said: "So walk."

"Walk!" That was a dirty word to a cowboy. "I come here to defend your honor and . . . and your propity and your employee's gunned-down life and you fire me or . . . or tell me I gotta work for you for three months for no pay, then you tell me to walk?"

"You didn't come here for those purposes and you know it, Cornelius," Arch shot back. "You knew what had happened between Billy Lee and Miss Black's men, yet you let Dallas Young-street lead you by the nose like the children he said . . ."

Cornelius hobbled another step or two closer. "Now, on top of ever'thin' else, you're callin' us snot-nosed kids? By gawd, Dallas was right!" He grabbed for his holstered pistol.

Even as Arch swung his Sharps to bear, Ben reached out, snagged the half-drawn weapon in Cornelius's hand, twisted it from the puncher's grip, aimed it left-handedly, and pressed the trigger. He watched the man plunge backward to the floor before he said: "Nobody pulls a gun on my father. Nobody."

And then, he passed out.

Chapter Nineteen

Whether Ben had slid directly from unconsciousness into sleep or just didn't recall any interim period, he'd spent the most peaceful, restful night he had enjoyed in a long time. He suffered no dreams, no discontent, felt no disturbance of any kind, and awoke to see brilliant daylight streaming through the open bedroom window.

Caitlan Black perched on the edge of the mattress beside him with a cup of coffee steaming in her hands. At that moment, he also discovered he was clean, bandaged, poulticed, and covered in sections to keep the greasy dressings over his shins and thighs from smearing the sheets, one folded over his feet and another from mid-thigh to armpit. Otherwise, he was naked.

"Good morning, Seth. How do you feel?"

He looked at Miss Cat smiling at him and assessed his person before he answered, lifting a tightly-wrapped hand to feel of the thick bandage protecting the bullet wound in his hair. Wiggling toes, finally deciding he was all there, he smiled back.

That hurt. He breathed—*"Argghh."*—and cupped a palm over his jaw and cheek, felt his split lip and swollen nose.

"Yes," Caitlan nodded seriously. "You look like something fierce hit you, but other than that, can you sit up and drink some coffee?" She set the cup on the floor and rose to grab the pillow. "You scoot and I'll fix this."

Groaning, he sat up. Cat stood the pillow on end and held it upright until he leaned back against it, then handed him the coffee cup.

He sipped gingerly—that also hurt. He swallowed, cleared his throat, and looked down at himself. The top sheet barely preserved his modesty. Hastily, he pulled it up around his waist. "I . . . seem to have taken a bath, but I don't remember doing that. I must have been really addled last night."

"Well, you were, but you didn't."

"What?" He frowned at her over the cup rim; what she'd just said didn't make sense to him.

She laughed. "You were unconscious. I couldn't have such a mess as you meeting my clean sheets, could I? So your daddy and I gave you a bath before we put you to bed."

He nearly choked on the coffee. "You washed me?"

Again, she laughed. "You're doing it again."

"What!"

"Blushing. All over. How do you do that, Seth? Even your knees are getting pink!" She touched a finger to his left kneecap. "And why? I mean, it's not like I've never seen your natural self

231

before. And I'm sure that when you lived with the Indians, you . . ." Her smile faded. "Or was that different?"

"Yes, that was different, and Injuns don't run around naked either, except for certain ceremonies when . . ." This was becoming too uncomfortable for him. To change the subject, he asked: "What time is it?"

"About ten-thirty."

"Ten-thirty! In the morning? I've never slept till ten-thirty in my life!"

"Well, you did today because you needed it! And you're staying right where you are the rest of the day."

"Like hell! Where are my clothes?" The coffee cup in one hand, the sheet bunched around himself with the other, he started to swing his feet off the bed, but abruptly grimaced and sagged back against the pillow.

"See?" Caitlan's palm against his chest kept him there. "Everyone else is handling things. You had quite a day yesterday, so today, you rest."

He heaved a heavy breath and decided not to argue, asked: "Where is everybody?"

"Mister Locklin has the men out rounding up my horses. He is leading one of the in-season mares that was still in the foal pen. If they can locate Ready Boy, the stallion will follow her, the other mares will follow him, the geldings will try to stay with the herd, and my men can bring them all back home."

"That's an Injun trick, using nature for their own purposes. I wonder where Arch learned it?" After last night, he was beginning to realize there was more to Arch Locklin than he had ever suspected.

Caitlan shrugged. "Don't know, but I'm grateful for his help. Umm . . . how do your legs feel? I made a mashed cat-tail root and lard poultice for the burns. Fortunately, you're only a little more than scorched . . . still, I'll imagine they smart some. I put the wrappings on to keep you from wiping the poultice away while you slept."

He said seriously: "Miss Cat, I'm real indebted to you. If it hadn't been for your help last night, I'd have been a damned sight more than merely scorched. About thirty seconds on, and I'd have been a chitlin'." He subdued a brief shudder.

She again sat on the edge of the bed and covered his bandaged hand with hers. "That was truly awful, Seth. It must have been . . . horrible for you, watching that fire leaping around you . . . unable to escape it."

He grinned wryly, didn't mention memories of the visions he had seen in the flames. "Would you think it unmanly of me if I confessed that I've never been so mortally scared in all my life?"

"Not at all. No, not at all, Seth."

He shifted his hand from hers and took her arm

233

to pull her gently to him, placed his lips as softly to hers, and kissed her almost too long because she didn't try to avoid him.

Still, when it finally ended, she breathed: "What was that for?"

"That was thank you, Cat. For last night. For some of the days past. Maybe . . ." Again, he grinned at her, and this time, there was nothing bashful about him. "Maybe for today and tomorrow, and . . . who knows? Now, where are my pants?"

Under the concept of, you kill them, you bury them, early in the morning, Arch had ordered what few cowpunchers remained with him to help inter Caitlan's horse wranglers who had died in last night's attack. He had sent Wayne back to his own ranch not only to bring Locklin horses to assist in the roundup, but also to call Reverend Mason to conduct rites.

The graves were dug. Mason delivered a fine, impassioned service, calling on God to have mercy on those who had died in defense of their home, whether that "home" was owned by someone else or not, and for forgiveness of those who had killed them, whether they were misbegotten or not. After the horses were rounded up and the dead put in the ground, Arch, still looking like someone else to Ben, with the black clothing and hat, and especially the way he barked orders and organized repairs, met Caitlan and Hawthorne on her front porch.

"Seth . . . good morning, Son. How are you?"

Ben now wore some of Cat's dead brother's clothes: a blue shirt and darker blue britches over a pair of Frank's boots, for his own were charred beyond repair. He was also armed with Black's gun belt, carrying an old but well-kept six-shooter.

He nodded and smiled back at Arch. "Well, I'm still alive, Father. I guess that's got to account for something."

Arch chuckled, stepped up onto the porch, leaned back against a post, and pulled a cigar from his shirt pocket—it had been kept dry during last night's deluge by gold foil wrapping. "Accounts for a lot. And Miss Caitlan had a hand in keeping you that way."

"Don't I know it! Still, if you hadn't appeared when you did . . . Uh, how come you did ride on over here ready for a fight?"

Arch lit the cigar and puffed. While he seemingly chatted with Ben and Caitlan, his eyes kept note of what went on in the yard. Out there, Reverend Mason hovered around punchers loading dead Locklin men onto their horses preparatory to transporting them off Cat's property. They would be buried behind Arch's house beside Billy Lee, Ev Ribble, and the whiskey-poisoned cook.

Locklin said: "Fred Perkins. It seems that Fred was as caught-up as everyone else and was headed here with the others, but about half-way, he cooled off and knew it was the wrong thing to do. He turned around and came back to let me know what was going on, so I left him looking after our interests there, and . . ." He shrugged.

"Thank God," Ben nodded. "I guess you could say he also saved my life by that, because along with Miss Cat, here, you saved my life comin' in when you did. Fred's a good man. Maybe you oughta promote him, Father."

"I'll think about it . . . and that's twice you have called me father instead of sir."

"I told you I would . . . when you earned it. And you've earned it . . . Father."

"Well," Caitlan said, as she had also been watching the activity in the yard, "if Seth hadn't come to warn us, we might all be dead now. In any event, my whole ranch could have gone up in smoke, so the most thanks should go to him, Mister Locklin. However, now is the time for me to take care of some personal business while you two are still here to back me up." She smiled ruefully. "Though I hope not, I may need your support. Reverend Mason and your men are about ready to take the bodies back to your spread, but if you can wait just a moment . . ." She stepped to the front of the porch and yelled: "PeeWee!"

The wrangler looked around from where he was in conversation with two other men. "Yeah, Miss Cat?"

"Call all our men together and tell them to come here, please. I have something to say to y'all."

"Yes, Miss Cat."

"Violet!" Ben scowled suddenly. "In all this mess, I near forgot her! Where's Violet?"

"Don't worry about her." Arch puffed a cloud of smoke into the quiet noonish air—there was no hint left of last evening's storm but drying mud and some errant wisps of steam rising from the manure pile. "I found her grazing peacefully back there by the fence and took care of her. She's in a stall in Caitlan's stable."

Cat's surviving wranglers approached in a group. It was obvious to Ben, looking at their expectant expressions, that they anticipated a well done from their boss lady, thanks, and maybe a bonus for their efforts during last night's altercation, and while what Caitlan said started out that way, what followed after her brief congratulations left all the men shuffling feet and shooting wary looks at each other.

She said: "I suppose y'all heard Les Moody order me back to the house where he thought I belonged last night, and saw him hit me, not once, but twice, when I didn't go. I also expect you heard him say that he and some of you, if not all of you, only work for me out of respect for my father and brother.

"Well, I also respect the memories of my father and brother, but they are both dead now, and *I* own this spread. *I* am the boss, and any of you who don't like taking orders from a woman are free to go. Pack up your gear and get out before the end of the day . . . do I make myself clear?"

The men glanced from Miss Black to Arch still leaning against the porch post, his eyes narrow and cold, at Ben standing with folded arms and legs akimbo beside and slightly behind Caitlan, his expression as hard and watchful as his father's, and they muttered various: "Sure, Miss Cat," and "You're the boss, yeah, Miss Cat."

She nodded once. "PeeWee, you are fired. Saddle up and move on . . . now. Right now."

His mouth fell open. "Wh . . . uh . . . why, Miss Cat? Whut call you got to fire me! I done . . ."

She cut him off. "For attempting to murder Mister Seth Locklin by burning him to death last evening. Reno Gootch and Les Moody were in with you on that . . . they both died for it, good enough . . . but I won't have someone on my ranch who can do something like that." Her voice sharpened. "You're fired. Get out! If you're still here at sundown, I'll gun you down myself, understood?

"And speaking of Mister Moody, he was my ramrod, and obviously I need a new one. I could

238

pick one of you myself, but I think it would be better if those of you who are staying choose one from among yourselves. I want to hear your decision by three o'clock. I also want a report from him at that time on the condition of my stock, both the horses and the cattle, and how many men he recommends we hire to replace those who died last night or who are leaving. That's all. You can go to work now."

As the wranglers bobbed heads and turned back toward stables and corrals, Ben grinned at Arch. "I like a woman who knows what she wants. I may seriously consider her as wife material one day, Father."

Caitlan jerked around to stare wide-eyed at him, gasped: "What?"

Arch laughed when Ben said: "Why, Miss Cat, you're blushing. I never saw anyone get so pink all over before . . . how do you do that?"

"Seth!"

Locklin came to her rescue. "Miss Caitlan, would you consider having dinner with my son and me at our place tonight about six? Call it business and pleasure . . . I want to apologize to you for all the discomfort my men caused you last night, and perhaps discuss . . . other things."

Both she and Ben cast him puzzled glances. Caitlan said: "I'll be pleased to dine with you, Mister Locklin, but . . . what other things do you want to talk about?"

He smiled off into the distance. "Oh, just . . . other things. I see my men have the bodies loaded and that Reverend Mason is also fixed. Seth, you up to riding home? Yes? Then, go get Violet and let's be on our way. Like Miss Cat, here, I have some firing to do."

The caravan of the dead, led by Arch, Ben, and Reverend Mason, was half-way home when Hawthorne said: "A band of Kiowas comin', Father."

"I see them." Arch turned to order the cowhands: "Be ready, but don't make any threatening moves. And no one is to fire under any circumstances unless I say so, understood?"

The men unclipped trigger guards and loosened weapons in holsters, eyed the oncoming Indians warily, but nodded. From the buckboard seat, Mason muttered nervously: " 'Yes, though I walk through the valley of the shadow of death, I will fear no evil. . . .' O Lord, protect us, I beseech thee. The heathen Kiowas have slaughtered more white men than any other breed of redskin has done, and . . ."

"Y'all just keep on goin', Father," Ben said. "I'll meet them and see what they want."

"All right, but be careful." Arch's fingers rested near the stock of the Sharps in its saddle scabbard by his knee; he could pull and fire the weapon almost instantly.

Ben nodded and kicked Violet into a canter toward the Kiowas. Shortly, he recognized Medicine Shield and the old shaman, Talking Buffalo, leading the group. He slowed the mare to a trot when they halted their ponies, lifted a palm in peace, and reined in beside Medicine Shield, grasping the chief's wrist in greeting, asking in their language: "What brings you onto This World Stealer's land, Father?"

Medicine Shield nodded at the shaman. "Talking Buffalo made fire magic for you last night to help you remember who you are, then called the rain to stop it. We come to discover if his healing was successful or not."

Ben smiled at Talking Buffalo. "You make strong medicine, holy one. Yes, I know who I am now, without question . . . but you nearly overdid your fire magic. You about burned me alive with it."

Talking Buffalo sighed heavily. "I did my best, Snow Fox. Since you were not close to me, I had to take extreme measures because I wanted to be sure you were cured and that all the Contraries were driven out of you. I see my rain quenched the prairie fires. I am satisfied." To Medicine Shield, he said: "We can go home now."

"Talking Buffalo, thank you." Ben leaned across Medicine Shield's pony to extend a hand to the shaman.

Talking Buffalo ignored the offered hand, but

turned sharp black eyes back toward Ben. "It was for your father, as well. But you are welcome. When you come to your father's camp to face Crow Runs, we will talk again."

Ben felt a jolt of surprise. In all this stampede, he had forgotten the young warrior's vow of revenge. He said nothing, merely nodded, tipped a finger to Medicine Shield and murmured "Father" before he reined Violet back toward where his other father waited.

Chapter Twenty

The dead had been put down and Fred Perkins accompanied Reverend Mason back to town. Now, candlelight glimmered softly against damask cloth and polished silver in the big house. Coffee steamed in fine china cups. Elegant plates were laden with beef steak and baked squash, but Ben hardly noticed what he was eating, for his eyes were irresistibly drawn—first to Caitlan, then to Arch. Neither looked anywhere familiar to him at the moment.

Because she was dressed in an ankle-length, high-necked, long-sleeved dress saved from being prim by its lustrous blue taffeta material, Caitlan had driven over in the buckboard rather than riding Picket Fence. Though the dress fit her well, she confessed it had once belonged to her mother; Ben didn't mention that he had seen rough, riding boot toes peeking from beneath her hem when she walked. Her fine floaty black hair was done up off her neck with a tall Spanish comb. Iridescent blue bobs dangled from her earlobes; he was more than enchanted by her tonight.

And then there was Arch Locklin decked out in white shirt, silk tie, a vest under his suit jacket with a gold watch chain draped from side to side, looking like Ben's vision of an Eastern banker when the man chatted as easily with Caitlan as though she was his own daughter. Trying to stack the dressed-in-black hardcase he'd seen last night against this soft-spoken man tonight almost put Ben's mind back to addled.

He was also gussied up. Since Seth hadn't been around as an adult long enough to acquire any, he wore one of David's suits. True, the fine duds were incongruous with the bandage still confining his hair, the one on his left hand, and the cuts, bruises, and other scrapes from his battle with Dallas Youngstreet marring his face, but he wondered briefly what Mrs. Inman down in Texas would have thought of him dressed like this—he'd been pleased enough to wear some of her boy, Jake's, outgrown clothing at the time, Jacob being a strapping man half again as big as he was. And now . . . ?

He actually said very little during dinner, but after the main course was done with, after Midge had brought the apple pie and then cognac to finish the repast, he couldn't stand it any longer.

"Who are you?"

Both Arch and Caitlan stared at him in puzzlement until Locklin scowled. "Seth, are you all right?"

"Yes! No! Yes! Maybe I should ask, who were you . . . once? I can't put together what I see here at this table with what I saw last night takin' men out right and left in the middle of a deluge! You're too . . . too civilized to be him! Where'd you come by that?"

Arch glanced at Caitlan briefly before he looked back at Ben. "You think I'm too civilized to have built all this?"

"Yeah. Like . . . like your daughter, uh . . ."

"Priscilla," Caitlan murmured.

Ben nodded. "Yes, like Priscilla's husband, whatever his name is . . . that I met the first day I was h-here . . . uh . . ."

"Todd Nichols." Arch's expression eased steadily into a broad smile. He fished out a cigar and clamped it between front teeth bared by the grin.

"Yeah, Todd Nichols. You said he had no interest in a spread this size nor the ability to manage it had he wanted to . . . yet here you sit, dandified like an Eastern tenderfoot . . . who were you before all this?"

Arch's smile took on a wry cast. He flamed the cigar before he said: "I was a highwayman."

Both Ben's and Caitlan's mouths fell open. They looked round-eyed at each other before Cat blurted: "A road agent?"

"Uhn-huh." Arch rolled the cigar between thumb and forefinger. "Took up the profession when I was fifteen."

"Wh-Where?"

"Back East. In a variety of places. My partner

and I did that for about five or six years. We were good at it, too. And frugal. Saved our gain. None of this doing a job then wasting the money on wine and women. I still take pleasure in the knowledge that while we robbed the rich, we never killed one person in the process. And no, before you ask, we didn't give to the poor. Kept it all ourselves."

He took another pull at the cigar. "One day . . . or, I should say, night . . . we hit it lucky, my partner and me. Stopped a real poorly looking, ill-guarded wagon. Oh, we hadn't even been looking for a target that night, we were on our way to a church social in town, but it was habit by that time, I guess, and it turned out to be a shipment of money to a bank. The authorities had evidently made a big to-do about sending the money by heavily armed stage, which was only a decoy. We accidentally got the real thing." His eyes fixed on candle flames. "A hundred and fifty-seven thousand dollars."

"Oh, my," Caitlan breathed. "So . . . so what did you do then?"

Arch tipped his head. "We were so over-whelmed, we nearly went crazy for a while. We knew we had to get ourselves together . . . pulled back into the forest, set up a hidden camp, got our minds calmed down . . . and finally, we came up with a plan. We had met two fine young ladies in church . . ."

"You went to church? Regular?" Ben gasped. Somehow, that didn't seem to fit the tale.

Arch also looked surprised. "And why not? Of course, we went to church on Sunday. After all, my father, your grandfather, Seth, was a minister. Even my older twin brother was studying to be a pastor. So why not?"

Again, Ben and Caitlan glanced at each other.

"Anyway," Arch went on, "we'd been courting certain young ladies off and on whenever we were in the territory, so we went to them, asked them to marry us and to move West with us. They said no."

"Oh, dear," Cat frowned. "So . . . ?"

"So we saddle-bagged our money and came West alone until we hit Pig's Eye, Missouri. We stopped off at a saloon there, and there we met two of the prettiest girls west of the Mississippi."

"Dance hall girls?" Ben scowled.

"Yep. We told them who we were and where we were headed and why. Asked them if they'd like to be wives instead of . . ."

"My mother was a whore?" Ben anticipated Arch's next words.

Locklin flared: "She was not! She was a waitress serving drinks and food there, a decent, hard-working girl who had to support herself because her folks were dead and she couldn't sew a stitch, so . . ." He swallowed, calmed himself with a sip of cognac and another puff at the cigar.

"Anyway, Cora and her friend said yes. And . . ."

"So you were a . . . criminal." Caitlan settled back into her chair, lids lowered over blue eyes. She appeared about to bolt. Her tone bordered on disgust when she finished: "A . . . a crook! A highwayman. And all this . . ."—her hand waved around the room—"was built with money stolen from honest folk who . . ."

"Don't get on your high horse, Miss Black," Arch grinned. "Who do you think my partner was?"

Her eyes flashed up to meet his. "Who? Wh-Why should I . . . why should I care?"

Now Arch's expression shaded to hard and watchful. In turn, he asked his own question. "Why do you think the Locklins and the Blacks have always been so close? Remember . . . think back to your childhood . . . you, Priscilla, Frank, Seth and David . . . your mother and Seth's closer than sisters. . . ."

She flared: "We were neighbors! The only white folks out here! Of course . . ."

"We were more than neighbors," Arch commented.

Caitlan was silent for a long moment before she said it. "My father was your p-p-p-partner?"

Arch knocked ash from his cigar into a tray. "There are two ways to look at this situation, Miss Black. You can run around beating your most excellent bosom crying . . . 'Oh, my God!

. . . I'm the daughter of a road agent and a saloon girl,' or, you can look at this ranch and yours, at the life we all have led out here, and say . . . 'My, look at how far we've come!' This generation is respectable . . . even though your mother and Seth's always considered themselves to be very respectable, and they were. They were good, hard-working, faithful wives and loving mothers. You have nothing to be ashamed of. Nothing."

A strained silence fell over the room. Ben watched Caitlan's expression pass through a series of emotions softening from chagrin to bemusement to a sudden, startling laugh. She flung her head back, opened her mouth, and howled a supremely unlady-like chortle.

Ben and Arch glanced at each other before Locklin asked: "What's so funny, Caitlan?"

She struggled to compose herself. "S-Sorry. I was just . . . Does Priscilla know this?"

Arch nodded understanding. "No. It wouldn't fit in with her chosen lifestyle. It wouldn't be acceptable for the daughter of an ex-highwayman to be the wife of an up-and-coming New York broker."

"No, I think not. Finally! Finally, I'm Priscilla's equal! I had to help Frank run the ranch while Pris went off to finishing school. I'm still running the ranch while she married well. To think that I've felt much less than Pris after she came back an Eastern lady. . . ."

"Miss Cat," Ben cut in, "you're not less than anyone, and after last night, I'll fight anybody who claims it."

She flashed her eyes in thanks to him, but murmured: "So . . . Jeremiah Black was also a . . . a road agent in his younger days. Oh, my."

"No." Arch looked at the table top.

Again, Cat's eyes met Ben's before she frowned at Locklin. "But you just said . . ."

"As long as we're baring all here, yes, your father was my partner, but his name wasn't Jeremiah Black." Arch sighed heavily. "It was your mother's idea . . . both the women's idea. Normally, when a man and a woman wed, the wife takes her husband's name. But in our case, the husbands were . . . fugitives from the law. Wanted men. Very wanted men. Our names were well-known. So your father, Seth McIntyre, took Margaret's father's name . . . Jeremiah Black. And I took Cora Locklin's father's, Arch Locklin. And we came here to start new lives. Fought Indians together. Opened the land together. Raised our children together, until . . ." He waved the cigar butt before he stubbed it out in the tray. "So now you know."

Again, a silence fell over the room, this one lengthy until Ben asked: "Then, I'm named after Caitlan's father? I got his real name?"

"Yes. Named for my closest friend . . . for a man who was more than a brother to me."

"Uh . . . just out of curiosity, Father, what was your name before you became Arch Locklin?"

Arch looked hard at him for a moment. Finally, he murmured: "I'm not sure you really want to know that, Seth."

Abruptly, Ben fought down a wash of shock. Both Arch and Caitlan leaned toward him in concern when he went white, but neither spoke, because they saw he was trying to say something.

Ben clutched table edges until his knuckles were as ashen as his face, and whispered: "You don't have to tell me. Your name was Ben Hawthorne, wasn't it?"

"Yes," Arch nodded. "My name was Ben Hawthorne."

Outside now, standing by Caitlin's buckboard, she said to Ben: "You must have heard your folks talking when you were little. Or your mother talking with mine. Or . . . or . . . And when you ran after Blue Glass Bead and your son died, maybe you were so crazy with grief you picked the first name that came to mind and it was Ben . . . Ben Hawthorne. After years of using it, when those men made you say it over and over . . . But now, you know you're really Seth Locklin, don't you?" Caitlan looked at Ben, anxious to go home before it got too dark.

It would have been so easy to say yes and leave

251

it at that, but Ben had the cold crawling sensation in the pit of his stomach that something still wasn't right here. In fact, something was terribly wrong. All right, yes, after the fire and his fight with Youngstreet, he'd been convinced he was Seth Locklin, but now he was just as sure that he, not Arch, was Ben Hawthorne.

Why did he know he was right? All the evidence pointed the other way. Why would Arch say he had once been Ben Hawthorne unless he had?

Everyone called him Seth, told him he was. Even Medicine Shield and Talking Buffalo, even Crow Runs seemed to have no doubt. He could discount Arch, because he had suspected early on that with David's accident and now death, Locklin searched for a son, even some other man's son, to fill the position . . . but Caitlan thought he was Seth. He admitted that the likelihood of some totally unrelated man resembling twins as closely as he did—if he envisioned a healthy David— was beyond the realm of probability, yet when Talking Buffalo had asked and he had assured the old shaman that the fire magic had worked, he had known at that moment that it indeed had. He was Ben, not Seth.

All the questions had been answered, right? No! No, they hadn't. There was still one remaining, and that was . . .

"Seth, you aren't answering me," Caitlan

prompted. "You *do* know who you are, don't you?"

"Oh. Yes. Sorry. Yes, I do. I . . ."

"No, you don't! I see that, now." She sighed softly before—in a move very forward but not unwelcome—she slid arms around him. "Then, let me put it this way. It doesn't really matter who you were, only who you are now. Just like our parents. We heard tonight that once our fathers were road agents, once our mothers were saloon girls. But they became pioneers . . . respectable wives and ranchers. Loving parents. You may have been Snow Fox or Ben Hawthorne, but now you're Seth Locklin. It's who you are now that's important . . . and what you make of yourself in the future.

"Good night, Seth. Thank you for an interesting evening. I have to get home."

He returned the hug briefly before he helped her into the buckboard. "You want me to escort you?"

"No. It's only three miles, and I know my way. Please, Seth, don't be a stranger. Come visit me."

"I . . . still have a couple of things to do. But then, you can count on it." He watched her ripple reins to start the carriage horse on its way, one blazing question still lingering in his mind: was his mother's name Cora Hawthorne or Cora Locklin? But there was that other memory, one of a tall man with white-blond hair, a God-fearing, Bible-toting, hard-working, laughing man named Eli Hawthorne. His father, Eli.

He had to find out who Eli was . . . or had been. Only then would this mess be resolved.

Chapter Twenty-One

The cowpuncher, hat in his hands, a perplexed look on his face, stepped from foot to foot in Arch's office doorway.

Locklin scowled up at the man. "Yes?"

"Uh . . . Mistuh Arch . . . uh . . . mebby it ain't none of my business, but . . . I mean, mebby you know about this and all, but . . ."

Arch leaned back in his chair. "Out with it, man! Is there some kind of a problem?"

"Well, we dunno. Like I said, mebby you know about it, but . . ."

"Spit it out, for God's sake!"

"Why is yer boy, Seth, diggin' up Cookie's grave?"

"What?" Frowning, Arch stiffened.

"Yeah. Uh . . . we know Mistuh Seth was raised up by the Injuns and all, and mebby it's some heathen religion he's got left over from it, but . . ."

"Oh, I doubt that."

"But it ain't decent, Mistuh Arch! Ain't proper to disturb no man's grave once he's put down!"

"And he's doing it right now?"

"Yes, suh! He's at it right now."

"Huh! Get on back to work. I'll see what's going on." Arch pushed back his chair and rose. The puncher put on his hat and retreated into the hallway, kept backing until he hit the front door, then whirled and leaped off the porch as if escaping something obscene.

The men had dug Cookie's grave the proper six feet deep. When Arch arrived, all he saw was a shovel tossing dirt up out of a hole. Shortly, a hand set a whiskey bottle on the ground beside a bucket of water waiting there. The container was followed by the shovel. Then the grubby, bandaged hand gripped the grave lip and Ben heaved himself into view. He nodded to Arch, picked up the bottle, dropped it into the water in the bucket, and again grabbed the shovel.

"Seth . . ."

"Yes, sir?" Ben began moving dirt back into the grave.

Arch indicated the hole. "You're giving the men fits by disturbing the cook's plot. May I ask what the hell you're doing?"

"Fixin' to solve a mystery. Please don't touch that bottle."

Arch had bent for the whiskey bottle bobbing on the water. He hesitated in mid-reach and scowled at Ben.

"Why not?"

Ben stopped refilling the grave and leaned on the shovel handle. "Well, sir, it appears to me that you're about to pay a lot of money to a murderer."

"What? Who?"

"That's what I hope to find out." Ben resumed shoveling. "You hired four bounty hunters to locate me. They did that. Promptly, one of 'em shuffled off this mortal coil with the aid of water hemlock in his vittles. Then, ol' Ev Ribble, he died of water hemlock poisoning that must have come from that bottle, because after Ev died, Cookie, here, killed off what was left in the bottle and *he* died.

"Now, takin' out a man in an honest gun battle or knife fight, that's one thing. But underhandedly doin' a man in with poison, that's another. I figger it was either Reuben Bettiger who did it, or Al Hoffs, but I don't know which. I'm fixin' to find out by usin' that bottle, because I take offense at you payin' forty thousand dollars to some greed-ridden, cold-blooded killer. When do you think your men will be back here with Bettiger, Hoffs, and the cash?"

Arch eyed the bottle distastefully. "Any day now."

"Good. I'd like to be present when you conclude your business with them, if you don't mind. And I'll ask that you follow my lead for a while, there, even though it's your house and your business."

"Sure. What do you intend to do?"

"You'll see." Ben finished replacing the dirt and patted the mound smooth with the back of the shovel blade. He nodded to the grave, said:

257

"My apologies for disturbin' you, man, but I hope to bring your killer to justice, so I figger you can forgive me."

"Seth, Cookie can't hear you," Arch frowned.

Ben grinned crookedly at him while he picked up the bucket. "Are you sure? The spirit life is very real to the . . . to some people. A little respect never hurts."

Arch watched Ben pull the cork from the bottle and sink the quart flask, carefully rinsing both the bottle and its stopper, then dumped the water. He followed when Hawthorne headed for the rear of the house with the cork and the bottle still in the bucket. Ben leaned the shovel against the wall by the kitchen steps, said: "I'll be right back." He vanished into the kitchen and returned almost immediately with a large, steaming teakettle.

He poured boiling water over the cork and into the bottle, gingerly picked up the bottle and emptied it onto the ground, repeated the process twice more, vigorously sloshed things, and finally satisfied that both the container and its stopper were clean, nodded at Arch. "I think that ought to do it. May I use some of your fine whiskey?"

"Of course." Fascinated, now, Arch again followed when, with the bottle and cork in one hand, the teakettle in the other, Ben reentered the kitchen.

Ben nodded to the house cook, handed her the

empty kettle, and passed on into the hallway toward the sitting room where the beautifully carved liquor cabinet stood. He searched through the supply until he located a full bottle, opened it, and carefully poured whiskey from the fresh container into Ev Ribble's washed one. He held the bounty hunter's bottle up to consider the level, added a little more until it was slightly less than half full, then returned Locklin's to the cabinet and corked Ev's.

He looked seriously at Arch. "I'm goin' to set this bottle over here in the corner of the cabinet, Father. Please don't drink out of it until Bettiger and Hoffs get here. Then, I want to be with you when you do your business with them. If I'm not here, I ask you to wait until I get back."

Arch tipped his head. "Agreed. But why wouldn't you be here? You going some place?"

"Yes, but with luck I won't be gone more than a few hours . . . at the most, overnight. I . . . have some . . . unfinished business to take care of at . . . Medicine Shield's camp."

"Seth . . ." Arch scowled.

Ben anticipated him. "No, I'm not going there to stay, if I can help it." He sighed heavily and fingered bottles in the cabinet for a moment, finally decided to tell Locklin the truth. He turned around and met Arch's eyes squarely. "Crow Runs, my Injun blood brother, blames me for Blue Glass Bead's death. I don't know why

259

he's so fierce about it, but he has vowed to kill me should I ever come into camp again."

"Then don't!" Arch almost shouted. "There's no reason for you to go there! You didn't cause her to . . ."

"I know it," Ben cut him off, "and you know it. But if I ignore it and just let it fester, one day Crow Runs is not gonna wait for me to come to him. Now that he knows I'm back, he'll maybe cry for a medicine dream, see himself comin' here instead of lettin' me go there, and do it. I can't spend the rest of my life wonderin' when a Kiowa arrow is gonna cut me short. No, I have to settle this one way or another, now, at a time of my choosing, not in the dark of some night when he chooses!"

"But I . . . I was the one who . . ."

"No, it wasn't you . . . or not just you. No, I have to go try to explain it to Crow Runs."

"But suppose he won't listen? Suppose he attacks you anyway, Seth. No, I can't let you go. If I lost you also . . ."

"Father . . ."—Ben stepped forward to lay a hand on Arch's arm—"I say again, I need to get this settled once and for all. If Crow Runs won't listen, then we'll have to do it his way, I guess. I hope it won't come to that, but until I face him, there will always be a shadow over me."

"Then I'll go with you. Together we'll . . ."

"No! If worse comes to worst, all you could do

anyway would be to stand on the sidelines with the others and watch, and neither you nor I need that. At the very worst, you might also die.

"Look . . ."—Ben turned toward the stairs—"I went to warn Miss Cat about the men comin' to burn her out. You came to help, and you did, but you let me settle the issue with Youngstreet on my own. Do me the same here. I'll be back one way or the other, either under my own power or Medicine Shield will bring my body to you . . . that's his way. Now, let me go, Father, while the day is still young. But do not . . . I repeat, do not follow me, understood?"

Locklin's expression went grim. Ben walked to the hall end of the stairs and waited, one hand on the banister, a foot on the bottom riser, until Arch nodded and said: "Then, I . . . wish you good luck."

"Thank you, Father." Hawthorne moved on up the stairs.

Arch was nowhere in sight when Ben came back down, but what cowhands were in the yard cast wall-eyed looks at the figure that crossed toward the corral where Violet was penned. Ben was again dressed in the loincloth, fringed leggings, and moccasins he had discovered stored in the camel-back trunk in his room. He had tied the eagle feather to his hair; because he had no roach spreader and his hair had been cut short with no scalp lock left to secure it, the

261

feather lay horizontally atop his head instead of standing upright. Also because in his years of living as a white man and clothing had allowed his tan to fade, he had put a cotton shirt back on to keep from getting sunburned between here and Medicine Shield's camp, though the elegant bib of bone and quill work showed through the unbuttoned front. His only weapons were a knife in the beaded belt at his waist, and the fine rifle in his left hand.

He caught Violet, bridled but didn't saddle her, and led her out of the corral. He noticed Arch standing on the house porch with a cigar in one hand and a glass of whiskey in the other, but neither waved nor really looked in Locklin's direction as he leaped astride the mare. With the rifle cradled in the crook of his left arm, he urged Violet into a running trot northward toward Medicine Shield's camp. He wasn't sure where the Kiowas were at the moment, but he would search until he located them; didn't know what he would do once he got there, or if he would live the day out or not, but if he was going to stay here and pretend to be Arch's son, he had to resolve all outstanding problems and tie up all loose ends. Otherwise, he had no future, either as Ben Hawthorne or as Seth Locklin.

He assessed his inner person. He wasn't afraid, nor did he anticipate anything. He found himself to be merely resigned to the inevitable. This was something over which he had little control, a thing that had to be done, a thing the spirits dictated, maybe an answer to past prayers.

An hour later, he noted a small band of riders approaching from out of the northwest and guided Violet toward them. His expression became faintly wry as he took off the white man's shirt and tied the cuffs to the mare's mane. It seemed old Talking Buffalo had visioned his approach and had sent an escort. The riders reined in their ponies, waited for Ben to reach them, then wordlessly wheeled their mounts and led him onward. Ben wondered what the shaman had said to Crow Runs in preparation for this confrontation. He would find out soon.

Chapter Twenty-Two

Ben had to admit that it felt uncommonly good to be back in Indian leather, wearing only the loincloth, leggings, and moccasins—he found "hairy-mouth"—as the Kiowas called the white man—clothing confining and ill-fitting, even after all these years. Still, he slid a look at the warriors riding around him and fought down a rising tension as he wondered whether they'd been sent as guides, as an honor escort, or if they were here to ensure he didn't escape now that he was this close to Medicine Shield's camp and Crow Runs's revenge.

Medicine Shield's people had set up their homes near a water-filled depression in the prairie—Ben didn't know whether the water was permanent or merely a residue of the recent storm. The teepees clustered in family groups, all their openings facing the rising sun, their tips—like the trees along Runoff Creek—slanted eastward to lessen the force of the prevailing wind upon them.

Ben's "honor guard" rode with him toward a certain teepee whose buffalo-hide walls were well painted to announce the deeds of its occupant. At their approach, Medicine Shield himself stepped out and nodded thanks to his men.

He said to Ben: "Snow Fox."

"Father." Ben again knew a brief flash of puzzlement that he found it easier to call a Kiowa "father" than to give Arch Locklin the same naming.

"Talking Buffalo said you would come today."

"He is wise and very powerful."

"That he is."

"Did he also tell you why I am here?"

"Yes. If Crow Runs takes his avowed revenge upon you, will you speak kindly of me to the spirits?"

"I will be honored to, Father." Ben slid down from Violet's back. The other men still sat their ponies, watching and listening with solemn curiosity. They edged their mounts back to give him room when, still carrying the rifle in the crook of his left arm, Hawthorne finished: "I have to prepare. Will you care for my mare for me, please?"

"Yes." Medicine Shield watched Snow Fox turn and walk toward the open center of the camp. Ben noticed a strange tingling coldness between his shoulder blades, not exactly fear, but as though the hungry eyes of a pack of wolves focused there, and it almost made him pause. He wondered, as he halted in the middle of the camp commons, just why he was doing this— certainly, even as Arch intimated, he didn't have to. Regardless of what he had said to Locklin, he could have stayed far away from Medicine

Shield's camp, could have merely surrounded himself with men whose presences and ready guns would have, might have, protected him, yet here he was. Why?

Moving almost as if someone else directed his body, he bent to lay the rifle on the ground, crosswise in front of his moccasin toes. All activity ceased around him; women called their children to them, men stopped gambling, caring for their horses, or chatting, and the camp became a silent waiting entity, the only sounds the wind whistling through crowning teepee poles, a dog's yip from somewhere behind one of the tents, or a pony nickering from far across the village.

All eyes in various shades of brown, from light hazel to pupil-less black, were focused on Snow Fox when he untied the knife belt and let it fall. Ben reached up and removed the bone-and-quill bib. Also let it drop. Now wearing nothing but his loincloth, leggin's, and moccasins, he lowered his arms to his sides, his hands open and empty, palms exposed, and waited, and he abruptly knew he hadn't come to fight but to make peace.

In the silence, he called: "Crow Runs, I am here!"

"And I am here."

Crow Runs had come so silently up behind him that Ben hadn't heard the warrior's approach. It was one of the hardest things he had ever had to do not to turn and face the man, not to move, not to flinch. He stayed motionless, looking straight ahead, his arms still down, hands still open and empty, until Crow Runs moved around in front of him.

The warrior wore only a loincloth and moccasins. He held a white man's steel knife in his right hand, wore three trophy feathers in his hair. Eyes wide, he reached to lay a palm against Ben's chest.

Still, Hawthorne didn't move, but he noted sweat on Crow Runs's brow and on his upper lip and saw that there was more fear than hatred in the brown eyes when the man whispered: "How is it your heart still beats? I killed you. The snow ran red with your blood. I know you are dead, yet you are here now and your heart beats. Are you a spirit grown man-flesh and come back to take revenge upon me?"

A jolt of surprise almost made Ben retreat a step, but he stopped himself. He said: "I do not recall you killing me, Crow Runs. When did you do that?"

Eyes even wider, the warrior leaned a little closer to study him. Presently, he gasped: "When Blue Glass Bead brought my son and left you to those whose ears stick out. When she tried to come home to me but the spirits rose against her so that you could follow her. Then, I killed you."

"Your son? The child she bore was yours, not mine?"

"My son. We loved, she and I. We had always loved. My son, not yours."

Now, Ben shook his head. He recalled that Caitlan Black had said a "friend" had visited Blue Glass Bead while the woman and her child had stayed at the Blacks' ranch, that she had reluctantly admitted the "friend" was a man, and abruptly knew the man had been Crow Runs.

He asked: "Then, if that is so, why did Blue Glass Bead wed me?"

"Even though you became Medicine Shield's son, you were once the eldest of This World Stealer. As such we knew that when This World Stealer died, his lands would become your lands. You wooed Blue Glass Bead. The women thought that if she wed you, we . . . all of us . . . would be able to regain the grounds your hairy-mouth father stole from us. And so Blue Glass Bead tried to sacrifice herself for the good of the people. She tried to do what was right, but our love was too strong. She divorced you and your white-man's ways, and was bringing our son home to me when the snows caught them.

"They were dead by the time I found them . . . by the time you found us. I killed you . . . buried you in the ground as is the hairy-mouths' way . . . yet here you are again, returned to confront me! Are you a spirit come to haunt me all the days of my life or are you a man I can kill again?"

Ben tipped his head. "Crow Runs, if you knew

I was dead, why did you vow to kill me should I ever return to camp?"

"To . . . to hide that I had already slain you! To . . ."

"But to best a rival in honest battle is an honorable deed! You could have claimed coup! You could have sung your victory song!"

The warrior cried in what seemed to be agony: "But you know we did not fight! You called me brother! I cut your throat from behind while you mourned the deaths of your wife and one you thought to be your son! I slaughtered you while you wept as though you were . . ." Crow Runs's voice choked briefly. "You were not the enemy! We were brothers, yet I . . . You had done no harm! You only loved Blue Glass Bead as I loved her, and when I cut your throat, you turned and looked at me in . . . in pity! I cannot bear the memory! I vowed to kill you should you ever return even while I prayed to the spirits that you would come and slay me to rid me of my guilt!" Crow Runs reversed the knife he held and offered it hilt-first to Ben. "Release me, Brother! Forgive me and release me!"

Hawthorne looked at the blade. Now he knew why Seth Locklin had never returned from his search for Blue Glass Bead and little Arch. He hadn't run, he had died. Now, he also knew why—despite all evidence to the contrary—he always came back to being Ben Hawthorne in his own mind. He was Ben Hawthorne.

He said: "I can't forgive you, Crow Runs, because it's not my place to do so . . . this is between your soul and the spirits. But I tell you that I will visit my father, Medicine Shield, at any time I so choose and at any time he desires. If you need to try to kill Snow Fox again, now is the time. Otherwise, I leave you to deal with your conscience."

Crow Runs made a harsh sound of frustration. He flipped the blade into the air, caught it by the handle, and raised the knife.

"You killed me once, Brother," Ben spoke before the weapon could fall, "you cannot kill me twice. I died for a wife who betrayed me. I died for another man's son. When I came back, the hairy-mouths did this to my body." His hands moved to indicate the branding iron burns healed but still pink over his chest, ribs, and belly. He turned his back on Crow Runs to show the fresh scars there. He continued his turn to again face the warrior poised to strike, finished with: "Talking Buffalo made fire magic for me so I could recall who I am, and his power is so strong, it nearly ate me." The effort it took not to defend himself from Crow Runs made his fingers tremble when he jerked the ties from the belt that held up his leggin's and let leather bunch around his feet. The burns on his legs were also healing, but still vivid. "And now you want to kill me again? Why, Crow Runs . . . why? What have I ever done to you, Crow Runs? You took my wife . . . you claim my son . . . you slew me once . . . why more, Crow Runs?"

The warrior darted a glance around the village at those watching and listening silently. He saw Medicine Shield, his mouth thinned into a grim line, still standing in front of his teepee. Over there, Talking Buffalo squatted on his heels by a fire; the shaman stared back with intent black eyes as he fondled the war lance he held in one hand, the red-dyed eagle feather he held in the other. All the rest, the men . . . women . . . children . . .

"For . . . honor," he gasped.

"Whose honor?" Ben snapped. "There is no honor in having to kill a man twice to make him stay dead! And I will not fight you."

"Then I will kill you as I did the first time, merely cut your throat as though you were a . . ."

"It's not a secret this time, Crow Runs." Hawthorne inclined his head toward the onlookers. "All our people are watching you . . . and me. They will see me die bravely and without flinching. I will sing my death song in your face. They will see and know what you do and how you do it, and your honor will be diminished."

Again, Crow Runs looked around. Ben tensed, frozen, when the warrior's arm twitched—despite his words, he knew that come an actual strike, he wouldn't merely stand here and be slaughtered.

But Crow Runs didn't finish the attack. Instead, he howled a terrible, wrenching cry, whirled, and bolted back into the forest of teepees.

Ben stood motionlessly for a moment longer simply because he couldn't move. Finally, aware that those who had watched both him and Crow Runs continued to scrutinize him, he slowly and carefully bent to pull up his leggin's, tied their strings, replaced his knife belt at his waist, picked up the rifle, and turned to look at Medicine Shield. "All right, now you know that I am not Snow Fox. Snow Fox died a long time ago. What are you going to do about it?"

"The thing is," Medicine Shield returned softly, "that now *you* know you are not Snow Fox. What are *you* going to do about it?"

Ben sighed and glanced around the camp briefly, before he turned his eyes toward the Locklin Ranch. "I don't know. I have to think about that. Are you . . . are you going to tell This World Stealer?"

"Not I. If anyone does, it will be you. Let me know your decision when you make it, and then we will discuss the future." Medicine Shield turned away.

Ben nodded. He headed across the area toward where the warriors who had led him in still sat their ponies and held Violet for him. As he passed Talking Buffalo, the medicine man held up the war lance.

"Here, young warrior, you will need this."

Ben's brows rose. Why would he need the lance . . . and for what? But he took the weapon, said: "Thank you, holy one." And passed on.

Just as he flung himself astride the mare and again nodded farewell to the Kiowas, a long, high, challenging cry rang from behind teepees far down to the left.

Everyone but Talking Buffalo jerked around to see what—or who—screamed what they all recognized to be a call to war. They saw Crow Runs mounted on a white pony, his shield on his left arm, a long lance readied in his right hand, urging his mount toward the visitor.

Ben's eyes widened. He hesitated briefly, until tactics practiced during his life with the Comanches, actions that had almost become instinct, took over. The rifle in his left hand, the lance Talking Buffalo had visioned he would need in his right, he kicked Violet into an instant run to meet the warrior.

They clashed in a headlong passage. Ben used the rifle barrel to deflect Crow Runs's weapon; still, he felt a burning pain in his shoulder when the lance blade slid up and over his back. His own lance plunged beneath Crow Runs's shield and between the warrior's ribs. Crow Runs flung up both arms, and with half the blade of Ben's weapon embedded in his chest, plunged to the ground. His riderless horse raced on until the group of mounted Kiowa warriors caught it.

Ben pulled Violet up sharply, wheeled her, and guided her back to where Crow Runs lay. He leaped to the ground to kneel beside the dying man, clasped Crow Runs's hand, but nearly cringed when the warrior whispered: "Thank you . . . brother . . . for h-honoring me in battle."

Ben looked up at Medicine Shield now standing beside them and gasped: "He let me kill him! He attacked me just enough that I had to defend myself, and then he . . . He made me kill him! Why?"

"He had lived a long time with his guilt," Medicine Shield murmured. "He saw that the time for lies was past. At least he died like a warrior."

"Shit," Ben breathed in English. "Shit! Shit, shit, shit!" He stopped saying it, stood, and looked from what was now a corpse to meet Medicine Shield's eyes. "Are you going to let me go?"

"Why would I not? You are not mine to hold."

"Then . . . I have a question. When you took Snow Fox from This World Stealer, did Mister Locklin give his son over willingly or did you have to fight him?"

The chief's hairless brows rose. "Did he not tell you of it, believing as he does that you are Snow Fox?"

"No. All he says is that you took Seth from him at spear point."

Now, Medicine Shield laughed. "Did he not say my lance had gone all the way through him?"

"No."

Medicine Shield made an expression of wonder. "I tell you, he fought me as fiercely to keep Snow Fox as I fought to claim the son . . . with knife and hand-to-hand. Not until my spear caught him and wounded him past resisting did he give the child up. But he fought so bravely that I could not kill him. I honor him as a warrior."

Ben nodded. "Then, you are both worthy to be called father. I will go now, but I will be back to visit."

Medicine Shield held out a hand. "If you cannot come here as a son, at least come as a friend."

Ben clasped the chief's wrist before he turned away. He was stopped by Talking Buffalo. The shaman indicated blood dribbling down Hawthorne's arm from the shallow shoulder slice.

"The red feather tells all you were wounded in honorable battle. You can go back to your hairy-mouth father in peace, because now you are as free as Crow Runs."

Ben nodded somberly, took the feather, and stuck it into his hair beside Seth's trophy before he whirled and dashed for Violet. He vaulted astride the mare and guided her southward at a run. He didn't go back to the Locklin Ranch. Instead, he went to see Caitlan Black.

Chapter Twenty-Three

It was a Kiowa warrior who entered Black Cat's ranch yard—at least, that's the impression the horse wranglers got when they saw Ben first ride in. But at sight of the pale skin and fair hair they recognized Seth Locklin, which kept them from grabbing their guns and shooting.

He came in at a slow trot and halted Violet in the middle of the area. He looked at the men staring at him with wide eyes and open mouths, and asked: "Where is Miss Black?"

One waved a hand toward the stable. "Uh . . . out back, Mistuh Locklin. Uh . . . uh . . . out back."

"Would you fetch her for me, please?"

"Uh . . . sure, Mistuh Locklin." The man whirled and strode swiftly toward the building. He was back shortly, followed by Caitlan wiping her hands on an old rag. Her hair was disheveled; she wore a sweat-stained shirt, a man's britches, and boots. She had obviously been working hard.

She frowned at Ben, asked: "Seth, what are you doing here . . . dressed like that? Oh! You've been hurt! There is blood on your arm! Come . . ."

He cut off her concern in mid-sentence. "Ride with me."

"To Bountiful Spring?"

"Yes."

She said to the wrangler who had called her: "Open the gate for us, would you please, George?"

"You sure you wanna do this, Miss Cat?"

"George!"

"Uh . . . yeah. Sure. Right away, Miss Cat." The man slid a wary look at Ben, but hurried toward the foaling meadow.

Ben slid the rifle under his thigh to free his hand, helped Caitlan up, then with the girl seated behind him and her arms around him, urged Violet back into a trot toward where the wrangler unlatched the gate. He nodded thanks to the man in passing and turned the mare toward the cut leading to Bountiful Spring glade.

Neither he nor Caitlan spoke. Ben was so deep in thought that he didn't really notice the beauty around them, but merely proceeded onward toward the pool. Caitlan only waited, because it was obvious from Seth's clothing—or lack thereof—and the attitude of his body that something important and perhaps disturbing had happened.

They reached the pool. Ben dismounted, helped Caitlan down, slipped the bit from Violet's mouth so she could nip grass if she so chose, lay the rifle on the bank, and went to kneel at the water's edge. Caitlan watched him wash blood from his arm before he turned to face her squarely.

He began: "You're takin' a real chance bein' alone here with me, Miss Cat, because I'm not who you think I am. You don't know me at all. We were never children together. My folks never knew your folks. I am a total stranger to you."

"Seth . . ." She leaned toward him, a hand out.

Again, he cut her off. "I'm not Seth Locklin. Seth is dead. He was killed the same day that Blue Glass Bead and the baby died in the blizzard."

"H-How do you know that?"

He walked a short way up onto the bank, took her hand, and pulled her down with him when he sat in the grass. With her perched cross-legged among the flowers and leaning toward him to catch his every word, he told her about his visit to Medicine Shield's camp, about Crow Runs, all he had learned there, and of what amounted to the warrior's suicide.

She listened in silence until he was finished, and his skin prickled when she murmured: "So Seth died for a . . . love that . . . never was. I thought . . . hoped . . . the Indian man who visited Blue Glass Bead when she lodged with me was her brother, or . . ."

"And not a week ago, I fought Dallas Young-street in Arch's front yard for callin' me a squawman." Ben laughed a sound, part grim humor, part bitterness. "I defended Blue Glass Bead's virtue, Cat . . . all Indian women's virtue when I was done fightin', and now I learn that

278

she betrayed Seth. Lay with another man when she was wed to him! Bore another man's son and told him it was his! Deserted him. . . ."

"But you said she only wedded Seth out of duty to her tribe. I believe she really loved Crow Runs. He proved that he surely loved her. When two people truly love . . . And all women, Indian or not, aren't like that, you know that. Most are honorable and . . . and . . ." Caitlan sighed and shook her head. "Umm . . . are you going to tell Arch who you are?"

"Not yet. There are still a couple of issues that need to be settled first. Like how come my name is the same as his real name was. And then, there are those bounty hunters to deal with." He sighed, and looked aside at the pool, at the silver cascade plashing under what was now late afternoon sun. "Maybe I'll never tell him. I . . . after seein' how David went . . . after all he's gone through . . . to have to tell a father he has lost both sons . . . I don't know."

"Ben . . ."

"No, call me Seth for the time bein', Miss Cat . . . at least until I make up my mind."

"All right. Seth . . . Seth, why did you come here instead of going straight back to the ranch?"

He grinned briefly and reached to take her hands in his. "Two reasons. One is because I needed somebody to talk to who could help me sort out what I should do next."

"Have I? Have you figured it out?"

"I'm . . . gettin' there."

"And the second reason?"

This time his brown eyes met her blue eyes and held. "Because I wanted you to know who you're dealin' with . . . wanted *you* to know me. Me . . . Ben." He released one hand, reached to cup her chin, and leaned to place a tentative kiss on her lips. Once again, he broke it off before she did. Watching her expression, he smiled. "That was from Ben, not Seth. Thank you for listenin', Miss Cat."

She leaned to him suddenly and this time her lips covered his, but only quickly. Her eyes sparkled above her own smile when she breathed: "And that was for Ben, not Seth. I know you have to go home now, but will you visit again soon . . . Seth?"

He nodded, rose, caught Violet, and replaced the bit. He helped Caitlan up, but sat astride the mare for a moment looking around the quiet glade. Talking Buffalo's rainstorm had washed the cañon walls and sluiced dust from the leaves. Everything sparkled—the water, the grass, the flowers. . . . Abruptly, Ben felt that a vast dark cloud had been lifted from over him.

He said: "We'll get started on the down-stream dam soon. Need to get it finished before winter."

Caitlan's eyes widened. She smiled a small,

secret smile, wrapped arms around Ben, and lay a cheek against his shoulder before she said: "Right."

"You been out doin' Injun business, Mistuh Seth?"

Ben nodded as he dismounted. "Yeah, I have, Fred. And I expect this is the last time you'll see me lookin' like this. Fred . . ." He leaned an arm wearily across Violet's back. He was tired. It had been a long, hard day. "How come, out of all the hands here, you're the only one who doesn't seem to take offense to me?"

Perkins looked surprised at his question. "Why should I? You never done me no ill, Mistuh Seth."

"But the others seem to cleave to Youngstreet's squawman namin' of me, and . . ."

"Hell, Mistuh Seth, you livin' with the Injuns wasn't your fault . . . you was just a li'l boy when they took you. Iffen I'd've been raised with nothin' but Injuns around me, I expect I wouldn't know the difference betwixt a purty li'l squaw and a white gal, neither. And, Mistuh Seth, now that ol' Dallas ain't raggin' 'em and all about you and your Injun woman, the men are gettin' used to you. They're calmin' down. I reckon, give 'em a li'l more time, and they'll forget all about it. Can I take your horse for you?"

"Yes. Thank you, Fred. Give her a good rub-down and an extra helpin' of oats, if you would. She's worked hard today."

"Will do." Perkins tipped a finger to his hat brim and led Violet away.

Rifle in hand, Ben headed for the house. His moccasins were silent on the steps and porch, and on the hall rug. He paused to look into Arch's office, because he saw Locklin sitting behind his desk, a glass of whiskey untouched before him, his face hidden by his hands. He was the picture of dejection.

"Father?"

Arch straightened with a jerk, and Ben had rarely seen such a look of relief in any man's expression. But it was quickly suppressed; Locklin almost grabbed at the glass, and Haw-thorne noted that the hand shook when Arch sipped and then leaned back in his chair.

Locklin asked: "How'd it go?"

Ben sighed. "I couldn't talk Crow Runs out of it. We had to do it his way. He's dead."

"You killed him?"

"He . . . ran himself onto my lance."

"And Medicine Shield? What's does he think about it?"

"It was an honorable battle between men. He witnessed it from start to finish. We are not at war."

"Good. Thank God! Then, it's over?"

"Yes, sir, it is. Excuse me. I'm goin' to go take a bath and get dressed for dinner."

"Seth . . . I'm . . . so glad you're home safe. I'm glad you're home, Son."

Ben nodded. "Me, too, Father." He passed on down the hallway.

Midge filled the tub for him and brought clean clothing—all of David's wardrobe was now Seth's. He let Arch's barber shave him and seal the shallow shoulder wound with ointment before he dressed in white man's clothing.

Upstairs in his room, he folded the Kiowa loincloth and leggin's and stored them, the bone bib, and the original eagle feather along with the beaded knife belt in the trunk; he doubted they would ever see daylight again. He stood twitching the red-dyed feather in his fingers while he stared at himself in the mirror. That first trophy feather had been won by Seth Locklin. It wasn't his. But this one . . .

He hardly saw his image in the glass because he was wondering how best to get that last piece of information he needed to settle the question of who he was, once and for all. He decided the best trail to follow was just to ask, and during dinner with Arch in the big dining room, he asked it.

"Father, there's a name running around inside my head that I can't . . . who is Eli?"

Locklin looked surprised. "Eli . . . Hawthorne?"

Ben stiffened. Carefully, his knife clutched in

283

his left hand, a bite of steak fork-impaled in mid-air in his right, he said: "Yes. Possibly."

"Strange that you should recall that name, because you never met him. I told you that before I came West, my name was Hawthorne."

"Yes." Ben still didn't take the bite of meat. He waited in a sort of suspended animation.

Arch grinned and reached for his coffee cup. "Eli was my older brother . . . my older twin brother. Twins run in our family, I guess. Our mother . . . your grandmother . . . was also a twin. Eli arrived in this world some five minutes before I did and never let me forget it.

"He was the . . . the good son. Never got into trouble. Never caused a problem. Never let me forget that, either. Unlike you and David, we never saw eye-to-eye, Eli and me. When you and David were boys together, you were inseparable. Two peas in a pod, as they say. When Medicine Shield took you, David cried for weeks. It took him years to get over your loss, if he ever did recover from it, but I think Eli was part and parcel to me taking up my life as a road agent just to prove that I could be successful at some-thing, even if it had to be crime." Arch shook his head. "I mean, our daddy was a preacher, you know, and Eli also took to the Bible. He could quote you chapter and verse no matter what the occasion."

I know, Ben thought. *But at least he was*

cheerful about it, not like Preacher Mason, all hellfire and brimstone. Eli believed the Lord was love, not punishment. "What . . . happened to him? Is he still back East preachin' the gospel?"

"Oh, no." Arch set down his coffee cup and again attacked his dinner. "Well, he may be back there now, but I don't know. I haven't seen him in over a quarter century. No, about a year before Jeremiah Black . . . uh . . . Seth McIntyre . . . and I made our unexpected haul, Eli married Cora Barker, and the two of them moved West to take the Word of God to the pioneers, to misguided Catholics, and to try to convert the heathen redskin." He shook his head. "My Cora and I used to laugh over that. A dance-hall girl named Cora wed an ex-highwayman named Hawthorne who moved West to . . . I guess you could say . . . hide out from the law. A pious church-going girl named Cora married a Bible-shouting would-be preacher named Hawthorne who moved West to lay down the law." Like Ben, he paused with a forked cube of meat uneaten before his mouth. "Never heard of them again. But I picture Eli with his own little clapboard church ministering to the settlers somewhere, maybe over in the territories."

Killed by *the Indians down in Texas,* Ben thought. But he didn't say it aloud, because hoof beats outside announced that they had company.

Arch scowled toward the front of the house,

threw down his fork, and snapped: "Shit, can't a man even have a peaceful dinner with his son without interruption? Who the hell . . . ?"

It was Ruffian Bullock and his men back with Bettiger, Hoffs, and forty thousand dollars in a wax-sealed string-wrapped, brown-paper package. His orange moustache was beige with dust, his hair carrot-colored and stringed with sweat. His clothes reeked with trail filth. Followed by his men and the two bounty hunters, his hat in one hand and the package in the other, Bullock waited at the door to be invited in.

Arch noted his condition. "Ruff! It's only been . . . what? . . . eight or so days! You look about done in, man!"

"Yes, sir, Mistuh Arch," Bullock nodded. "We rid hard to get there and harder comin' back, but here's the item you ordered." He stepped into the dining room and offered the package.

Arch rose to take it from him. "You have done exceedingly well for me, Ruff . . . men. There's a bonus in it for you. Go on to the cook shack now, have dinner, get cleaned up, and rest. Take tomorrow off . . . with my thanks."

"Thank you, Mistuh Arch." Ruff grinned. He turned to herd his men out, and vanished into the early evening.

Reuben Bettiger and Al Hoffs watched them go, but stayed behind.

Bettiger nodded at Ben, grinned. "Glad to see

286

you're still here and gettin' settled in, Mister Seth."

Ben lifted brows coolly back at Reuben; this was the man who had printed up a bogus Wanted poster on him and had besmirched his good name with it, the man who had hired three others to hold him prisoner and to addle his brains with a hot running iron and a bullwhip. He said shortly: "I am."

Bettiger looked back at Arch. "So, if you're satisfied we done our job, Mister Locklin, we'll just take our pay and be on our way."

Ben darted a hard warning glance at Arch— neither of them had come armed to dinner; both Bettiger and Hoffs wore sidearms and knives. Reuben carried a rifle slung over his shoulder.

Arch caught the look. He smiled, flourished the package, and said: "Yes, I'm satisfied. Like my hands, you did well. But also like the boys, you've had a long hard ride today. It's late. Why don't you go on out to the cook shack, get yourselves some food, find a couple of spare beds in the bunkhouse for the night, and get a fresh start in the morning."

Hoffs scowled at the package. "Uh . . . that's a awful lot of cash to have just layin' aroun', Mistuh Locklin, sir. Don't you think . . . ?"

"It won't be merely lying around, Mister Hoffs. I have a strongbox in my desk drawer in my office, and I am the only one who has the key.

This has come here across some rough country, it will be safe in my box overnight."

"Uh . . . that's the desk in your other room, there?" Al asked.

"Yes. Why?"

Hoffs looked at Bettiger frowning at him, muttered: "Yeah . . . well . . . yeah, it ought to be O.K. there, I guess. We'll just go eat, collect ol' Ev, and . . ."

"Ev Ribble is dead," Ben said abruptly.

"No! How?" Hoffs shot a shocked look at Reuben.

"Went just like your other partner, Murry Harding," Ben said. "Had a heart seizure or the like the day after y'all left for town. We buried him out back."

"Dead!" Bettiger gasped. He and Hoffs eyed each other.

"Yes. A most unfortunate thing." Package in hand, Arch stepped around the table and headed for the door to put the money away. "As Seth said, your other man died about the same way. Strange. Damned odd, if you ask me."

Ben rose from his chair to tag along when the two men followed Arch down the hallway to his study; he wanted to make sure neither of the bounty hunters shot Locklin in the back, grabbed the money, and ran for it. The men hesitated in the office doorway long enough to see Arch secure the package in his desk drawer lock-box before they said good night and left the house.

Ben and Locklin watched them go. Presently, Arch said: "They look like two tomcats wondering which one of them is going to scratch first."

Ben chuckled. "That's because we muddied up their water a mite, Father. Neither one of 'em is totally innocent . . . after what they hired done to me, after the way they just shot down their men instead of payin' them their bounden wage . . . No, no matter which one of 'em poisoned Harding and ol' Ev, they're both guilty as sin. Well, we've set the stage, as it were." He turned to look speculatively at Locklin. "You know, we seem to work uncommonly well together!"

"We do at that, don't we!" Arch grinned. He slapped Ben's shoulder fondly. "Must be family."

"Yeah. Now, all we can do is wait and see what happens next, but I suggest you keep a weapon close at hand till we're rid of them."

"You do likewise, Son. You do likewise. I don't want to lose you now."

Chapter Twenty-Four

Except that he had exchanged his boots for moccasins, Ben was still dressed and now wearing a sidearm. He stood by the window in his room and waited until he heard Arch retire before he moved to the hall door, opened it, slipped out, and headed silently down the stairs to the ground floor.

At the bottom of the stairs, he walked along that corridor toward the kitchen, where he located a full bull's-eye lantern. He lighted it, turned the wick down as far as he could without killing the flame, and returned to the hall. He went into Arch Locklin's study.

First, he checked the drawer in Arch's desk where Locklin had stored the money. It was tight and undisturbed. Then, he moved a chair into a far dark corner, shut the metal shield on the lantern before he set it onto the floor behind a thick table leg so no light would show, drew his pistol, and settled himself in the chair to guard Mister Locklin's money. Arch was paying forty thousand dollars for a son—any man's son—and, by God, he wasn't going to let someone get away with the money before its time.

It had been a long, hard day. The night was quiet, summer warm, and very dark—the full moon had disappeared along with the storm a couple of days ago. Ben had no idea what time it was when something awoke him, but he opened his eyes to see a darker shadow at Arch's desk. What sounded like metal splintering wood, and then a crisp snap, made him reach slowly for the shielded lantern beside him. Recalling how easy it had been to pick off men carrying torches through the darkness at Caitlan's place, he held the lantern out at arm's length before, simultaneously with thumbing the hammer on his weapon, he flipped open the lantern's metal panel.

He was almost more surprised than the would-be thief when he saw who stood behind Arch's desk with an iron crowbar in his hands. He had expected it to be either Bettiger or Hoffs; instead, it was Ruffian Bullock who held a pry-bar in one hand and grabbed for his gun with the other.

"Hold it!"

Bullock froze his reach when Ben aimed his own pistol. Ruff's eyes were huge in the lantern light while he slowly lifted his hands to shoulder height. He gasped: "What you doin' here, boy?"

"Lookin' out for my pa's interests, and it seems my hunch was right, except . . . Mister Bullock, what the hell are you doin' here? You were fixin' to steal Mister Locklin's money, weren't you! Why? You're his most trusted man! Seems I heard you been with him longer than any of the other hands . . . why are you doin' him this way?"

Ruffian licked lips below his moustache. His eyes darted from Ben toward the ceiling and back before he hissed: "Quiet, or you'll waken Mister Arch!"

Ben murmured: "That's just what I'm fixin' to do. Think he needs to see this."

"No! No! Lissen, boy, don't be a idjit! Think about it, boy! There's a powerful lot of money here! We can't let it go to them low-life bounty hunters . . . we can split it, you and me, yeah? Right down the middle, boy!" Bullock nodded hopefully.

Ben's lip curled. "You think his most trusted hand and his son stealin' from him is gonna set better on his table than payin' off some men who at least earned the money?"

"I earned it, by damn! I been workin' for Arch Locklin for near twenty years, and what have I got to show for it? Not very damned much, I'll tell you! I'm gettin' on, boy! I gotta think of my old age, here. Look, I ain't greedy. Mister Arch has got twenty thousan' acres of prime grassland and forty-seven thousan' head of cattle, and all I got is gray hairs and saddle sores! He can afford this. You take two-thirds, and . . ."

"I don't want Arch's money! All I want is a father and a home, and I got both now, so you just stand there, keep your hands up, and wait till I call my pa down here. Then, we'll see what . . ."

292

Bullock snarled a curse, and before Ben could pull the trigger, flung the crowbar at him. Hawthorne ducked. The heavy bar crashed against the wall behind him, and even as he brought his gun back to bear, two shots rang out.

Bullock's sidearm had been half drawn, but he didn't get to finish pulling it; he plunged to the floor and lay still. Ben had seen the fire of a pistol discharge from across the room, swung both the lantern beam and his weapon to target who else was in the office with him and Bullock, and his mouth fell open when he saw Arch sitting grimly in a chair there with a smoking gun in his hand.

"F-Father! How the hell . . . ? How long have you been there?"

"Long enough, Son. And you said it . . . I would never have believed it of Ruff, of all people."

"Jesus! You must move as good as any Injun I ever met! I never even heard you come in! My God, Father, I could have plugged you, you sneakin' around like that! Thank the Lord you didn't come over here and sit in my lap, thinkin' I was a chair. What a mess *that* would have been!"

"Yes, and I might have shot you had I known you were there." Arch rose and went to check Bullock's body just as footsteps pounded the porch and fists beat on the front door amid cries of concern. He murmured: "Dead. Never would have believed it of Ruff. Never."

"Me, neither. I figgered it would be Bettiger or Hoffs, but not him. Father, you better calm those men out there else they bust the door."

The front door wasn't locked, but good sense—and the fear of being shot down—had kept the hands from intruding until invited in. Bettiger and Hoffs were among them. Mrs. McPhee, in her nightgown and cap, was half-way down the stairs when the men hurried into the vestibule.

She gasped—"Oh, dear!"—and beat a hasty retreat to the room she had once shared with David.

Arch looked at the maids, the cook, and the barber poking heads into the hallway from the rear of the house, and snapped: "Everything is under control. Go back to bed! You men . . ."—he beckoned the punchers—"come with me." He led them into the study, showed them the crowbar, the damaged desk drawer, and Bullock's body. He explained what had happened, and finished: "I am devastated. I trusted Ruff completely. Please . . . take him out and we'll bury him in the morning." He shook his head. "It seems we've done nothing but hold funerals recently!

"Uh . . . I obviously need a new ramrod. Fred . . . Fred Perkins . . . if you want the job, it's yours."

"Yes, sir," Fred said seriously. "I'll do my best for you . . . and for Mistuh Seth and the ranch and all."

"Good. Get Ruff out of my sight! Then, get some rest. I . . . also need to go to bed."

Ben watched the men pick Bullock's body off the floor and cart it out. He followed to close the front door after them. When he returned to the study, he saw Arch holding the strongbox.

Locklin smiled ruefully. "I guess I'd better sleep with this under my pillow, eh?"

"Yes. And brace a chair at your doorknob, too, Father."

"Seth . . ." Arch put a hand out to stop Ben when Hawthorne started to turn away. "I heard what you said to Ruff when you didn't know I was listening . . . that you didn't want my money, you only wanted to be my son. That means everything to me, Seth. It means it has all been worth it. I know I'm not the most . . . demonstrative father in the world, but . . ."

"I meant it, Father. I would have said it to your face had you asked." Most amazing to Ben was, he knew he spoke the truth.

Arch was looking like a dime-novel bandit to Ben again while he ate breakfast with the strongbox on the floor at his feet. Not that Locklin was dressed in total black today—he wore a pale gray shirt, blue and white bandanna, and brown pants over his bent-heel boots—but he had black leather and silver buckle twin holsters strapped on and thigh-tied like a gunfighter. More than that, it was the attitude, the look in the dark eyes. The best Ben could come up with was that an air of grim humor hovered like a cloud of cigar smoke around him.

It came to Hawthorne that though Arch hid it very well most of the time, Locklin had probably always been and still was a downright dangerous man. Well, he guessed you had to be that to carve a ranch such as this out of a wilderness, wrest the land from the Indians, and survive it all. Which brought to mind what the Kiowa chief had said of Arch yesterday.

Ben himself wore a buff-white shirt, blue britches, Indian moccasins, and Frank Black's old but hair-triggered pistol in the single-gun belt. He downed the last of the fried spuds and onions, scrambled eggs, and bacon, and reached for his coffee. "Medicine Shield mentioned you with high respect, Father."

"Oh?" Arch lifted brows at him from over the rim of his own cup.

"Yeah. He told me about the day he took . . . me. He said you fought him near to the death, even after he'd run you through with his lance. You said he held you at spear point. You *didn't* say the business-end had come out your back side. He considers you to be a real warrior and so do I. I want to give you this in . . . appreciation." Ben reached down to where he had put it and picked the red-dyed eagle feather off the rug.

He handed it to Arch. "The red says you were wounded in honorable battle. You may not think much of it, but a feather like this counts for a lot to a Kiowa warrior . . . or especially to a Sioux or just about any other plains Injun . . . and it means a lot to me."

Arch took the feather, said somberly: "And to me, Seth. Thank you. I'll wear it with pride when I . . ." His voice cut off sharply as his gaze flashed past Ben and toward the door.

Hawthorne turned to see Reuben Bettiger and Al Hoffs standing there looking like they were ready to hit a long trail.

Arch grinned, lay the feather beside his water glass, leaned back in his chair, and fished a match from his pants pocket. He produced a cigar from his shirt breast pocket and started peeling gold foil while he said: "Well, gentlemen, come in. I expect you've come for your money."

Reuben nodded. "Yes, sir, if it's all the same to you, we have. Our job is done and it's time for us to move on."

"Agreed." Locklin nipped the end off the cigar, spat the piece onto his plate, lighted up, and puffed contentedly. "You men had breakfast?"

"Yes, sir. Ate in the cook shack with some of your hands." Bettiger slid a look at Hoffs. "If we can have our pay, now . . ."

"Got it right here." The stogie between his front teeth, Arch bent to retrieve the metal box from under the table and put it on the cloth beside his plate before he said to Ben: "Son, this is an occasion. Why don't you go to the liquor cabinet, bring back a bottle and four glasses, and let's see these men off with one for the road."

Ben grinned and mentally thanked Locklin; Arch hadn't forgotten. He said: "Yes, sir, I'll do that." He rose, sidled past the bounty hunters, and hurried on down the hall. In Locklin's office, he picked Ev Ribble's washed and refilled bottle from the corner of the cabinet, gathered four glasses, and returned to the dining room to set all before Arch.

Locklin said: "That's all right, Seth, you pour." Silently, Ben nodded. He uncorked the bottle, sloshed a healthy portion into each glass, handed one to Arch and one to Reuben and Al before he picked up the last glass, and raised it. He said: "You men, you started out four of you lookin' for me. Murry Harding, he died on the trail. Ol' Ev, he passed on here. Here's to Murry and Ev, wherever they may be and however they got there." He hefted the bottle as he watched the two bounty hunters lift their drinks in salute.

Hoffs said—"I'll amen to that."—and tipped his glass.

Reuben also raised his.

Ben noted: "This here's ol' Ev's bottle. I expect he'd take real kindly to sharin' his last drink with his good friends and partners."

Reuben Bettiger nodded and finished the whiskey. Hoffs spit his mouthful back into the glass. He crouched slightly when Ben grinned. "Ah, it was you! I thought so when you lost the coffee pot in the river, but I wasn't sure."

Bettiger looked perplexed. "It was Al what?"

"Who poisoned Murry and Ev. Doctored that same whiskey with water hemlock, I might add." Ben's smile grew. "You'll notice neither Pa nor I drank any of it."

Bettiger swung a glare at Al. He shouted: "You killed Murry and Ev and just stood there and let me drink poisoned booze? You wantin' to kill me, too? Why? Wasn't twenty thousand dollars enough for you?"

"No, it wasn't!" Hoffs's crouch deepened. His hand hovered near his sidearm. "You were always the one sayin' do this, do that, givin' orders like you had so many more brains than the rest of us it'd make a man sick just to lissen to you! I need pay for puttin' up with that all this time! Ol' Murry was just excess . . . he din't count! Ol' Ev was nothin' but a drunk, but you lordin' it over us all, you . . ."

"You son-of-a-bitch!" Reuben grabbed for his gun.

Hoffs had also started his draw, but he was torn between firing at Arch, who already had his pistol out and aimed at him, Ben whose hand likewise dipped toward his holster, or Reuben, and his fleeting hesitation let Bettiger complete his motion. It seemed Hoffs made his decision too late—his gun fired, but a fraction of a second after Reuben's. They were standing nearly face-to-face; at that close range, neither could miss. Al plunged backward to the carpet, arms and legs sprawled, a bullet in the heart. Bettiger lurched into a chair and toppled it. He and the furniture fell to the floor.

Neither Ben nor Arch had pulled triggers. As Hawthorne checked each man for signs of life and found none, Locklin jammed his pistol back into its holster and puffed furiously on his cigar for a moment before he snapped: "My God! Just what I need to start my day off right . . . a shoot-out in my dining room and two more bodies to bury!" He sighed heavily. "Too bad one of them couldn't have lived to enjoy their wage, but I guess you just saved me forty thousand dollars, Son. Yes, yes, we're all right!" Again, a crowd of the concerned had gathered in the doorway. "Somebody get a shovel!"

Ben was scrubbed, shaved, combed, dressed in fresh clothing, and carrying a picnic basket when Arch called from behind his desk: "Where you off to, Son?"

Hawthorne halted and felt himself getting red around the ears. He said: "I'm goin' . . . courtin', if it's all the same to you, sir."

"Ah-hah!" Arch leaned back in his chair and laced fingers behind his head. "And since Miss Caitlan Black is the only eligible woman within fifty miles, I guess it's safe to assume it's her you're going to woo? Or are you headed for Medicine Shield's camp?"

"No, sir, it's Miss Cat. Does that meet with your approval?"

"You bet it does! Have a nice day, Seth . . . and good luck."

"Thank you, Father." Grinning, Ben moved on out to saddle Violet.

He tied the basket to the saddle horn and rode at an easy trot westward along Runoff Creek toward where the stream was born at Bountiful Spring. Half-way to Caitlan's ranch, he halted the mare and looked out over the land.

Miss Cat, my name is Ben Hawthorne. Will you marry me?

My name is Ben Hawthorne. . . .

He now knew that Arch Locklin was his uncle, not his father, and that his own resemblance to Arch's boys was that of close family. He, and Seth and David, were the sons of twin brothers. They had been first cousins, and since there weren't that many white families out here, that relationship wasn't too strange.

He held no lingering doubts about who he was, where he had come from, and who his parents were. Regardless of what Arch thought of his own twin, Eli had loved his younger brother deeply enough to name his first-born son after him. Because Eli and Cora Hawthorne were dead, and Seth and David gone, there would be no purpose whatsoever in informing Arch that he had lost both his sons. No, he would never tell.

He thought about how very lucky he was. He, Ben, had the unique privilege of having had several men claim him as son. There was his birth father, Eli. There was his Comanche father, Nighthorse, who had loved him as his own—that was one of several coincidences here, that both he and Seth had been taken in their childhood by Indians, but then, things like that happened in this country. Mr. and Mrs. Inman had accepted him into their family as though he was one of their naturally born. There was Medicine Shield, who welcomed Ben as his adopted son. And there was Arch Locklin, who would be his final father.

He scrutinized the land. Twenty thousand acres. Forty or fifty thousand head of cattle. As Seth Locklin, this would all be his one day. He didn't feel that he was misrepresenting himself or stealing from Arch, because except for Priscilla and her Eastern husband, he was the only family Arch had left. As such, he would keep the ranch in the family.

Besides, he had fought for this. Even though he was another man's son, he had earned his place here.

Last, but not least, over there to the west was a fine woman who might become his bride one day soon. If she said yes, together he and Cat would give Arch the grandchildren Locklin yearned for to continue the family line and preserve their holdings.

No, he wasn't stealing from Arch. He would do his utmost to be the best son any man could want, then while he and Arch made the living, Caitlan and those babies would make the living worth living.

Humming a Comanche—or was it Kiowa?— love song, he patted the picnic basket and urged Violet onward.

About the Author

S.I. Soper was born in a remote valley in Washington state and has lived in Oregon, California, Arizona, Texas, and Missouri, before returning to the shores of the Puget Sound. Soper, who worked for IBM for twenty-three years, came late to writing Western fiction, producing in the early years science fiction and fantasy novels. *Remittance Man* (2015) was Soper's first Western.

Center Point Large Print
600 Brooks Road / PO Box 1
Thorndike, ME 04986-0001 USA

(207) 568-3717

US & Canada:
1 800 929-9108
www.centerpointlargeprint.com